Being Sapphire

New Atlantia, Book One

Sylvia Ryan

LYRICAL PRESS
Kensington Publishing Corp.
www.kensingtonbooks.com

Lyrical Press books are published by
Kensington Publishing Corp. 119 West 40th Street New York, NY 10018

All Kensington titles, imprints, and distributed lines are available at special quantity discounts for bulk purchases for sales promotion, premiums, fund-raising, and educational or institutional use.

Special book excerpts or customized printings can also be created to fit specific needs. For details, write or phone the office of the Kensington Special Sales Manager:
Kensington Publishing Corp.
119 West 40th Street
New York, NY 10018
Attn. Special Sales Department. Phone: 1-800-221-2647.

First Electronic Edition: February 2014
eISBN-13: 978-1-61650-196-9
eISBN-10: 1-61650-196-0

First Print Edition: February 2014
ISBN-13: 978-1-61650-757-2
ISBN-10: 1-61650-757-8

Printed in the United States of America

Torn between two zones. Torn between two men.

Patrick O'Connor is a soldier in the army that keeps the Zones separated. Though he does his duty, he is one of many who do not agree with how the Gov is operating. His twin is ripped from the family and dumped in the Amber Zone, but Patrick finds a way to join the Resistance to reconnect with his brother. Once he's in the Zone, Jordan Ford runs straight into his arms. Instead of arresting her for setting off a bomb in a Gov building, he does the unthinkable...he offers her his assistance.

Jordan Ford has struggled against all odds to become third in command of the Resistance, whose goal is ousting ending the Repopulation Laws. She is both attracted to and suspicious of Patrick's assistance. She ends up acting liaison between the Resistance members in the Amber Zone and those in the Sapphire Zone, bridging the chasm between the sectors.

Attraction sparks between Jordan and the two brothers, leaving her wondering if she can survive her next mission, the revelation of her darkest secrets, and being torn between two men who love each other more than they love her.

Books by Sylvia Ryan

New Atlantia Series
Being Amber
Being Sapphire

Friday Afternoon

Published by Kensington Publishing Corporation

To the only person who really knows me.

Prologue

The first cases of the deadly influenza were identified January 22, 2050 in New York City. The spread of the virus proved aggressive and unstoppable despite the declaration of martial law and mandatory quarantines enforced by the National Guard. Death of the infected occurred within seven days of the first signs of the disease.

Mortality rates grew exponentially and government services collapsed sixty days after the first identified cases. By that time, there were not enough people alive for society to carry on as normal. Millions of dead were left unburied and made cities uninhabitable for the few uninfected by the virus.

By the time the pandemic was over, an estimated ninety-two percent of the world's population had not survived. The majority of the deaths were caused by the virus, but some were a result of being cut off from food and water or from the chaos reigning in the aftermath of the pandemic. Those who survived were left isolated throughout the world. Suddenly, mankind was an endangered species.

In the United States, remaining government and military leaders rallied quickly in an effort to save surviving citizens. The skeletal remnants of military forces concentrated on making three US cities--Chicago, Los Angeles and Atlanta--habitable.

In New Atlanta, the densely packed skyscrapers of the downtown area were left untouched and loomed like ghosts haunting the new city hastily constructed in its shadow. In outlying neighborhoods where the population had been less dense, corpses were buried in mass graves so their homes could be assigned to the thousands of people that descended in hoards in a last-ditch effort to survive with others instead of dying alone.

In the years that followed, martial law ruled with brutal authority. Everybody participated in the rebuilding, except for the very young and the very old. Those who didn't fall in line were exiled outside the safety of the tall walls that surrounded the "new" cities. The area outside the walls, what would later be named the Onyx Zone, was unlivable and lawless.

As the population gathered, and the momentous, uphill struggle of rebuilding society began, it became clear that some genetic traits in humans, like blond hair and blue eyes, were on the verge of disappearing altogether. In an effort to propagate these endangered genes, and eliminate unwanted genes as well, the government decided that the repopulation of the US would occur slowly and under their supervision. Backed by a heavy military presence, the Repopulation Laws were enacted in 2052.

The Repopulation Laws mandated significant and difficult restrictions on the pandemic survivors all in the name of saving the unique and diverse qualities of the human race. Segregation of the population into zones and sterilization of those who possessed unwanted genes linked to chronic illnesses and mental-health diagnoses, eliminated propagation to the next generation. That, hand in hand with mandatory birth-control implants and heavy policing made the following of the Repopulation Laws nonnegotiable. Any type of relationship between citizens of different zones was illegal and the punishments for breaking that rule became more severe as the years passed. In time, leaders reasoned, the US would be completely populated with humans who had near-perfect genetic profiles. People who were smarter and disease free. People who would someday rule the world.

By the end of 2053, all citizens living under government control had submitted to genetic, psychological and intelligence testing and were classified according to the results of those tests. Four classes were established and given corresponding color marks. Every person was required to bear the color mark of his or her class, follow the Repopulation Laws established for that classification and restrict their movements to their own zone. Those with impeccable genetics were classified Diamond. The ruling class and those determined to possess significant talents or have made significant contributions to society, were designated as Emeralds. The overwhelming majority of people were classified as Sapphires or Ambers, with Ambers being the lowest and most restricted of the classes.

The Sapphire Zone had substantial restrictions to their freedoms as well. In the beginning, those designated as Sapphire lived happy and oblivious to the atrocities the Amber population was subjected to. However, when leadership of the National Guard changed, life for the Sapphire population changed as well. The changes were subtle at first, but over time, more and more Sapphire citizens became afraid of the Gov that "protected" them. By the time the Sapphire population began to realize there was a monster within, they'd already waited too long. General Morgan was entrenched as leader in his position of power with one hundred percent control over the Guard that policed them.

The Sapphire people were pumped with the Gov's propaganda about the crazy and diseased people in the Amber Zone, reminding them regularly how much the Gov did for them and reinforcing the mindset that they should be grateful to be alive.

The Repopulation Laws accomplished what they were set up to do. Genetic traits like blue eyes and blond hair were snatched away from eminent extinction. Yet the Laws continued, serving a different purpose from what they were originally intended. They had evolved into nothing more than a way to control the population so that the Gov could maintain absolute power over all the citizens of New Atlanta.

Objections against the Gov's rules were no longer voiced for fear of consequences that befell those who spoke out for change. As a result, fear increased in direct proportion to the military tyranny of the Gov, and the Constitutional rights American's fought to preserve in countless wars were denied in the name of improving the quality of the next generation of Americans thus maintaining the Gov's total control.

Slowly, people in every zone of New Atlanta were waking up to the fact that failure to act would doom them all.

Chapter 1

Triumph exploded out of Jordan Ford as she gazed at the fireball rolling up into the black sky of night. The Amber Zone Sterilization Center burned out of control and she stood mesmerized by the orange maelstrom of roaring flames while her heart hammered out a frantic beat in response to what she'd just done.

She felt compelled to stop and look, to revel in the satisfaction of the moment. The inferno's heat bathed her face. She didn't think she would ever experience a prouder moment than this one.

Her throat tightened as she mentally ran down the names of women victimized by forced sterilizations performed in that building. This was their retribution and her narrow escape. In less than twelve hours, Jordan was due to report for her next ten-year-birth-control implant. Now, there was nowhere to report.

"Come on, Jordan." Xander's voice emanated from the darkness behind her.

She turned to glance at him for just a moment before returning to the mind-blowing sight holding her captive.

"Go on, I just want to watch for a few more seconds."

"Now. Let's go!"

It was an order from her superior officer, plain and simple, yet she couldn't turn away.

"I'm right behind you. Go."

She waved a hand at him and registered his retreating footfalls while she took in several more seconds of the conflagration.

This was a pivotal event for the country. It was the Boston Tea Party of the twenty-first century. She wondered whether history would remember it as such. Or would their act of rebellion be a forgotten glitch in the heavy-handed reign of the current Gov? She shrugged. Only time would tell.

Reluctantly, Jordan finally turned away and ran into the darkness. The night was like tar, black and sticky from the unseasonably hot and humid September air. They'd picked this moonless night on purpose. But now, away from the fire, it was impossibly dark, and she was forced to slow her gait until her eyes adjusted.

The escape plan for their first act of sabotage was perfect. The Amber Zone police cruiser waited less than a mile away and instead of driving away from the scene of the crime, she and Xander would approach the disturbance together in the police cruiser, as if responding to the emergency.

After taking the time for her eyes to adjust, she moved in the shadows toward the rendezvous point, her black police uniform giving her excellent stealth in the deserted commercial district of the Amber Zone.

When a hand shot out of the darkness and tugged her into an alley between two massive buildings, Jordan gasped, startled by the unexpected new direction her body took. She hadn't seen who grabbed her, but she was pretty sure it wasn't Xander. The man's arms encircled her, holding her tightly and pinning her arms at her sides. She attempted to twist away from the hard male figure behind her, but he didn't give her an inch of leeway. He remained still and silent while his calm, slow breathing rustled her hair and warmed her scalp where his lips rested so very close to her ear.

She shifted slightly and gripped the butt of the gun holstered at her hip. The shadow behind her lowered his arm, grabbed her wrist and then restrained it against her abdomen. A sexy chuckle vibrated against her back and floated over her, raising the hairs on the back of her neck.

"Shh." The sound was the slightest whisper through lips that skimmed the shell of her ear. "They're coming."

Just as the stranger finished his sentence, Jordan detected the Guardsmen up ahead, by the subtle uneven rhythm of boots stomping the pavement. She stood in the slip of real estate, uncertain of her next move.

Her breathing heaved out of control, an unfortunate side effect of the run to escape combined with the panic of being caught. She was breathing too loudly. No matter how much she tried to regulate it she continued to bellow great, uncontrollable swells of air. One of the flock of National Guardsmen jogging by would hear her, turn his head and spot her there. The same thoughts must have run through the mind of the man at her back because the arms that caged her tightened and he held his breath, releasing it only after they'd passed.

A moment after the stomping of their boots had completely faded in the distance, the man lowered his grasp from her wrist to her hand and tugged her out from between the buildings. He navigated away from the gathering emergency responders but away from her rendezvous location with Xander as well. They rounded a corner and the border gate to the Sapphire Zone lay straight ahead, lighting up the entire area.

In the increasing light, she gaped at the man dragging her behind him, and dread dropped like a boulder in the pit of her stomach. He wore a green camouflage uniform and carried an automatic rifle by a strap over his shoulder. He was Guard.

Stricken, she attempted twist away from him, pulling hard against his grip.

He paused to look back at her. "Jordan. Stop."

When she got the split-second look at his face, recognition was instantaneous. Patrick O'Connor.

The National Guardsman who currently dragged her behind him was at the border guard station *that* night, the night Emily was killed. The night that started everything. She had spent a couple of hours passing the time with him while she waited for Jaci to cross back over into the Amber Zone. He'd liked her. It wasn't hard to tell. He hadn't been able to hide it very well. Months had passed since then, and he still remembered her name. The first time she'd heard him say it with his slightly off cadence syllables and the slight roll of his R made her name sound lyrical coming from his lips. She raised her eyebrows in surprise because she remembered his name as well.

"Come on!"

He pulled her again. And again, she resisted.

"There's no place to hide out here. They've already established a perimeter and are flooding the area with Guard for a grid search." He leaned in close until they were almost nose to nose. "I can hide you."

He smiled at her. The gleaming white of his teeth cut through the darkness and her reservations.

In a leap of faith Jordan quit resisting his pull and nodded. She followed him willingly then, as he led her into the small, brilliantly illuminated building that held the turnstiles used as the checkpoint for people traveling between the Amber and Sapphire Zones.

"Hands and knees," he spat, pushing her to the floor as he positioned himself in front of her. "There's a camera sweeping our way in a second. Shit," he cursed under his breath.

His tone of desperation had heightened to that of a man who was dangerously close to coming face-to-face with his own demise. Jordan looked around and saw them, too, a group of four Guardsmen getting out of their vehicle on the Sapphire side of the border. Patrick's body blocked their view of her as he moved around the checkpoint desk and pulled out the chair. "In you go," he mumbled.

She scooted into the small square of leg space under the desk and Patrick sat, rolling into her and pressing her tightly between his legs and the front panel. She knelt carefully, making sure no part of her body stuck out the six-inch opening at the floor and trying to hear the men enter the building over of the thundering of her heart.

"Stay quiet. If they catch you, we're both dead."

He was scared, too. Scared of the Guard, a group he was part of. Moments later the hard raps of boots hitting the tile floor sounded inside the building and got louder until they stopped directly beside her. The men were literally less than a foot away, just on the other side of the desk.

"We've been instructed to move in and help secure the area around the fire." She heard the familiar beeping sound of the code scanner, reading the numbers tattooed on the Guardsmen. Every Amber's palm held a numerical code that kept track of all their movements and their credits as well. She wasn't surprised that the Guard had codes in their palms too. The Gov would want to keep tight control over their personnel, tracking the where, when and with whom of each soldier.

Without further discussion, the group proceeded through the turnstiles and exited into the Amber Zone. She shifted, waiting for Patrick to roll backward and let her out. He didn't. His shins pressed tightly against her side, unmoving.

"Take it easy. We're not clear yet," he mumbled.

Jordan groaned softly and rearranged herself into a more comfortable position, throwing an arm over Patrick's thighs to steady herself and rested her head on his thigh. Seconds later, more soldiers streamed through the building and for the next half an hour or so, there were only snippets of time when they were in the room alone.

"You can make yourself useful under there, beautiful," he said, during a short span of silence in the building. The smile on his face clearly audible in the words he spoke, bringing a smile to her face too. It was a balm to her fear. Jordan responded by pinching the sensitive skin behind Patrick's knee. "Ow. Jesus, woman."

"Where's your partner?"

"He's sleeping in the break room, like he does every night."

"Why are you doing this?"

"I'm a sucker for a damsel in distress--"

His words stopped abruptly as another stream of soldiers and members of the New Atlanta Fire Department crisscrossed between the Sapphire and Amber Zones.

The next time they were alone, she asked again, "Why?"

"What else is a red-blooded American man supposed to do when a gorgeous shadow is coming at him at breakneck speed."

"Do you take anything seriously?"

"Oh, Jo…"

For a moment she thought they were going to be joined by more Guard traipsing through the building. Instead, he moved a hand under the desk and ran his palm over her forearm, then gave it a brief squeeze. His Sapphire wrist tattoo looked almost black in the dim space.

"I don't think we can get more serious than this." His voice was sober, and she agreed with his statement. So far this had been the most satisfying and most dangerous night of her life. "Very soon we're going to have to take our chances getting you out of here. My shift will be ending soon and my partner is due up from his good night's sleep anytime now."

Another group passed through the building. The foot traffic appeared to have turned the tide, with most of the soldiers and firemen crossing back into the Sapphire Zone.

Jordan's legs ached from being forced into the unnatural position for so long. "I've got to go. I'm dying under here."

"Come see me again, tomorrow," he whispered. "I can help your cause. I usually step out to get some air after my partner goes beddy-bye, normally around twelve thirty. Look for me then? In the alley?"

Apprehension churned her insides. Trusting this man was risky at best, and deadly if the trust was betrayed. But he already knew who she was, and if he had any brains at all, what she'd done that evening. Yet he still reached out to her, wanting to help. There was no way this man was ignorant of the fact he was risking his life by seeing her again.

"Why would *you* be interested in helping the resistance?"

"We don't have the time to get into that now," he said with a hard, cold tone of voice that told her, despite his uniform, he was not a fan of the Gov.

Or, he was a spy.

"It's dangerous."

He snorted. "So is setting a Gov building on fire."

Jordan stayed silent. She wasn't going to openly admit to that. Surely he didn't think she was that stupid. "I'll talk to my people. If they okay it, I'll be back tomorrow."

He sighed. It was a sound of both resignation and confession. "I'd like to see you again either way." His hand slid softly over the arm she had slung across his lap. It only took a split second to decipher his nonverbal cues, and her sharp intake of breath accompanied the true meaning of his words.

She didn't know what to say. She was thrown. The whole purpose of the Repopulation Laws was to keep people like him away from people like her. A little flirting was one thing, but what he proposed was forbidden, and they'd both be swiftly and brutally punished if they were caught.

"Since the first time we met, I've hoped to see you again, and I'm going to keep hoping after you leave tonight." Before she could develop a train of thought as answer to his statement, he spoke again. "Think on it. I'm here every night, Monday through Friday."

He cleared his throat. "Okay, this is what we're going to do. I'll slide away from the desk. When I tell you to go, you'll have a window of about seven seconds to get out the door and back into the Amber Zone." He squeezed her forearm again. "I'll be looking for you tomorrow night."

Suddenly, he rolled back a bit, leaving Jordan crammed into a slightly larger little box. She shifted to her hands and knees and groaned as her usually limber form creaked complaints at being compressed into a human brick for so long. She lifted her chin and looked up at Patrick O'Connor. Their gazes met for a split second. The color of his eyes drew her into their indigo depths. They sparkled with mischief as he grinned down at her. "You look especially beautiful down there on your hands and knees."

Yes, and he looked absolutely delicious towering over her.

He chuckled, as if he were reading her mind.

"My ma says I'm incorrigible." He said the words as if he was proud of them while his deep blue eyes flashed with more than mischief. Shadows of erotic acts and silent promises leapt at her from the mesmerizing, heart racing gaze. "It's just a part of my charm. You'll get used to it."

He scooted back away from the desk a little farther. "Are you ready?"

"Yes." She hitched a breath, bracing herself for the sprint she'd execute at his signal.

His attention shifted to one side of the border and then to the other. He rolled away from the desk a few inches more. Seconds passed.

"Go."

Jordan bolted from the shelter of the desk and ran out the glass door of the brightly lit building into Amber, into the night.

She'd gotten about fifty feet from the building when a crowd of Guardsmen turned a corner and spotted her. Still in her police uniform, she composed herself and smiled at the group. "Hey, you guys need any more help over there?"

She called the question across the twenty or so feet that separated them, hoping she didn't look as caught as she felt. Her blood whooshed loudly in her ears while she viciously fought the impulse to look away from the Guard's direct eye contact. Straightening her spine and locking her teeth together, she steeled herself and looked the man directly in the eye.

"No. Everything is under control now. Get on back to where you belong." The order was riddled with the superior attitude and disgust that those from a different zone parroted when in the presence of an Amber. Jordan gave the man a quick salute and turned, heading back on foot toward Amber Zone Police Headquarters.

The farther she walked away from the border guard station, the more relaxed she became. Her solitary steps echoed outward into the gathering fog of early morning, punctuating the rapid-fire thoughts shooting through her mind. They'd done it. The resistance was a reality, now. And already, there was someone from a different zone reaching out as an ally. If she could trust him.

Jordan thought back to the night she met Patrick, waiting for Jaci to cross back into the Amber Zone after Caroline had tried to kill her. She'd spent over an hour talking and flirting with him and his sleazy partner on the night shift. She'd flirted with the men because she wanted to keep them off-kilter, not questioning why she was there or why her friend was crossing back into Amber at such a late hour. It had worked, but she'd never looked back after they made their escape from the border guard station.

That wasn't really the truth. She'd thought about Patrick a couple of times since then. He was attractive, and she'd picked up on his attraction to her.

But there was something about him even more memorable. She didn't sense any disapproval or superiority usual during contact with people of other zones. He'd been fun, cracking jokes and tossing out sexual innuendos, which of course, was taboo because of their difference in designations. A flood of confidence swelled within her. After only a couple hours of contact months ago, Patrick remembered her name, both first and last.

She found it hard to believe, because she wasn't a bat-her-eyelashes-and-wrap-men-around-her-little-finger type of woman. She'd never even tried that wholly female ploy before that night, and when she thought back, she was still shocked it worked. Maybe the years since she turned twenty-one and moved into Circle City allowed her to pick up some of the basics, but she was still way behind the learning curve in the feminine wiles department compared to the rest of the women in Amber.

Her upbringing in the Amber Zone had been different from other girls. She didn't grow up doing the things they did. She never found comfort and acceptance through the touch of someone else. Never had pretty clothes, or spent hours figuring out the best way to do her hair, and never had a friend or had sex until after she turned twenty-one and moved to Circle City.

She was definitely different and keenly aware of her shortcomings. She wasn't feminine. She kept her hair supershort, didn't wear makeup and only recently put herself out there enough to make a friend, her very first girlfriend.

Overall, she'd characterize herself as tough, and tough wasn't generally what men looked for in a woman. But, being tough was what led her to tonight. It almost made every other miserable moment of her life worth it. She shook her head bringing herself out of the reoccurring negative train of thought. No. Not tonight. Tonight was everything good and lucky and right.

The sun rose ahead of her, painting the smattering of clouds pink and orange. The colorful spread only spurred the ridiculous grin she couldn't seem to erase from her face. When she turned the corner onto the final leg of her trek, she spotted Captain Rush sitting on the entry steps to Police Headquarters.

He was waiting for her. When he caught sight of her approach, she pumped her fist in the air and flashed him her best hell-yes expression. He released a long breath and his shoulders slumped, slowly releasing the tension they held. He'd been worried about her.

As she approached, she noticed he was definitely starting to show his age now that he'd lost most of his hair. He looked more like a bald eagle with every passing day. But he was still sharp and smart and everything to her. God she loved that old fart.

Rush stood when she finally reached him and they wordlessly walked alongside each other into the building. In his office, he rounded his desk and Jordan closed the door behind her before sitting across from him.

His chair squealed a complaint as he leaned back and crossed his arms. "What happened?"

Jordan reported the entire evening from the time Xander left her, to her close call after she fled the border guard station. "I assume Xander got here okay?"

"Yeah, but he wanted to go back and look for you instead of following the plan. I had to order him not to go."

"I'm sorry, Cap. I couldn't stop myself from just...taking it all in."

That feeling, that irrational joy, resumed its excited flutter in her belly, tickling like brushes of butterfly wings on her interior organs. She squashed it down the best she could but still couldn't hold back the smile curving her lips. "It won't happen again."

"Go home. Get some sleep. We'll debrief before the meeting tonight."

Jordan nodded and stood. "Cap?"

His eyes softened at her soft inquiry. "Yes, Sergeant?"

"We did it."

He shook his head. "No. You did it."

Chapter 2

Patrick's mother would be able to tell something was up with just a glance of her always-assessing gaze. Neither her husband, nor her sons could hide anything from Kate O'Connor. The short, strong-willed redhead was the undisputed matriarch of the O'Connor household. She ran a tight ship and was always keenly aware of how her boys were doing emotionally. Patrick didn't know whether she saw it in their eyes or if she read body language. Maybe it was just a woman's keen intuition, but she knew.

As he prepared himself to enter his parent's house, he schooled the expression on his face, trying to avoid a discussion with his mother before he crashed for the day.

Like everyone else in New Atlanta, Patrick was assigned an apartment at age twenty-one. But he'd never truly moved in there, choosing to spend most of his free time at his childhood home. He just didn't have the heart to leave.

His mother had been absolutely devastated when his identical twin Shane had never returned from the Designation Center that day. He'd been designated Amber and taken away.

Because he and Shane had been born with deep blue eyes, the entire family had assumed they would be Sapphires like the rest of their clan. But Shane hadn't been. They arrived at the center together and left separately.

Shane's testing determined him to be infertile. The most likely reason was the mumps and high fever he'd had as a child. Infertility resulted in an automatic Amber designation, and just like that, with no fanfare or remorse, their family had been ripped apart.

The robust, funny mother he'd grown up with transformed into a woman he barely recognized. She deteriorated into a shadow of her former self. The brash love that flowed from her, affecting everyone in her path, was still expressed in her actions, but heartbreaking anguish shone in her eyes. She was less. Thinner in both heart and body with one of her boys gone. After that, he couldn't bring himself to leave the family home. His apartment sat mostly empty.

Patrick and his dad, Aaron, surrounded her, cushioned her from the pain as best they knew how. They kept her busy with never-ending requests for favorite dinners and help with one task or another. They made her feel needed. It seemed like the best way to divert her attention from the hole Shane's designation created.

Since then, Patrick had been consumed by the drive to act against the regime that struck such a powerful blow to his family. His mother was not the only one who suffered Shane's loss. For years, Patrick stumbled through life feeling like a part of himself was missing. From the moment of conception to the day they turned twenty-one, he'd spent his life with a living, breathing duplicate of himself. He and Shane had an innate connection, a visceral bond so strong it was as if they were two halves of the same whole.

In the Sapphire Zone, there was a growing unhappiness with a Gov that left women childless, ripped family members away from those they loved and strong-armed every one of them to conform or reap the consequences.

A growing fear of the Gov's tightening grip on all parts of their lives was beginning to give the population in the Sapphire Zone fearful pause, and as the population's discontentment increased, Guard patrols on the streets of Sapphire increased as well. Both subtle and not so subtle messages by the Gov were heard loud and clear. Dissention would be crushed.

When he walked through the back door to his family home, his mom was in the kitchen making breakfast like she did for him every morning. The yellow kitchen was bright with early morning sun and the windows were open allowing a slight breeze and the sound of birdsong into the room.

She glanced over her shoulder and smiled as he closed the door behind him. "Breakfast will be ready in a minute."

He stood next to her, washing his hands at the kitchen sink when she peered over at him and cocked her head. "What is it? You've got an imbecile's grin on your face." He turned away from her omnipotent gaze, drying his hands. "And don't you dare say 'nothing' to your mother now. Not when she knows it's an outright lie."

Patrick snorted. "No, Ma, I wouldn't dare."

She set a plate of eggs and toast on the table in front of him, pulled out her chair at the opposite side of the small, square dinette and sat with a steaming cup of coffee.

He kept his eyes on his food in a lame attempt to avoid her scrutiny. "I've got some things to talk over with you. Where's Da?" He glanced up at her and her gaze turned serious.

"He's getting dressed."

"Let's wait to talk until he comes down."

Patrick continued to shovel food into his mouth, carefully avoiding his mother's inspection and trying to figure the best way to tell her he was diving headfirst into deep water.

Aaron O'Connor, was a big man with dark hair and midnight blue eyes, just like his sons. When he entered the kitchen, he was surly as always. His mother rose and served up a portion of eggs to his father and popped bread into the toaster.

"Patrick's got something to talk to us about, Aaron." She set the plate in front of her husband and sat again, looking expectantly at Patrick.

"Jeez, Ma. Relax." He was stalling, and his mother knew it.

"Well, come on. Out with it." She sat with her blue-eyed gaze fixed on him.

When he'd eaten the last bite of food on his plate and glanced up at her, the worry in her eyes gave him pause. He felt as if he was going to tear her heart out with what he was about to say, but he forged ahead and proceeded to tell them about Jordan and the events of his overnight shift. When he'd finished, his mother sat tight-lipped and pale.

"What's your plan, boy?" his father asked.

Patrick shook his head. "I don't know, I--" He stopped short. "I guess that's why we're all sitting here," he said quietly, looking at his mother. "Ma, I don't want to spend the rest of my life living two miles away from my brother and not being able to see him. It's time to act. I wouldn't be the man I want to be if I turned away from what's right because of fear. It's time for me to choose a path I can be proud of."

He paused and gentled his tone "And...well, Ma, I really like this girl. I know I don't know her very well, but...I don't know. There's something between us, some kind of chemistry. I need to see her again."

Kate O'Connor sucked in a breath and a tide of alarm rolled over her face, turning it ashen. "Patrick, no! You're going to be caught if you try to spend time with this woman. I forbid it. It's too dangerous."

"Ma--"

"Patrick, I said no. I won't have it. Things are getting worse. Every day is a little more dangerous. People are disappearing into thin air. Children are reporting their parent's private conversations to the Guard. Neighbors are spying on neighbors. Anything out of the ordinary is scrutinized and questioned." She shook her head. "No. All it would take is one person noticing something different and reporting you. I'm not going to lose you to the Gov, too." A sob hitched in her throat, and Patrick knew his mother was within an inch of losing it. She turned her face away from him and covered it with their hands.

Patrick glanced over at his father, who was staring cold-faced right back at him. Aaron O'Conner couldn't abide one of his boys making their mother cry.

"Ma." He knelt next to her and grasped her hand in his. "It's the right thing, on so many levels. What's going on here is wrong. I surely don't have to convince you of that. Organization against the Gov is inevitable. At some point, we have to join those who are working to change it.

"That woman, Jordan, risked her life last night to stop Amber women from being forcibly sterilized. She's brave and--" He sighed. "Ma, I don't know why, but I need to see her again."

His mother lowered her hands. She had tears in her eyes as she slumped, looking defeated. Then, finally, she gave him a slight nod. "Okay, Patrick. You've got my blessing." She looked up at him, with bright eyes full with unshed tears. "Far be it for me to prevent you from following your heart and fighting for what you believe."

"Thanks, Ma," he whispered, squeezing her hand tightly before returning to his chair.

She nodded at her son, looking resigned. "If you're going to do this, you might as well do it right."

He froze with a glass of orange juice halfway to his mouth. Alarm rose from somewhere deep in his gut when a look of determination passed across her face. "You're going to need some help." She pointed at him. "And I won't be takin' 'no' for an answer." She stood and headed toward the threshold that led into the rest of the house. "I'll call the kin," she said over her shoulder on her way out of the kitchen.

Patrick met the pacific blue of his father's gaze.

"Don't bother," Aaron O'Connor said with his distinct Irish-hued English.

"What?"

"Don't bother tryin' to talk her out of it. It would be wasted breath." His father rose. "I'm proud of you, son." They shared a moment between them before he nodded once. "I've got to get to work." He turned and followed his wife's path out of the kitchen.

"I want to meet this girl who's caught your eye, Patrick," his mother said a few minutes later as she breezed back into the room with her ear bud already in.

And just like that, Kate O'Connor, the woman he grew up with, was back. The small hope of maybe having Shane with them again seemed to put her sound footing and iron-clad composure back in place.

He laughed and rolled his eyes, pushing his chair away from the table as his mother sat back down. "I'll see what I can do, Ma."

Kate O'Connor grabbed his forearm to stop his retreat from the table. "You're a fine man, Patrick."

He leaned over and pecked a kiss on her cheek. "I'm going to bed."

Patrick made his way to the bedroom he and Shane used to share and sat down at the desk instead of flopping into bed as per usual. There were so many things he wanted to express to Jordan. So many ideas running around in his brain. He felt like a dumb-ass, giddy teenager instead of a grown man.

He reflected on the facts that led him to this crossroads in his life and acknowledged there was so much more that landed him in this moment of time. Shane's designation wasn't the only reason he'd made this sharp turn, rushing full speed toward a head-on collision with a regime fast becoming an unstoppable machine. It was that. And more.

When he'd been recruited to the National Guard seven years ago, he'd been proud of his job and held total loyalty to the Gov. Since then, leadership changed and his loyalty had eroded.

National Guardsmen, and their leader, General Morgan displayed an increasing sense of superiority toward the population. Small infractions of the law were being met with punishments of progressively disproportionate intensity. Rumors about the execution of people who wanted to leave New Atlanta to try to make it on their own in the Onyx Zone were frequent. And the massive number of surveillance cameras being installed throughout the Sapphire Zone was hard to dismiss. They were a tightly controlled population.

He'd heard General Morgan speak many times. The man delivered powerful speeches that drew the listener in and swayed them to his point of view. But lately, the speeches more closely resembled rants and his words reeked of racial superiority and the elimination of those who didn't measure up to standards that were getting harder and harder to meet. Every year, more genetic conditions were added to the list of Automatic

Disqualifiers that sent a person to the Amber Zone, and for the first time in almost a decade, the number of people being designated Amber had increased.

He was on the wrong side of what was right. He was a small cog in an authoritarian government reeking from the putrid decay of ideals the United States was built on.

Patrick sat, staring at the blank piece of paper sitting on the desktop in front of him. It took about thirty minutes of thought to sort out how he wanted to approach this first contact, this first admission of hope that there'd be something more between them. He had to address his personal feelings, his need to get to know her better as well as the cooperation and coordination of their groups. But he wanted to keep the two separate. He didn't want to embarrass her in front of the others of her group by putting her personal business out there for all to see.

He decided on two messages: one for Jordan alone and one for the leader of the resistance. The notes would have to be in code, but not so vague the reader wouldn't know the true meaning of what he was trying to say. He didn't want Jordan to be caught in possession of communications that implicated her as anti-Gov. He picked up a pen and began to write.

Chapter 3

At eight PM, the members of the Amber Zone resistance filled the activity room of the Wellness Center to capacity. During the day, the room was used for dance and yoga classes. It contained the standard wall of mirrors and a hardwood floor. To Jordan, the presence of the large crush of men with their rough edges and hard hearts were out of place in a room intended for little ballerinas and pregnant women learning childbirth methods.

The turnout was exceptional, all of them wanting to hear the firsthand account of how the previous evening's mission fared. Jordan made her way toward Captain Rush and Xander to take her place next to them on the raised platform. She was unbelievably proud to be third in command and in charge of guerilla missions and covert operations.

Xander's jaw clenched when he saw her approaching. Obviously, he was still a little ticked about her loitering to take in the fire last night. Trying to avoid the inevitable ass chewing she was sure to get before the night was over, she mouthed "sorry" from across the room and shot him her most ingratiating pout. It was about as close to a real apology he was going to get, and he knew it. He got the message and shook his head, his grimace turning into a reluctant smile.

The solidarity in the room was potent, charging the air and giving significance to the moment. The walk through the crowd was one she'd never forget. Large hands landed hard on her shoulders in rough congratulations for the success of her first act of sabotage. Their enthusiasm was going to give her bruises.

Captain Rush stood and quieted the crowd as Jordan sat down next to Xander.

"Hey," she said, under her breath.

He grunted an unintelligible response, and she knew her small lapse in judgment was forgiven.

"Okay, let's get started," Rush said, and the white noise of a hundred voices fell silent. "As everyone knows by now, our mission last night was successful."

Shouts and applause forced the Captain to stop the briefing.

"I guess we should congratulate Xander and Jordan on a job well done."

The crowd continued to whoop and cheer. The joy in the room overwhelmed Jordan, and she was at a loss as to how to behave in response to the recognition. She forced her gaze away from her clasped hands on the table in front of her and looked out over the crowd, humbly accepting the accolades.

Experiencing the surge of pride and accomplishment that went along with her success felt unfamiliar and awkward. Her throat tightened with emotion. She was deeply moved by the display.

She'd had a lot of practice reacting to her defeats. Failure was an old friend, and through the years she'd become accustomed to picking herself up, dusting herself off and trying again.

Success. That was altogether different. It was completely unfamiliar and totally scary on so many levels. People were counting on her to be successful.

She looked out over the celebrating men. This was the exception. She liked the feel of it, though, and she aspired to become what everyone in the room thought she was.

She soaked up this giddy, bubbling feeling of success. She'd save the memory of it for later, when she needed it.

"Okay, okay, let's get on with business," Captain Rush said a few times before he got relative silence in the room.

"The Sterilization Center is gone. We have to focus on the next item of business. During Jordan's escape last night, a guardsman saved her from running into a group of them heading her way and hid her until she was clear. He offered his assistance to our cause."

The hum of the crowd increased in volume as men discussed the revelation with others around them.

"All right, quiet down," Captain Rush shouted over the escalating din. "Xander and I have discussed how to proceed in this matter. An alliance like this could be an extremely valuable addition to our group and jump-start our efforts. It would be shortsighted of us to reject his offer, so we've decided to forge ahead in a way that will have minimal risk to our ongoing operations. For the time being, the only access this man will have to us is through his contact, Jordan. She's volunteered to be the liaison and is already developing a working relationship with the contact. The rest of our identities will be withheld. It's a risk, but we think it's a risk worth taking. Questions, comments, concerns?"

There were low murmurs here and there, but no objections. "Okay, that's settled. Any committee heads want to give updates before we adjourn until the next meet?"

Xander stood and stepped around the table, taking the floor. "I'd like to give updates on a couple of projects. Digging the tunnel to the Onyx Zone has been slow, backbreaking work and we're looking for a few men who can help with the load."

A few shouts from the crowd answered his call for help, and he nodded his thanks. "Meet with me after the meeting tonight for the details." He looked over the crowd. "I also have a firearms update from Stan's unit. We just received another bundle of side arms and ammunition from our over the fence contacts. I want to thank all of the men and women who are consuming less so we have the commissary food to fund our acquisition of arms."

As the room began a round of applause, a barrage of gunfire sounded from somewhere outside the building. A scream and then the sound of multiple weapons and prolonged automatic fire had every person in the room springing to action at the same time. More muffled screams ensued as the room emptied with thorough efficiency. Jordan followed the crowd out the front doors of the Wellness Center and into Circle City.

As Jordan ran toward the heart of the disturbance, she noted the retreat of a large group of National Guard. Most of them were already through the tall barrier that ran from building to building, enclosing Circle City.

The world outside the doors was chaos. Masses of people spilled out of every doorway, making an accurate assessment of the situation difficult. Jordan followed the screaming and crying ahead of her. When she finally got a good view of what had happened, the shock of it stopped her cold.

Hundreds of people had been sprawled out over the park-like, sloping green in the center of Circle City, staking their claim of real estate for the evening so they could sleep in the cool night air instead of the stifling-hot buildings. The multicolored blankets sprinkled against the dark texture of the grass looked like small, colorful squares of confetti. Dozens of people lay dead. Bullet wounds riddled the ones closest to her. The guard had shot them all. The living searched for those they knew, flowing and swerving around the dead in the same way water parted around objects in its path. Wails of grief filled the air.

Stopped dead in her tracks, she was a lone, still person in a swarm of movement and noise. The ruthless extermination of innocent Ambers detonated a cache of rage that always lurked inside her. They'd done nothing wrong.

But she had.

A realization struck with brutal force. This was her fault. These people were dead because of what she'd done the night before. They'd expected swift retaliation by the Gov if the fire was suspected to be arson instead of an accident. But she'd never imagined they would murder indiscriminately. That assumption had been naive and the awkward feeling of success she'd experiences minutes before transformed into the familiar pall she was used to.

Jordan pulled out her handheld and began recording a video of the mayhem while there was still some light from the rapidly setting sun. She focused on her screen and walked through the carnage with the weight of her responsibility for the massacre skewing her perspective.

She found herself automatically gravitating toward the spot where she usually slept with her roommate, Dennis. Her mind ran through all the reasons he wouldn't have been waiting for her to join him on the lawn, but that small part of her life experience had forged and shaped already knew he was dead. It was the same part of her that knew she'd been too happy these last few months. Her new friendship with Jaci and the important position she held in the resistance had given her instances of joy, of hope. The feelings were new to her. It was all too good to be true.

Her throat closed tight for the second time that evening, making it difficult to breathe. It felt as if she was barely taking in enough air to be conscious as she walked through the gore to where she'd been sleeping with Dennis during these hot nights of late summer. Then, on the video screen of her handheld, she found him.

His hands were cradled under his head as he looked up into the sky. For a split second, in the fading light, he looked alive. But in the melee of the moment, he was too still.

Jordan dropped the handheld and fell to her knees beside him. "Dennis."

She looked him up and down and spied the bloody bullet hole a few inches below his armpit. The sounds of the frenzied throng around her faded while her own panic and grief sharpened.

Laying her head on his chest, she listened. There was no heartbeat, no rise and fall of his breaths. He was dead.

The world fell away and agony detonated somewhere deep inside her chest. Grief came at her from all sides. Her nose burned and her eyes watered as she denied her body's demand to cry.

She closed Dennis's vacant eyes and rested her head on his chest. She wouldn't survive this loss. This would leave utter devastation in its wake.

Dennis had been her champion. He protected her, saved her from the mental illness that plagued the life she tried to build in Circle City. He fought side by side with her, helping her to overcome her issues and took on the fight alone when she didn't want to fight for herself.

Her thoughts were dismal and self-centered. She needed him for everything. There was no recovery from this.

Sometime later, Jordan became aware of Xander standing over her. Concern was blatant on his face. She knew what she must look like with her tear-filled eyes and devastated heart. Her skinny body, pale skin and round eyes made her resemble a waif when she cried. She knew because she'd seen it in the mirror more times than she could count. It was not a side of herself she let people see.

"Say your goodbye, Jordan, and then I'll take you home."

Jordan pressed a chaste kiss to Dennis's forehead and rose.

"Would you rather stay with Jaci and me?" He squeezed her with a muscular arm around her shoulder while turning her in the direction of her building.

"No," she said numbly. "I've got to meet with the contact. He told me to be there tonight."

"It can wait a day."

She looked up at Xander and nodded and then squirmed out of his grip. "I'm fine. I can walk home by myself."

She turned and walked away from him, hoping he wasn't following her.

Instead of going up to her apartment when she entered building twelve, she walked straight through the lobby and out the front entrance.

It took a tremendous amount of repression to turn her thoughts away from the scene she'd just walked away from, and she was utterly unsuccessful at it for any length of time.

The hole Dennis's loss would leave in her life was massive, and the ramifications were starting to circle the outskirts of her mind. Her life was a perfect example of why every female had a male roommate assigned to her. She needed the created link of family because she had no one else. Dennis had been better family to her than the people she'd been born to.

He was someone safe to touch and be touched by without expectation of anything more. She could be herself when she was with him.

He knew everything and cared for her anyway. She was bereft.

It took a good half hour of walking before her brain started to emerge from the fog, and then during the next half hour, her grief turned into anger. She fumed as she finished her hike to the border gate station. Those miserable fuckers would pay. She would have her revenge.

In the pitch-dark of another moonless night, Jordan's feet took her where she needed to go while her mind worked, trying to assimilate the drastic changes of the last twenty-four hours.

Jordan stood outside the circle of light surrounding the border and hid in the shadows, watching intently. The windowed building was a brightly lit fishbowl with every detail of the interior easily visible. Two Guardsmen stood talking next to the row of turnstiles. Neither one was Patrick.

It was incredibly stupid not to have backup for this meet, but there was something within her that trusted him, and that was a rare occurrence.

Minutes later, Patrick walked into the building from the Sapphire side of the border. She absorbed every detail about him. He was average weight, average height with brown hair.

His eyes. They were extraordinary. She remembered flashes of the bluest eyes she'd ever seen. They had startled her the night before. Growing up in Amber, she was accustomed to being surrounded with brown-eyed gazes and hadn't remembered how startling it was to be regarded with indigo eyes. Having them pointed at her, scrutinizing her, increased her heart rate and shortened her breathing. They were a constant reminder he was forbidden to her. There was no mistaking the flashes of desire or the air of playfulness she'd seen in them the night before. It was as if a tiny devil sat on his shoulder, whispering in his ear, because when he looked at her it was very clear the things running through his head would land them both in Hell.

He had affected her on some level during their first encounter several months before because a short time later she experienced a jolt of excitement when she thought she'd seen him in a crowd. She was actually changing direction to walk toward him when she realized there were no National Guardsmen living in the Amber Zone. She distinctly remembered a momentary twinge of disappointment at the revelation but never thought of him again after that. Until last night.

She closed her eyes and mentally put herself back under that desk. Just thinking about his hand running up and down her arm fluttered her insides and made her part her lips so she could take in more air. She swallowed and raised her lids to look again at this man that made her pant just a little bit every time her mind wandered to him.

In the cluster of four men wearing the same uniforms, she was able to easily identify which was Patrick O'Connor. He was--

She shook her head, having a hard time putting words to the vibe he gave off. Inviting. It was as close an adjective she could bring to mind. The expression on his face and the way he moved his body was warm, relaxed. He possessed an easy leisure, from his gorgeous narrow-hipped, sweet, tight ass to the slightly off-kilter canter of his words. She felt it even from this distance away.

He was not like the men she knew in Amber who, because of their life experiences, grew to be stoic and imposing, needing to control everything.

Jordan frowned into the darkness. She was sure by the way he carried himself that Patrick's life had been easy. He had no reason to be angry and stoic. She forced herself to remember he was on the wrong side of this fledgling war, and she should be terrified of him. But when he looked at her, she felt the opposite. Somehow this liaison felt right inside.

She silently regarded the change of shifts and continued to watch while he talked with his partner. A few minutes later, she moved to the alley he'd pulled her into the evening before.

She walked deep into the shadows between the two buildings and sat against a wall, bringing her knees up underneath her chin. It was a familiar position she felt compelled to assume when she was scared or threatened.

As a child she'd realized when she tucked her head and covered the back of her neck with her hands, she could easily withstand the most severe of beatings. She was sure reverting to this protective pose was a reaction to losing Dennis, because she hadn't given in to the compulsion to assume that position in several years. She spent the wait rocking slightly and rebuilding her defenses.

It seemed to Jordan like several hours had passed before Patrick stepped into the gap and sat on the ground beside her. She hadn't heard him approach, and she jumped at the sudden shadow man sitting shoulder to shoulder with her.

She held her breath, waiting for him to make the first move, waiting to find out whether her judgment about him was good or if this folly would ultimately result in her demise.

He grasped her hand and whispered, "I have to make this short. Tonight hasn't been a usual night. There's been a lot of traffic back and forth. Did you talk to your people?"

"Yes."

"And?"

"We're a go. For now, you're on a need-to-know basis with me as your only contact."

He nodded. It was an almost imperceptible acknowledgement in the darkness of the night. "I have two messages." He pushed paper into her palm. "One of them is for your eyes only."

"Okay." She shoved the papers into her pocket.

"Jordan?"

She turned her head, trying to meet his gaze. She wanted to get a glimpse of that blue, but, even though they sat shoulder to shoulder, it was too dark. "What?"

"I know what happened in Circle City tonight. I'm glad you're okay."

She tried to swallow down the swelling lump in her throat but she couldn't clear it enough to utter her thanks for the sweet sentiment. He leaned into her. "You are okay, aren't you?" His hands roamed the darkness until they found hers and held them tight. "Jo, what is it?"

His kindness shattered the thin veneer of normalcy she'd worked so hard at. Before she could stop it, an unexpected sob ripped free.

"My roommate was killed tonight." She choked the words through a rough throat.

"Dennis?"

She gaped at him. "Yes. How did--"

"I'm so sorry." The words whispered to her through the darkness, and the warm air they traveled on wafted past her cheek. He stood and pulled her to her feet, wrapping his arms around her. The small kindness meant so much and was a poignant reminder they were all built the same. Experienced the same emotions, faced the same fears, no matter the designation.

His warm hands lay flat on her back. Her breasts pressed against the plane of his body. It felt unbelievably good to be comforted by him.

He was so close. She tilted her head up so they were face-to-face, and his step forward pushed her closer to the wall at her back. There was still a small part of her that remained perched on the brink of panic, waiting for the strike that would kill her. It screamed to be heard. He stroked her tenderly and shushed her before she had the chance to voice an objection. She stayed alert and skeptical of his motives. Nothing this sweet ever happened to her, not without strings or unforeseen ramifications that would surely become apparent to her way too late in the game.

But as time elapsed in that intimate embrace, the rigid muscles poised to make a fight-or-flight decision, relaxed. And with the realization he wasn't the enemy and wasn't going to hurt her, the hug of consolation crumbled her defenses even further. Another partially choked sob shot out of her before she could stop it.

"Oh God, Jordan, please don't cry."

She straightened her spine and inhaled a big gulp of reality. "I don't cry, Patrick," she said between clenched teeth. "Crying is for the weak, and I'm not weak."

But she couldn't find the strength to pull away. They stayed there for several minutes, relative strangers breaking the law with a gentle embrace.

Their hearts thundered against the other's chest. Their breathing synchronized.

Then Jordan spoke again. "I'm sorry for being so emotional. It's just that I'm partially responsible for all those murders." She shook the pall of her feelings away and tried to rebuild the facade of the strong woman who was third in the resistance's chain of command. She composed herself and tried to pull away from the large male holding her. "I have video. Do you know someone who can post it undetected?"

He nodded. "Yeah."

She removed her handheld from her pocket and handed it to Patrick. "Take the whole unit. I'll get it back from you tomorrow." He stuffed her mini-compad down the front of his pants.

He must have gotten some hint of her horrified expression because he shrugged his shoulders and said, "You can't be too careful." He rumbled a low chuckle. "Plus, when I give it back, I'm hopin' you'll think about where it's been every time you pull it out of your pocket." He followed with an eye wag and a Cheshire-cat grin.

Exasperated, she rolled her eyes at his shadow. He was like no man she'd ever met. He let it all hang out. He knew how he felt and wasn't afraid to tell the world.

She shook her head. "You're crazy."

He grabbed her hand, brought it up and pressed his lips to the top, then didn't let go. They stood, connected, in a suspended moment in time. A million thoughts cascaded through her brain, following all possibilities of proceeding with this attraction to their ultimate conclusion. Imprisonment, torture, death.

But the ultimate conclusion in his mind was not only positive but probable. She saw it in his eyes. So naive and idealistic.

It made her smile.

"I'll see you tomorrow. Same time. Hopefully it will be more like a normal night."

"Yes, okay." She nodded.

He peeked his head out from between the two buildings to see if the coast was clear. "Wait until I'm back in the building before you pass by."

"Okay," she whispered.

"Jordan?"

"Yes?"

"Stay safe." Patrick bent and placed a kiss on her forehead. "Tomorrow," he whispered, and then turned and walked back toward the brightly lit area of the border guard station.

Jordan waited a couple of minutes and then moved under cover of darkness back toward Circle City. When she passed the border station, Patrick sat alone at his desk working on a compad. She wondered if he would be the one posting the video. It would be ironic if the damning footage was posted by a Guardsman. She was strangely satisfied at the thought.

Despite the fact she wasn't wearing her jogging shoes, Jordan ramped up her walk to a light jog. She needed to burn off all of the emotions of the day. She needed to be very, very tired in order to accomplish the task of falling asleep in her bed without Dennis.

An hour later, sweat dampened her shirt as she approached building twelve. It was the middle of the night, and she was exhausted.

When she opened the door to her dark apartment, the room was heavy with hot, stagnant air. She closed and locked the door behind her and walked further into the room, unbuttoning her shirt and then toeing off her shoes. Remembering the papers Patrick gave her, she fished them out of her pocket and turned right, into the bathroom, flicking on the light.

She looked down at the two folded squares of paper resting on the flat of her hand. One displayed a J on the outside. She opened the other one and read Patrick's message to the resistance leader and then noticed her hands were tinted the rusty brown of dried blood. She shifted her gaze and found more stains on her shirt and knees.

She dropped the notes on the vanity. Knowing she wouldn't survive waking up tomorrow morning with Dennis's blood on her skin, she turned on the shower, letting it warm up while she removed her panties and bra. It took an enormous effort to gather up the strength she needed to take a five-minute shower.

When Jordan finally climbed into the tub, she sat under the spray, letting it hit her back while she soaped up her hands. The lather was the color of the red New Atlanta clay, and after doing a cursory wash, she dropped the soap and let the hot spray hit her. Relaxing even further, she closed her eyes. She slumped and her mind drifted. She was almost asleep when an internal signal forced her awake.

She stood, turned off the water and wrapped a towel around herself barely able keep her eyes open.

When her gaze landed on the folded note with the J penned on the top, she grabbed it and, leaving the bathroom light on, walked the few steps out of the bathroom to her bed. Hands trembling, she unfolded the paper and read the short sentences that Patrick had written to her.

Jo,

I was hooked the first night we met and I've looked for your beautiful brown eyes ever since.

You must think I'm crazy. I'm not.

I'm an optimist.

It will work.

I think everything we do together will work.

PO

Jordan stared at the paper, reading it a few times and then set it on her night table. She flopped back onto the bed and couldn't find the energy to swing her legs up to join the rest of her body.

She'd been poised on the edge of sleep again when a tap on the door sounded. She groaned. "Go away, Xander." The tap sounded again.

She was getting pissed off. She needed some time to recoup. A silent rage triggered inside Jordan's head as she sprung to her feet and stormed to the door. She knew she was losing it. She shouldn't be ready to rip him to shreds just for knocking on her door. Unlocking and pulling it open, she yelled, "Dammit--"

But when she caught sight of the person standing on the other side of the threshold, the tirade she'd been ready to rain down on Xander disappeared.

She gasped. "Patrick."

Chapter 4

Shane ignored the tone that sounded from his earbud, signaling an incoming com. His hands were busy pushing Trent's face into the mattress while savagely thrusting his cock into the man's exquisitely tight ass.

He took in the view of the sweaty male form laid out before him. It was his to rule, use and discipline as he wished. Trent was his conquest for the evening. He was physically larger than Shane, but submitted so nicely.

Shane ran his hand over the reserve of lube puddled just above the crack of Trent's ass. Then, lowered himself so his body covered him. His nipples slipped over the sweaty skin of the man beneath him with every brutal thrust Shane delivered. He reached around and grabbed the man's bobbing cock. It fit heavy and diamond hard in his fist. Trent's soft groan of protest drifted through the sweaty air.

"You'll hold it until I say, or you will be disciplined again," Shane growled, pumping his hips and fist in unison.

He knew Trent was trying hard to hold back that impending explosion of ecstasy, hoping to please Shane. Hoping Shane would consider taking him on, even though he'd been straight with Trent from the beginning, cautioning him he would never take a male as his own.

Shane wasn't gay, but sometimes he was forced to take satisfaction where he could get it, and sometimes the only way he could get it was with a man. He didn't mind as long as it didn't happen too often. Truth was, he got a bigger high from dominating a man, but he wasn't sexually excited by them. With a man under him, it was all about the dominance, power exchange and control. When he found the right person, it would be about both, domination and sexual gratification. Plus, he didn't think he'd ever feel the compulsion to take care of a man like he would a woman. But it was sweet of Trent to try anyway.

"Please," Trent cried, seeking permission to come while so near orgasm.

He was rigid with the effort to hold back the bursts of relief. Shane delivered another brutal twist of the wide cock head at the apex of his stroke and Trent's back curled upward, like a cat. Then, crying out, he thrust hard and fast within the tunnel of Shane's fist. Cum spurted and rolled, warm on the outside of his hand while Trent rode his orgasm to the very end, shooting cum onto the clean, white sheets. And when he was completely done shooting his load without permission, Shane covered Trent's mouth with his cum-slicked hand.

"Bad."

He thrust hard and Trent whimpered.

"Boy."

He thrust again and came in Trent's ass. "Fuck yeah," he spat with a wild, uncontrolled series of pumps that continued his orgasm, coating Trent with his cum, both inside and out.

Shane stayed with Trent only as long as he needed to before he made a beeline for the door. When he reached the courtyard, he knew something wasn't right. Crowds of people milled about, yelling and crying. He stilled, taking in the commotion, and then remembered the com he received earlier. He tapped his earbud. "Play."

"Hey, bro. I need a favor…"

* * * *

Jordan's jaw dropped open a second before she lunged forward and pulled Patrick over the threshold into her apartment, closing and locking the door behind her. Her knee-jerk reaction to protect him from being seen outside her door was significant. Apparently, her subconscious had already made its decision whether Patrick was dangerous or not.

She turned and eyed him by the light spilling from the bathroom and attempted to clarify her confusion.

"No. Not Patrick," she said. "Who are you?"

The man smiled at her. "Shane O'Connor. The older and more handsome version of Patrick."

She couldn't prevent her lips from quirking up at his remark. "Also the slightly skinnier version."

"Ah, yes. I miss my ma's cookin'."

"Twins?"

He nodded, smiled and then gave her an obvious once-over. "Patrick was right. You're very pretty."

She looked at the floor, not sure how to respond to his compliment. In her life, compliments were few and far between, and when one was given, it was usually related to work, not the way she looked.

Realizing she stood there wearing only a towel, she walked to her dresser and pulled out a nightshirt.

"Now don't be getting dressed on my account," he said with a more serious tone than she'd ever heard Patrick use, even when they were in danger.

"Ah, and there it is, that O'Connor humor. It must run in the family." She noticed his Amber designation tattoo and the slightly more aged patina his face presented compared to his identical twin. "Why are you here, Shane?" she asked softly, assuming he was there at Patrick's request, but not knowing exactly why he stood in her apartment in the middle of the night.

"Patrick commed me. His message was cryptic, but I got the gist. Your roommate was killed?"

Jordan nodded and looked away from him, not wanting to reveal weakness. It was an automatic behavior more than an indication that she didn't trust Shane.

"Patrick wanted me to stay with you and make sure you're okay." He shrugged. "He didn't want you to be alone."

Jordan sighed, then nodded. "Thanks. I was settling in for the night." She motioned toward the far side of the bed. "You can sleep on that side if you want to join me."

As she climbed under the covers, she didn't care whether Shane was friend or foe. She was too tired.

Shane sidled over to Dennis's side of the room and removed his shoes.

"I don't know what I'm going to do about that brother of yours," she murmured into the shadows created by the wedge of light escaping through the partially closed bathroom door.

"Can you fill me in on exactly what's going on? Like I said, our communications are kind of cryptic."

Jordan lay on her back, looking at the ceiling. She didn't know where to look while he got ready for bed. God, already she missed Dennis with a desperate urgency that scared her. With him, awkwardness about that kind of stuff vanished years ago. The two of them were comfortable with each other. He was the only person in the world she ever experienced that odd sensation of comfort with. Jordan's throat tightened and she swallowed hard to push down the fear that was already returning.

The bed dipped as Shane slid in beside her. He reached out and clasped her hand in his.

Her breath caught and her heart squeezed. He couldn't possibly fathom how grateful she was for that tiny span of his skin touching hers.

"Okay. Enlighten me on my brother's escapades." His voice was rough and his words didn't echo that almost nonexistent accent of Patrick's musically lilting speech and ever so slightly rolled pronunciation of the letter *r*.

"I'll give you the headlines. We can fill in the rest tomorrow morning." She turned to look at him." Your brother has just joined the Amber Resistance. I'm his contact."

Shane unclasped their hands and lifted himself on his elbow. "He did what?"

"He saved me the other night after the Sterilization Center fire. He kept me from getting caught. He likes me, I think." She sat up. "I got a note. You can help me decipher it."

"No problem, Patrick's encrypting is my specialty."

She handed him the paper and watched him squint in the low light, reading the small script.

"Okay, translated from cryptic to English, it says, Don't eliminate him because you're an Amber and he's a Sapphire. He thinks the resistance movement will be successful, and the two of you will be successful. That's what this…" He pointed. "I think everything we do will be successful means." Shane lifted his gaze to Jordan's. "He's got it bad for you."

He handed the paper back to her and lay back down. Jordan returned the paper to her stand and then returned her attention to Shane.

He had a big grin on his face, like Patrick's. "I bet Ma's going to tan his hide when he tells her." His grin turned wickedly evil. "Oh, what I wouldn't give to be a fly on the wall when that happens."

"When he tells her about me or about joining the resistance?"

He chuckled. "Both."

"It didn't occur to me that there'd be any family to approve or disapprove." She yawned and could no longer keep her eyes open. "This is a conversation we'll have to save until morning. I need to sleep," she murmured. "Would you mind rolling over to face the window?"

"No, lass, I wouldn't mind at all."

After he rolled to face away from her, she cautiously slid closer, bringing her knees up to her chest and tucking her head under her arm. How quickly she reverted back to the way things were for her before Dennis, when she found shadows of intimacy and comfort in unconventional and covert ways because she gave her heart away too quickly, thinking that the touch meant more. She'd been totally new at all of it back then. Now, she steeled herself against the false intimacy. Tonight it would be so easy to succumb to the illusion that the man lying beside her cared about her.

She'd done that when she first arrived in Circle City. But to her, the closeness between Ambers was all a cruel joke, because the intimacy was a fleeting sensation that left just as easily as it appeared.

* * * *

It was early when Shane slid out of bed. The sun was just starting to lighten the eastern sky from black to a deep blue. He turned to look down at Jordan. She was curled in on herself, reminding him of a fetus.

He stooped for a moment so he could peek at what the arm over her head was hiding. Her face was softer when she slept. There was no mettle, no boldness there in her features without her will to guide them, just an innocent face with pouty lips.

He shook his head. What was Patrick thinking?

Grabbing his pants, he treaded to the bathroom and locked himself in. He immediately recognized the handwriting on the tan square of paper lying on the counter. It was a note from Patrick. He picked it up and read it.

Hedman,

Me and some of my friends were hoping to be invited to your next party. I'm thinking you may have already met my brother. If not, look him up so you can invite him, too. As I've already mentioned to Jo, I'll be around again tomorrow if you want to hook up and maybe fill me in on what's happening. You'll have to let me know what you want me to bring to the table for your next blow out, and I'm there. I won't bail on you. Promise.

PO

Huh. Patrick had a group of people willing to help. That meant Ma already knew about everything he'd gotten himself into. Shane smiled at the thought of his mother giving his twin what for.

God he missed her. He missed everybody he grew up with in the Sapphire Zone. Because of the empty, lonely feeling he experienced when he let his mind wander to them, he'd become good at redirecting his attention to something else before his thoughts gained a foothold and submerged him like they used to.

Turning his attention back to the note, he continued. Patrick wanted him to join the cause on this end. He wanted to meet Jordan again tonight. He was willing to do what they need him to, and he wanted them to know they could trust him.

Shane turned on the water in the shower and pulled his earbud out of his pocket. Putting it in, he activated it.

"Com Patrick."

When he heard the tone indicating he should leave a message instead of his brother's voice, Shane sighed. "Sorry I missed you, bro. Just shooting you a com to tell you our friend is okay and sleeping now. I'll keep an eye on her, but I'm not sure what else you want me to do. I just wanted to let you know. *I* prefer we're on the same page. So...that's it. Later." Touching his earbud again, he disconnected.

After his shower, Shane began cooking breakfast in the standard galley kitchen along the rear wall of the apartment, by the door. Jordan slept without moving while he clinked and sizzled in the kitchen. When the powdered scrambled eggs and potatoes were done, he turned the burner off and went to the bed.

He gently touched her arm to shake her awake, and she jumped up with wide eyes, swinging her fist.

Shane jerked out of the way of her right cross and caught it with a firm grip around her wrist. It only took a split second more before she gained her bearings.

"I'm sorry I startled you." He loosened his clasp on her arm and caressed her forearm to her elbow before letting go completely. "Breakfast is ready."

He walked back to the kitchen, filled the plates with food, and brought them to the small, two-person table on the other side of the kitchen counter, separating the cooking area from the rest of the apartment.

Jordan sat on the edge of the bed.

"Go on, before it gets cold," he said, back on the move into the kitchen. When he returned, he set out two cups of tea and then sat down in front of one of the plates of food. Jordan looked at him from her perch on the bed. She smiled and moved to the table. "Thanks."

He nodded and shoveled a congealed lump of eggs into his mouth. "I've been thinking about things this morning. The group that's willing to help will be my mother's people."

She cocked her head and picked up her fork. "People?"

"Yeah. My parents are Irish, from Ireland. They were in the States for their honeymoon when the virus started spreading. They were stranded here when the Gov shut down the airports in an effort to contain it. Anyways, early on, before even the walls were completely finished, my ma quickly made friends with other women of Irish descent. They flocked to her, actually. I think her accent reminded a lot of them of their mothers or aunts whoever they'd lost in the pandemic.

"In the last two decades she's fought hard to keep the customs and history of our ancestry alive. Every person with even a molecule of Irish descent has been absorbed into the Sapphire Zone's Irish Heritage Club.

"She'll contact those she trusts completely. I'd say you have a good-sized group of people waiting to do their part. One person, my cousin Kyle, pops to mind because when I left, his job assignment was as a tattoo tagger in the Sapphire Zone Designation Center. Once every few months or so, he was called to the Peacekeepers Compound in the Emerald Zone to tattoo palm codes in new Guard recruits. He'd also have access to official ink colors and a tattoo machine if you ever needed it."

"Access to the Peacekeepers Compound. That's where General Morgan spends his days."

"He's the one who's ultimately in charge here in New Atlanta. The people we vote for are his puppets."

"I agree," Jordan said. She stared off as if in another world for several moments before her serious gaze met his. "So really, our ultimate goal is to assassinate General Morgan and hope everything else will fall with the dictator."

"If we wait until Kyle has access to the Peacekeepers Compound, he can drop an innocent-looking package with a bomb inside in the right place and walk away. They wouldn't even know it was him."

"Maybe, but we'd have to know where the right place is. I have a friend, Rock, who's an Emerald. He may be able to help with that. I think the first step is to have Patrick contact Rock." Jordan ate a few more bites before she set down her fork and pushed the plate away. "How did Patrick know where I lived?"

"There's a citizen database on the compad in the border guard station."

Jordan nodded. "He can look up anybody?"

"I think so."

"Okay. The first task is to have Patrick and Rock connect and see if Rock can get intel on General Morgan's office location and his routine-- like what days he's there, usual hours, if he's in his office around the same times each day. And if there are any times when he thinks Morgan has substandard or no security.

"It's a good place to start. I'm also going to assign you as my protection duty on all future meets with Patrick."

He looked up from his food. "What makes you think I want to join you?"

"Patrick assumed you would. You don't?"

"I didn't say that either. I have to talk to my brother first. Don't you have to check with the resistance leaders before you start making decisions like that? Let them know about me, and see what the higher ups want me to do?"

She scowled at Shane. "No."

Shane sat silent for a minute, weighing the possible reasons why she didn't want to tell the resistance higher-ups about him. Either she *was* a resistance higher-up, or the resistance was a bunch of dreamers with no real experience or knowledge of what it would take to topple the Gov. He wanted to know which of those options applied, because he wasn't going to put his ass on the line for a ragtag, disorganized effort to overthrow a military dictatorship.

"No. Why?" He looked at her straight-faced and silent.

"Don't worry about it, Shane. This is not an amateur operation."

"If I'm going to do this, I need to know some details. Only an idiot would follow blindly, and I'm no idiot."

Jordan sat back in her chair, eyeing him. The pros and cons, checks and balances of the situation were displayed in her expression like a vignette. She pressed her lips together and tapped her fingernails on the table in front of her.

He was just about to react to her drawn-out silence when she sat back and sighed. "I'm third in command of the Amber resistance. I'm in charge of the liaison meetings with your brother, and I command all offensive missions like the sabotage the other night…and assassinations when the time comes. You'll be introduced to my superior today, but that will be it for now until I feel satisfied you and your brother aren't setting me up. Until then, it's me and my boss. That's it."

"I'm impressed. How'd you get so high up in the chain of command?"

"You mean being a girl and all?" She stared him down as much as a little peanut like her could. But when their gazes remained locked after several long seconds, she handed over the dominant position in their exchange and looked away.

"Yeah." He smirked at her. "With you being a pixie-sized little girl and all."

"I'm a cop."

She spoke those three words with pride but it took a moment for it to sink in. "Ahh, I didn't know that." But, as the information penetrated, he saw it in her. He smiled. "It suits you."

"What's your job assignment?"

"I work the landscaping crew and waste removal for Gov buildings and parks."

Jordan picked up the empty dishes from the table and walked around the counter to enter the kitchen. "Can you help me encrypt a note for your brother?"

"Sure."

"I honestly have no clue how to get all of this information down in a way that won't compromise him if the paper is found on his person," she called over her shoulder as the dishes clinked in the sink.

"I wouldn't write anything down except for maybe that Rock guy's last name. The less written down the better."

Shane stood and wandered around the living area of the apartment. It was oddly bare, especially on Jordan's side of the room. No photos, no girlie baubles, nothing personal at all.

Just as she'd finished the dishes, there was a knock on the door.

Jordan glanced over at him and smiled. "Good money says that's my boss."

The buzz of conversations from the crowded hallway resonated through the apartment when she opened the door. "How are you doing?" It was a woman's voice.

"I'm fine," Jordan murmured.

"Good." This time it was a man's voice. Shane heard the apartment door close and lock as the man and woman walked into the living space of the apartment. The man was tall, dark and serious. Recognition played over his face as he focused on Shane. Shane recognized him, too. They'd been in the same class at the Wellness Center many years ago.

Jordan introduced Xander and Jaci. Shane shook Xander's hand and nodded to Jaci. The two women sat at the table, and Xander leaned back against the wall with this arms crossed. Jordan filled Xander in on the meeting with Patrick she apparently wasn't supposed to have last night, according to Xander, and she gave him the written message from Patrick.

They discussed their thoughts about assassinating General Morgan, and both agreed that Morgan's assassination would be Jordan's next mission.

Xander seemed galvanized when she told him Patrick would be able to contact Rock. "After he makes contact, let me know. It sounds like you've got everything under control." He looked over at Shane. "You're going to have to teach Shane how to use a gun. We're having an in-service on shooting at the meeting tonight, but you'll have to do it with him one-on-one for the time being."

Shane whipped his head around to meet Jordan's gaze. "You have guns?"

Xander nodded. "Only about twenty-five so far, but if you're protecting Jordan I'm going to have to insist you have one during the meets."

"No problem."

Xander put his finger up to signal him to wait a minute and touched his earbud. "Yeah? When? Did you see it? This will be good for us in the long run. We're working on contacts outside of Amber so if we need internet we can probably use one of them. Alright."

Before Xander even had a chance to fill her in on the call, Jordan said, "I forgot to tell you, I gave Patrick digital footage of the massacre last night."

Xander smiled. "He posted it on the net. People outside the Amber Zone are making comments and asking questions. Nice job, Jordan. He put an arm around her shoulder "So…you're sure you're doin' okay?" His voice was soft.

"Yeah. Shane spent the night with me. So far, dealing with this has been easier than I expected. With everything that's going on, my mind has been on other things."

Xander looked to Shane. "Are you staying again tonight?"

"Yeah. I'd planned to."

Xander nodded. "Good."

"I'll send someone over with a gun for him. Teach him to shoot before you leave for the meet," he said, facing Jordan. "I need to get going. I have a lot of stops today. I'll want to be briefed tomorrow on how things go tonight." Xander looked over at the woman he'd brought with him. "I'll meet you in the courtyard, sweetie." Then he motioned to Shane. "Come on, I want to talk to you." Shane followed Xander down the crowded hallway and caught up to him in the elevator, but the ride to the ground floor was silent.

When they were out of the building and standing off to the side in the courtyard, Xander finally spoke. "I want to make this perfectly clear so you can make informed decisions and act accordingly."

Shane nodded and studied the man standing in front of him. He was grim-faced and carried an air of intimidating authority. "First, every member of the Amber Resistance believes we're fighting for the freedom so many soldiers before us have given their lives to protect. We're all willing to give our life for our beliefs. This is going to turn very ugly, very fast. So if you're just hanging around with Jordan to get your dick wet, I'd take a moment to reconsider your plan. Second point." He held two fingers out in front of him. "You are subordinate to Jordan. Outside resistance business you can behave as you wish, but when it comes to making decisions and following orders, she is the general, you are the grunt. Do you have a problem with that?"

Shane glared at the man standing in his personal space. Because of the class they'd both taken, Xander knew he was a dominant, knew he'd have difficulty giving up control. "No. I'll respect her authority."

Xander nodded. "Point number three, and this is the most important one so listen closely. If you or your brother are spying for the Gov, I'm giving you the opportunity to walk away, right now, no questions asked. Later, if I find out you're really not on our side, I will kill the both of you." Shane watched a muscle work in the Xander's jaw before he spoke again. "It would be easy enough. Patrick's a sitting duck in that bright fishbowl every night. And if Jordan gets hurt because you're a traitor," Xander growled "I'll kill your fucking parents too." He leaned in toward Shane until they were in each other's face. "Are we clear?"

Shane nodded once and then gritted between his teeth, "Crystal."

He didn't like the insinuations and was not accustomed to being treated as if he were under the authority of any man. But Xander, he'd indulge. They were similar, running neck and neck on the dominant-male scale.

"Good. You're her shadow until she or I says differently. Keep her alive."

"Don't worry about her. She'll be fine during the meets with both me and my brother watching out for her."

Xander nodded. "I'll see you tomorrow then."

He walked away from Shane without another word. The man was a force to be reckoned with, but needed help with his people skills because now, after the threats, Shane was pissed off.

Chapter 5

Jordan stood at the apartment door, hugging Jaci goodbye, when she saw Shane striding down the corridor toward them. Their gazes locked and she instantly felt his demeanor had changed. He looked...meaner, harder in some way.

What had Xander said? Because clearly, a different man from the one who left the apartment minutes ago was walking toward her. Jordan said her goodbyes to Jaci and followed Shane back to the dinette table.

"You look different. What did he say to you?"

He didn't answer, just sat there with that peculiar look on his face. He was in a serious stupor of the hit-with-a ton-of-bricks variety.

She recognized it. Months earlier, after the first resistance meeting, she'd seen it in her own reflection after she realized she was chest-deep in some serious fucking business. It was time to transform from a dreamer of freedom to a fighter of freedom. The time for talking, wishing and planning ended and the transition from conversation to action eventually had to include the inevitable slap in the face of reality.

It wasn't too late to back out. She hadn't done anything that would get her killed yet. Was she in or out? Every person had to make that final decision on their own, weighing the ramifications.

All of that had settled on her shoulders at once. On that night, she had to acknowledge some dire facts. She would probably have to kill and may even be killed for the decisions and choices she was making. It was on that day, after she'd made the decision to fight for what she believed in, she understood that she was a soldier at war.

After a long pause, Shane shook his head and smiled. Then, his deep blue eyes flashed mischief. "He said you're the general and I'm the grunt."

"Ahh." She laughed. "Let me return the favor and decipher that message for you because I've had a lot more experience with Xander-speak than you have." Jordan thought for a couple of seconds before she spoke. "He's afraid you won't take me or what we're doing seriously because you're new and have no clue as to how big or how organized this revolt is. I'm betting he gave you a very clear picture so you know exactly where you stand with him."

"Yeah, I'm completely filled in," he said, drily.

She looked into his serious eyes and furrowed brow. "Good, because he means what he says." She walked to her chest of drawers and began to rummage through it. "Now, I need to take a shower. You hanging out?"

"No. I have to go back to my apartment and pick up some things."

"Close the apartment door behind you when you leave. I'm not going anywhere so you can come back any time you want. We won't leave to meet Patrick until eleven."

Jordan tucked the clothes she'd gathered under her arm and locked herself in the bathroom.

The conversation with Xander had freed up enough of her brain cells that her thoughts wandered to Patrick while she showered, and she couldn't wipe the ridiculous smile off her face. He had to be a little crazy to want to pursue any connections with her, romantic or otherwise. Even if she were optimistic, it would be some time before she and Patrick would be able to openly associate with each other.

And what happened when Patrick found out she wasn't the woman his imagination had conjured up? Heartbreak for her. She would be the one to suffer.

But right now, it felt so good. The flirting and sexual innuendos were new and thrilling and even though her intellect told her nothing good would come of what was between them, her insides fluttered with excitement at the thought of seeing him again.

After she'd exited the shower and dressed in her uniform, she searched the apartment for paper, with no luck. Finally, she pulled a label off of a can of chicken broth in her cupboard and hunted around for something to write with. This paper-and-pencil thing was way past old-fashioned, rapidly advancing on archaic. She carefully ripped the label into four pieces and tucked three of them away.

With a twinge of disappointment, Jordan forced herself to be realistic as she wrote her response to Patrick. When she was done, she slipped it into her pocket and sat in the quiet room, thinking about the past few days and feeling slightly unhinged without her usual routine, without Dennis.

It was starting to get dark by the time Shane returned. He left the apartment door open when he arrived, and the constant background chatter of the crowd in the hallway brought life into the silent dreariness

Jordan settled into during the long, lonely afternoon. He looked like he had things on his mind as well and stayed in the kitchen preparing food instead of spending time with her.

Later, Xander's runner, Journey, walked through the open door. Jordan smiled as Journey turned and looked into the galley kitchen adjacent to the apartment's entrance and then leaned back checking the number on the door, verifying she was in the right place. "You're not Jordan."

"I'm at the table," Jordan called out.

Journey closed and locked the door behind her and walked in looking shy, as always. "Xander wanted me to give this to you." She pulled a handgun and a box of ammunition out of her bag and set them gently on the table. "Can I sit down for a minute?"

Jordan looked up, surprised at the request. "Sure. Want something to drink?"

She shook her head. "No, thank you." She swallowed and then took a deep breath. "Xander told me that you're going to try to make contact with Rock."

"Yes." Jordan made the connection, and she kicked herself for not realizing it right away. Journey had been Rock's roommate for many years before he got transferred to the Emerald Zone.

She and Rock were the most unlikely pairing she'd ever seen. Journey was delicate and fragile, like fine china, and Rock was the proverbial bull in a china shop.

"If I write him a letter, can you get it to him?" Her voice was always more of a whisper than normal speaking volume.

Jordan straightened. "Your letter would actually be a big help in opening the door for our Sapphire contact. Rock's not likely to trust just anybody approaching him. This might help to smooth the way. Do you think you could have it done before eleven tonight?"

Journey beamed. "Absolutely. Bring it back here?"

"Yes. It would help if you could put something in the letter Rock would know could only have come from you."

"Done."

After Journey headed out with a promise to be back before eleven, Shane turned to Jordan. "What's your plan?"

"No plan. Just a way to soften Rock up a little. He's going to be suspicious that this is some kind of trap. Journey's letter will be an excellent way to confirm to Rock that Patrick is working with us."

"Good idea." He gave her a flat, serious stare. It was overwhelmingly apparent something was still bothering him.

"Now let's eat. You can teach me how to shoot after dinner."

Shane was quiet while they ate, and he was all business while Jordan taught him the features of his sidearm and how to aim and shoot it. Then they repeatedly reviewed protocols for possible scenarios during future meets.

It was close to eleven when Journey came back to drop off her letter. "He'll know it's from me," she said to Jordan as they left the apartment together. Journey grasped her hand and held it in hers while they walked to the elevator together. Shane followed behind them.

When they landed on the ground floor, they went their separate ways, with Jordan and Shane walking left toward the Amber Zone, and Journey walking right to reenter Circle City.

She and Shane set off into the night. Not a word was spoken between them during the long walk to the border guard station. The man beside her had not been the same since he left the apartment with Xander.

The night was quite dark again, with only a tiny crescent of the moon shining. They waited in the alley for less than a half hour before Patrick slipped into the hidden sliver of safety.

"Jordan," he whispered as he continued to close the space between them, backing her toward the building. "I've got time tonight. Everything is back to normal, slow and boring," he whispered, still advancing on her until her back was against the wall.

"No hello for me, bro?"

Patrick's spine straightened as he turned. "Oh, God! Shane."

Jordan witnessed a profound moment between the men as they hugged each other and had a soft conversation while in the long clutch. The long, shameless embrace between the two men illustrated just how intimate their bond was. It was as if two halves became whole.

They were together and for them, the rest of the world fell away. They were in their own reality, frozen in time, like a scene in a snow globe, with a flurry of wild emotions filling the space around them. When they finally separated, Patrick grabbed Shane's upper arms and looked him up and down. "You're getting skinny."

Shane skipped the pleasantries. "I'm about ready to beat your ass for what you've got us mixed up in."

Patrick chuckled. "What? Overthrowing the Gov is an inconvenience to you? Or are you turning into a pussy over there in Amber." Even with the low light, Jordan saw Patrick's dancing blue eyes and the mischievous grin. "I can't wait to tell Ma. She'll finally have her proof of which one of us is the brave one."

They both laughed out loud and finally Patrick dropped his arms, breaking the contact between the twins.

"Let's get the business out of the way," Jordan said, fishing out Journey's note to Rock. "I want you to contact a friend of mine. His name is Rock. Last name Rodgers with a D. He's an Emerald now, but he's on our side and can help us quite a bit once we make a connection with him. Here's a letter from his former roommate. They were very close, and it will give you proof that you're working with us. Don't let him intimidate you. He's a nasty bastard, but he'll definitely want to do anything he can to help us. You need to establish a secure way to exchange information with him. I'll leave that up to the both of you.

"We'll figure something out," Patrick said in his musical, almost but not quite Irish accent.

"Here's the roommate's letter." She leaned in and lowered her voice. "And there's a small note for you folded inside."

The broad grin that transformed his expression from all business to boyishly charming was immediate. He stepped closer to her. "Is it good news or bad news?" he asked as he took another step closer and wrapped his arms around her. Then, with his lips next to her ear, he whispered, "I hope it's good."

Never before had Jordan ever lost the ability to speak. She didn't lose her head or panic in dangerous situations, but at that moment, she did all three. She swallowed, willing her mind to work and think of something adequate to say.

He ran a hand from the small of her back up to the nape of her neck. "Jo, please tell me it's good news." The breathy whisper raised gooseflesh on her arms.

"It's not bad news," she whispered back.

He let her go slowly and reached into his pocket.

"Here's your handheld." Jordan didn't need to see his face to know it held a playful grin as he slowly slipped it into her back pocket with wandering hands, taking full advantage of the fact she was rattled and couldn't put two coherent words together.

"Okay, okay, back to business," Shane interrupted.

Jordan nodded and snapped out of the slow-motion trance she'd just been in. "Shane's right. The longer we're here the more dangerous these meetings get. Shane told me about Kyle. Is he still a designation tagger?"

"He is."

"You need to contact him and find out whether he's willing to be a part of this. Let him know up front that this will be dangerous. He'll be putting his life on the line."

Patrick nodded. "Will do."

"How long before you want to meet again?"

"Give me forty-eight hours. I hope to have news from both of those men by then."

Jordan nodded. "I'm going to give you two some time." She looked at Patrick and then to Shane. "I'm pulling back to our safe position. Don't be too long." A second later she was out in the night, leaving the two men behind.

* * * *

"She's a beauty, ain't she, bro?" Patrick said after Jordan slipped into the night.

"I'll agree with you on that point, but I'm having problems with the rest of it."

"The rest of it?"

"These people are organized. They have weapons. They are going to try to overthrow the Gov and assassinate General Morgan."

"I know. I'm countin' on it, Shane, or I wouldn't be pressuring Jordan so much to give me a chance. I've got some serious chemistry with that girl. Plus, you need to come home. Ma's not the same since you've been gone."

The carbon copies faced each other. "What are your reservations? Maybe I can put them to rest."

"This is going to be very fucking dangerous, Patrick. It's the kind of shit that will get you killed. It won't help Ma to have your corpse being delivered to the ovens," Shane admonished in an angry whisper. "Are you willing to put everybody's life on the line? Because you need to know that the leader of the resistance, threatened to kill our whole family if I was spying for the Gov," he went on in an urgent whisper.

"You're not, are you?"

"Of course not."

"Then you have nothin' to worry about, do ya?"

"They are balls-to-the-wall serious about this, Patrick. You need to be too."

"I am."

With a huff of exasperation, Shane brushed his fingers through his hair. "They're planning a coup."

Patrick leaned into him, placing a palm on his brother's shoulder. "So am I." Patrick made sure he was close enough to Shane that the determination in his eyes was apparent. "So am I."

Shane glared at him in the dense silence that followed and then, eventually, he released a long held breath and nodded. "Alright. I'll do my part on my end. I've been assigned to protect Jordan, so at least we'll be seeing each other regularly." Shane edged toward the opening of the alley. "I don't want to leave her alone too long."

"I'll see you in two days then?"

"Yeah." Then he smiled. "It's good to see you. Tell ma that her favorite son says 'hello.'"

Patrick nodded. "Yeah." His throat closed with emotion. It was as if being in Shane's presence brought precise focus to what he'd been missing these years since Shane left. His brother's Adam's apple bobbed up and down. The two of them had always shared the same thoughts. It seemed time had not changed anything. Their gazes met and grief reflected back at him. "I know. I feel the same."

Shane nodded, turned and fled into the night.

Patrick waited a minute, and then he headed out from between the buildings toward the brightly lit border. Jordan's note weighed heavy, like a rock, in his pocket. By the time he entered the building and sat at the desk, he felt near crazy not knowing whether this particular rock was the cornerstone of a new relationship or just the rubble of his hope. She'd given no indication what it might say during their meeting, and that made him nervous.

In the eerily silent room, it was easy to hear his heart pounding in anticipation of Jordan's return message. After he'd unfolded Rock's letter and found the tiny note from Jordan to him, his hope faltered. It was too short, only one sentence.

PO

Explain to me how you're expecting this to work.

Jo

Sitting back in his chair, Patrick smiled. Now, he could work with that. He had forty-eight hours and endless ideas. Then he read the letter to Rock Rodgers from Journey. He entered Rock's name into his compad and the screen filled with the man's vital information.

Patrick thought for a moment, then touched his com. "Send com Rock Rodgers-Emerald."

He waited for the tone signaling him to start his message. "Rock, my name is Patrick O'Connor. I have news from an old friend. I was hoping you'd make the *journey*"-- he stressed the word and then paused for a few beats-- "to meet with me tomorrow in the Sapphire Zone."

Patrick touched his earbud to disconnect and began to identify other things he needed to do before he saw Jordan again. He was startled a few moments later by the tone signaling he had an incoming com. He touched his earbud. "Play." The reply from Rock was terse, almost a growl. "Where and what time?"

"Reply." He paused. "Sapphire Zone library nine AM. How will I know you?"

Thirty seconds later, he got his reply.

"I'm an Emerald and I'll definitely stick out."

That was easier than he'd thought it would be.

When he got off work, Patrick walked into the brisk morning air. He enjoyed this time of year. It brought the slow departure of the oppressive summer heat in New Atlanta along with a show of leaves to appreciate in the perfect sunny daytime temperatures.

He felt on top of the world, with hope and excitement consuming him, as he walked the mile from the border guard station to the library. Jordan had not shut him down. The chemistry between them was conspicuous, and their second meeting smacked of serendipity. He didn't believe in happenstance or coincidence. Those concepts were for the faithless. Jordan was plopped right into his lap and he had to believe there was a reason for that, and for his intense need to have her as his.

The long, lonely hours of the night shift had given him plenty of time to hammer out a plan that would make both of the women in his life have hope. And Jordan *was* officially in his life, whether she knew it yet, or not. He wasn't going to let her go, wasn't going to give up. It felt right. His body hummed from the flood of destiny that coursed though his veins whenever she was in his presence.

The library was still closed when he arrived at the steps of the old building with carved pillars in the front. It was one of the few building that retained its original function after the pandemic. The inside was just as detailed with crown molding, antique tables and study carols. The first time he'd been there as a child, he was awestruck with the sheer volume of paper books. It gave him a weird sense of being connected to the past when reading a book someone held in his hands half a century ago.

He strolled another two circuits around the area, killing time and watching for indications something was not as it should be when he became preoccupied with the thought there may be some useful knowledge in that building.

Everything on the intranet the Gov considered subversive was purged, and they heavily monitored and controlled the news feeds, minimizing radical ideas and information. But…how thorough had they been with purging the library? Surely it would be much harder to censor information secreted in the millions and millions of pages inside these walls.

Patrick was the first person through the doors after they were unlocked. He roamed the nonfiction shelves, trying to get an idea if there was any usable information there when he happened upon an area that had military themes to the titles. He found a book on developing and cracking codes, pulled it from the shelf and walked to a table that provided a good view of the library entrance.

Less than two minutes later, a huge, dark-haired man with tattoos on his neck and arms entered behind a mother with two small children. The mother walked one direction and the man in another. The man's Emerald tattoo shone boldly on his skin. This was Rock. He was right. He definitely stood out.

Rock stood still for a moment and scanned the room, just as Patrick had done earlier. He was nonchalant about it, and even though the man's gaze scanned Patrick, he gave no indication it made any difference to him at all that there was a Guardsman there. He grabbed a book after his initial investigation and sat down at the complete opposite end of the large reading and study table area. Rock obviously wasn't expecting his rendezvous to be with him, a man in a National Guard uniform.

Patrick stood and approached Rock's table. When he sat down, the man's eyes widened for just a moment before he regained his blank facade. Patrick slid the letter across the table toward Rock and watched as he picked it up and read. His expression was different while his gaze skimmed over the words. He almost looked sad. When he finished, he folded the paper carefully, as if it was a treasure, and leaned to one side so he could slide it in a back pocket.

He looked to Patrick. "Who did you get this from?"

"Jordan."

Rock nodded. "Thank you." He moved to get up.

"That letter was not why I contacted you. It's a verification that I'm on the right team."

Rock hesitated. "Okay, now I know you're on the right team, what do you want?"

"I was asked by the Amber Zone resistance to contact you. Jordan believed you would want to be involved and help out where you could. Is this true?" he asked in such a quiet whisper that it had Rock leaning in to him to hear the words.

Rock nodded. "The Sterilization Center fire, was it theirs?" he asked in an equally hushed tone.

"Yes."

"Who's the resistance leader?"

"I don't know. They don't trust me enough to tell me that information yet."

Rock smiled. "You've got balls contacting an Emerald like this."

"They may not trust me, but I trust Jordan not to lead me into a trap."

"They'll trust you soon enough."

"Right now, all she wants me to do is make contact and set up a safe way for you and I to exchange information. Here in public like this is too dangerous. We need something more secure for ongoing meets."

Rock nodded and looked down at the open book in front of him for a while and then asked, "Where are you stationed?"

"Amber Zone border crossing, gate one."

"That's pretty far from where I live, and it would cause suspicion if I started regularly crossing into the Sapphire Zone when I haven't been before. The Gov watches me closely when I'm in the city. Most of the time I'm in Onyx."

"You're on the recovery team?"

"Yeah."

"That may be useful to us. There are a lot of things you have access to in the Onyx Zone they may need. I think we're going to need a way to transfer items as well as information."

Rock nodded. "When are you meeting Jordan again?"

"Tomorrow night."

"I need some time to think about this. It's important we get this right. Our meets have to be secure." He rubbed a finger over his bottom lip, appearing lost in thought. "The morning after your meet with Jordan, come back here. I should have worked things out by then."

Patrick nodded his assent

Rock glanced down at the book lying on the table in front of Patrick. "Codes--smart. When you decide on one, pass the key on to me. It doesn't hurt to have extra security if we're forced to write on paper. Two days." Without another word, Rock rose and left Patrick sitting alone. Jordan was right. He was an intimidating SOB.

After Patrick exited the library, he pulled Jordan's handwritten note from his pocket and read it again. Oh she of little faith. Showing her how this was going to work was the easy part. He smiled and he knew exactly how to prove to her. It would be as easy as falling, and if he had his way, that's precisely what she'd do--right into his arms.

Chapter 6

A wall of hot, stagnant air collided with Jordan's cooler, sweat-dampened skin, as she and Shane walked into the dark apartment. She was exhausted and wanted to flop onto the bed and hibernate, just insulate herself from the outside world in oblivion.

But, she could actually smell herself and needed to rinse off before she climbed between the sheets. "I'm taking a quick shower," she said as she made a right turn into the bathroom, already unbuttoning her uniform shirt.

Only a drizzle of water escaped the shower nozzle when she twisted it on. Something was wrong with the shower…or the water. She opened the bathroom door, catching Shane in his boxers, and walked to the kitchen. When she lifted the faucet handle, barely a trickle escaped from there as well.

"What's wrong?"

"I think the Gov has shut off our water." Jordan lifted a shaky hand to her temple. "People are going to be panicked when they wake up in the morning and nothing but a slow dribble comes out." She walked back into the room and touched her ear bud "Call Xander."

A second later he answered. "What."

"My water is off."

He grumbled. "Hold on. I'll check mine." Jordan heard the rustling of sheets in the background. "I'm getting just drops here. Dammit." The thud she heard on his end was no doubt his fist or foot slamming into something. "I'll call Rush. The PD can release a statement. This is not resistance business."

"Yes, I know that. But it's happening because of what we did, what we're doing."

"We expected shit like this to happen. We talked about it, Jordan." A long pause passed between them. "Have you slept yet?"

"No."

"Go to bed. I'll make sure you're not called for extra duty. And don't forget to call me when you wake up to debrief me about your meet."

Xander disconnected before she could say another word.

The slow uncoiling of senses when the brain stopped processing and will was not enough to continue against the strain of fatigue crept up on her. She didn't have enough left in her to deal with everything that had happened. Each event in the past two days wore away at her stamina and her sanity. She was empty, totally depleted. With a sigh, she closed her eyes.

She became aware of Shane as he picked her up and turned to move toward the bed. His strong arms cradled her and she allowed herself to nuzzle into his chest for a moment.

He tenderly laid her down and then walked away from her toward the exit. Her anxiety spiked and then two full seconds of panic ensued until he turned into the kitchen at the last moment. For a second, she thought Shane was going to leave.

Jordan watched him move around on the other side of the counter. He was bare-chested, and she took in the subtleties of his musculature when he turned to face away from her. She was a fan of the male back. She appreciated the way the muscles and bone moved and shifted under the skin, how the broadness of his shoulders tapered to narrow hips. The biggest benefit of the male back was she could admire it when the owner had no clue they were being ogled.

She sighed and closed her eyes as her mind began to roam into the fog of presleep. Her ears tracked Shane's movement when he came out of the kitchen and sat down on the edge of the bed beside her. He pushed the hair away from her face and smoothed cool heaven over her forehead, cheek and neck. Then he pressed the water soaked cloth on the opposite cheek.

She sighed again. "Thank you."

She opened her eyes when he stood, and she watched as he unfolded the dishcloth. "Take off your shirt," he said as he returned to the kitchen.

She ignored the demand and closed her eyes again instead. She had almost succumbed to the sleep beckoning her when Shane unbuttoned the last two buttons of her shirt. Jordan didn't open her eyes. She just let him do it. His hands skimmed over the sensitive skin of her chest and abdomen when he spread the shirt wide. The sensation of the cool cloth as he laid it over her bare torso relieved her heated, sticky skin.

She groaned at the exquisite relief his ministrations provided. The sound was intimate and reeked of sexual pleasure even to her own ears, despite the fact that it wasn't her intention. She opened her eyes to find Shane's stunning gaze gliding over her. She attempted to cover her bare skin, but he caught her hand. "It's a hundred degrees in here. I'm planning to sleep in my boxers. There's no reason for you to wear all these clothes.

She shook her head. "If Patrick knew we slept in the same bed with barely anything on. Well…I don't want to hurt him."

"Neither do I. He asked me to be here. He knows how it is in Amber, the touching, the boy-girl roommate and sleeping arrangements. That's why he sent me here last night. He knew you'd be alone, and he didn't want that for you. Now relax. I'm almost done."

Shane left the bed to rinse out the cloth once again, and Jordan let her body go limp. She was so tired, even the touch of unknown hands couldn't raise enough alarm within her to object any more than she already had.

When Shane returned from the kitchen, he unbuttoned and unzipped her pants and peeled them away, and then he finished wiping her down without a word. His hands were gentle and innocent, staying away from sexual places. Her thoughts wandered while he cleaned her and Jordan found herself hoping his hands weren't so innocent. She knew sex wouldn't change how she felt inside. It wouldn't pacify the raging anger and grief.

Only one thing could do that and now that Dennis was gone, she had no idea how to get it. Jordan's eyes began to fill with tears she fought to hold back.

Jordan fell asleep with silent sobs trapped in her chest and turmoil ravaging her to her very soul.

When she woke at nine AM, she flicked on the video feed before going to the bathroom. She crawled back into bed and pulled the sheet up, tucking it under her arms while sitting back against the headboard. Printed words scrolled across the bottom of the screen, breaking the story that the viral video of an Amber massacre was a fake. The crawling words reported it was a sick joke staged by some unstable Ambers in order to gain attention and sympathy from the other zones. The report of arson being the cause of the Sterilization Center fire also crawled across the screen and indicated the Gov had a high level leader of the terrorist group identified.

Jordan and Shane looked at each other after reading that tidbit. "Who do you think it is?"

Shane shrugged. "Your guess is as good as mine, but it will be someone they want to get rid of."

At ten AM, the General was scheduled to make a statement regarding the arson and fake video. Shane and Jordan sat next to each other on the bed watching the podium, waiting anxiously to hear what he had to say.

When Morgan stepped onto the podium, his ice-blue eyes looked with distain at the people assembled before him. His flashy uniform displayed rows upon rows of medals pinned to the front. He looked as if he'd waited for this moment his whole life. Even though it was well known that the press reported their news from the Gov's prepared statement, reporters still played the game and yelled out questions.

Morgan leaned in toward the microphone. "Good morning." Then he cleared his throat and looked down at the minions yipping at his feet like dogs begging for a bone.

"Yesterday morning, the Amber Zone Sterilization Center was destroyed by a terrorist group gaining support in the Amber Zone. Not since the time of our grandparents have US citizens been forced to suffer through the ever-present threat of terrorism on our own soil. We didn't back down then, and we won't back down now."

He paused for a moment, allowing the audience to clap in reaction to the rousing statement. "These domestic terrorists are a rising threat to our way of life here in New Atlanta. There are a growing number of Ambers that want to do away with the Repopulation Laws and strip away the system that has allowed us to rebuild and thrive."

Morgan raised his voice as he went on.

"I say to them, Ambers are not the only people who have sacrificed during this rebuilding. We've all sacrificed. We must remember we've done it for a reason, the most important cause of all, restoring our great nation to its former supremacy and reclaiming our standing as a world power.

"Only through our painful sacrifice will the US return to its rightful place in the world community, and we will do it with stronger and smarter citizens. Our recovery from this global disaster has excelled compared to the rest of the world because of our forethought and planning. While other countries have returned to the dark ages where anarchy rules, where stealing and killing for food is the norm, we've survived and thrived. We've maintained a modern society with laws and technology, and we've proved our exceptional ability to sacrifice for the greater good. The success we've had rebuilding our society has been difficult for all of us, not just Ambers.

"Your country recognizes the sacrifices of all the people of New Atlanta We've only been able to get this far because of the heart-wrenching suffering of those around us. Future generations will remember everything your generation has given up to make them healthier, smarter, stronger."

He paused for a moment and looked down at the faces tilted up with rapt attention. "Now, I'd like to address the hoaxed video posted yesterday. I ask all of you, did those terrorists really believe the smart people of New Atlanta would fall for their staged massacre? They're so simple, they don't understand the citizens of the other zones easily see through their ruse.

"I urge every man and woman to be diligent. Only with your help will we be able to find the anarchists and protect the infancy of our way of life and punish the sick individuals who think they're doing us a service by committing crimes and subverting our ideals. So today, I tell all of you--if you are not part of the solution, you are part of the problem. Do not hesitate from alerting the Guard of suspicious activity. We must all work together to ferret out this new threat. Show these dangerous Ambers we won't allow them to dupe trusting people like our neighbors and friends who've fallen for the rhetoric of the terrorists. Justice will find those who remain unaccountable for their crimes and, no doubt, are planning their next."

The urgency and volume of his words escalated to the point he was almost shouting. The man was insane, rabid with fanatical thoughts and spreading those insane ideas with charisma and a tone of certainty and authority that would play on most of the population's paranoia regarding the Amber population.

"They must be stopped. If we let this attack go unanswered, the good work of the Repopulation Laws will be spoiled. It's not popular, but the truth remains, people are designated Amber for a reason. They are a collective of diseased, mentally ill and ignorant people, and they are dangerous to us all. Ambers are like curdled milk added to the most delicious recipe. One cannot undo the damage after the spoiled liquid has been mixed in. If we allow Ambers to intermingle with the rest of us, they will quickly spoil the superior genetic pool of Americans we have achieved over the past two decades. We must not allow it!"

He pounded his fist on the podium. "How can we in good conscience let the sick and feebleminded grow in numbers again? As before, they will become burdens to the Gov, requiring social-welfare programs like the days of old.

"History has shown these people are a weight around the neck of the country. They will destroy us from the inside. We cannot allow imbeciles and the diseased to procreate unchecked. We cannot give them the option of choosing whether they want to utilize birth control because it is the stupid who procreate irresponsibly, not knowing or caring what the consequences of their behaviors might be.

"Until I can assure citizens of their safety once again, our courageous Guard will be stepping up patrols of all zones. They will be enforcing new curfews in all zones as well until this threat is neutralized.

"It is unfortunate that good people have to suffer for the actions of a few, but for now it will be assumed anybody caught outside their homes after nine PM, are terrorists and they will be arrested regardless of their designation.

"Only together can we fight this insidious menace. And together we'll create the best country this world has ever seen."

He took his hands off the podium and stepped back. "Thank you and God bless America."

He waved and smiled at the audience as they applauded him before the news feed cut out.

Jordan glanced at Shane. "He's very good at what he does."

He nodded and let out a long sigh. "Yes, he is."

Chapter 7

It took Patrick two full days to arrange everything the way he wanted for his next meet with Jordan. He'd barely slept since the meeting with Rock the day before, and after finally getting some quality sleep before his shift, he was energized and felt as ready as he was going to. Excitement built within him as he went about his business straightening up his apartment to pass the time before work. Chuckling, he shook his head. He didn't know if he was more excited about seeing Shane or Jordan. Soon they would all be together.

It felt weird driving his parent's car to work instead of riding the transport as per his usual, but it was all a part of his grand plan.

The first hour and a half of work was excruciating, waiting for his doofus partner to go take his nap. But finally, he was alone with only the soft hum of the fluorescent lights filling the stark space. It was time. He reminded himself failure was not an option during this pivotal encounter with the woman who called to his destiny.

He surveyed the Sapphire side and then the Amber side of the border. When he was satisfied the area was clear, he shot out the Amber door and made his way quickly to their alley. This time, he was the first to arrive, and his heart sank. More waiting. He didn't think he could take another minute of it. His adrenaline surged and he didn't know if it was in anticipation or aggravation. It didn't matter because his blood pressure rose either way. He was a basket case.

He considered returning to the station because the longer he waited for her, the greater the chance someone would notice his absence, although he'd already worked up a story in case that happened. He would not be the man caught red-handed sleeping on the job like his partner. He'd be the Guard bravely leaving his post to follow someone suspicious he'd seen in the shadows.

Jordan and Shane slipped into the darkness next to him seconds later. He took them both in. Jordan was out of breath and Shane didn't look as angry as the last time they'd met. He hugged his brother. "You okay?" he asked, slapping Shane's back.

"Yeah. It's all good."

When they separated, Patrick turned and gave Jordan a quick kiss on the lips. "Hello, Jo," he whispered and then laughed at her wide eyes as he pulled away. "Can you give me a minute with my brother?"

A moment of disappointment played over her features. He smiled reassuringly at her and then pulled Shane aside and told him his plan in the lowest of whispers.

The revelation contained in the short conversation finally did it. Shane grinned at him with delight. "I never thought I'd see the day you got so stirred up over a woman that you put yourself directly on the path toward Ma's wrath. On purpose no less." Shane clapped Patrick on the shoulder, smiling. "It's going to be epic." With that, Shane made eye contact with Jordan and then turned and strode into the darkness.

Patrick returned to Jordan. "Are you ready?"

Her expression was quizzical. "Ready for what?"

"For me to answer your question." Patrick watched the slight shake of Jordan's head and the crease between her eyebrows. "You asked how I expected this to work. I'm going to show you. Are you ready?"

She appeared wary. "What are you going to do?"

"I'm going to walk you through to the Sapphire side, and you'll sleep the rest of my shift in the back of my parents' car. I've got a blanket there for you to cover up with, and I parked the car away from the building. Nobody will get close enough to see you sleeping in there."

"Are you crazy? I'd be a sitting duck."

"Not with me watching out for you. I'd never let anything happen to you." He leaned into her. "What's wrong, Jo? You chicken?"

Her eyes spit fire and Patrick knew she'd cave to his will if he questioned her courage because she may be a lot of things but chicken definitely wasn't one of them. He smiled at her, watching while her mind worked through the scenario.

"This is crazy."

"Yes. It is." Not letting her hesitate for another second, he grabbed her hand and pulled her out from between the two buildings, toward the border guard station. They didn't go into the building. Instead, he dragged her over the border through the automobile checkpoint and headed directly to his parent's car. "Try to get some sleep. We have a busy day tomorrow.

And don't worry. Nobody is going to get near this car." He opened the back door and turned to her. She was breathless and looked unsure.

Patrick leaned in, cupped her face in his hands and kissed her hard on the mouth before shoving her into the back and slamming the door behind her.

* * * *

Jordan woke with a start to the sound of Patrick getting into the driver's seat and slamming the door closed. He didn't look her way or say anything until he'd driven away from the border. They rode that way for several minutes before Patrick patted the seat next to him. "Come on, climb up front." Looking over his shoulder, he grinned a wide smile at her. "Don't worry. No one can see you're an Amber from inside the car."

Reluctantly, Jordan climbed between the seats.

"First time in the Sapphire Zone?" he asked as if they both weren't risking their lives.

What the hell was she doing? "I'm not sure this was such a good idea."

"Don't worry. I'm not going to let anything happen to you." He reassured her again, taking her hand. It was such an Amber thing to do. She smiled at him and then studied his face in the light of day. His profile was very Sapphire-esque. To her, the few Sapphires she's seen seemed to have the same bone structure. Their faces were elegant, with higher cheekbones accentuating the fair skin they all seemed to have in common. This, along with their pretty-colored eyes, made them fairly identifiable as a designation even if they didn't have blond or red hair.

Patrick's qualities fit within that standard. She absorbed every detail of his face while he drove and her heart thumped long, loud beats like time was slowing down. *Thump...thump...thump.* Like the heavy steps of a giant shaking the earth beneath her feet, her world tremored. "Jesus," she whispered.

He turned his head for a moment to look at her with those dangerous blue eyes. "What?"

She closed her mouth and shook her head, flying back into the present. She swallowed and took a breath. "Where are we going?"

"We have a packed itinerary. I scheduled as much as I could in the two days you'll be here." He glanced at her with his ridiculous boyish grin.

"Two days? I can't be here for two days!"

"You're going to have to because I don't work for the next two nights." He appeared so very satisfied with himself. It didn't look like he would easily let her go now that he'd gotten her there. The thought didn't bother her as much as it should.

"The resistance leader is going to make mince meat out of Shane if I disappear. They're going to think he did something to me."

"Don't worry about him. Shane can take care of himself. Now here." He handed her a jacket. "Put this on, it will cover your wrist."

This man was crazy. She wasn't going out in public. "Where are we going that I have to cover my color?" She stared at him while he drove. He was still grinning like an idiot.

"To the library." He reached over and placed a hand on Jordan's thigh and momentarily traded his idiotic grin for an expression that more closely matched Shane's, intense and brooding. "Now's a good time to start trusting me, Jo. I'm just as dead as you are if you get caught here with me."

Patrick pulled into the library parking lot, and they waited in the car until the librarian unlocked the door to the main entrance. They were the first visitors of the day, and the gigantic room was still and quiet. He took her hand again, leading her to a table and they sat down next to each other.

She looked at him. "Well?"

"What's the matter, Jo? Don't like sitting with me?" He curled an arm around her shoulders and drew her closer. He turned his head into her hair with his lips brushing the shell of her ear. "Go find a book that interests you. We still have a few minutes."

"I don't want to go anywhere." Jordan laid her head on Patrick's shoulder instead and they sat together quietly for another minute before someone rounded their table and pulled the chair out across from them.

Jordan looked up and gasped. "Rock." Jordan leaned forward and stretched her hands across the table. "Oh my God."

Rock clasped both of her hands in his. "Jordan."

He looked the same dressed all in black with tattoos showing up over the collar at his neck and below the edge of his short-sleeved t-shirt. As usual, he sported a mean son-of-a-bitch look on his face. She traced a finger over the emerald tattoo on his wrist. "Are you okay?" she whispered, staring into eyes that more resembled black holes than windows to the soul. He was not the same man. He looked dead inside.

He squeezed her hand a bit too hard but his mask was in place. He did to her what she'd watched him do to so many others--shut them out. She was no longer in his inner circle. No longer privy to what was going on inside the man.

"When am I not okay?" He was straight-faced. "It's good to see you, Jordan. Now what the fuck are you doing in Sapphire?" His voice was a dangerous growl. He was angry and staring at Patrick as if it were his fault she was there. Well it was his fault, but Rock didn't know that.

"Quit it, hard-ass," she hissed.

He let go of her hands and sat back in his chair.

"Okay, before I forget, I have the key we discussed last time." Patrick broke the tension and slid a piece of paper across the table toward Rock. "From now on all written communication will use that code."

Rock nodded. "I think I've figured out a way to get items in without having to openly meet you, like we are now. If I'm right, there's already a tunnel emptying out into the Onyx Zone?"

Jordan nodded. "It's not complete yet."

"From where to where?"

"From the back of the Wellness Center. We don't know exactly where it's going to end since it's not finished yet and nobody's been on the other side. The digging is very slow going, but people are working on it night and day."

"Okay. I'm in Onyx regularly. Our first stop is always at a rest stop set up for refueling and stocked with food. It will be a long way, but once you get a car running on the other side it should be no problem for someone to drive and pick up the items I've collected and stashed for you. I'll pass on the location and directions to Patrick." Rock looked over at the other man. "On agreed upon days, I'll close the library the night before, leaving the coded message taped underneath this table. You come first thing in the morning to retrieve it. That way we don't have to meet in person."

"Sounds good," Patrick said.

"Rock, can you get onto the Peacekeeping Compound?" Jordan asked.

He nodded. "Why?"

"We need intel on Morgan--the whens and wheres of his days."

Rock raised his eyebrows. "Ballsy."

Then, he smiled at her. It wasn't a stupid grin like Patrick's. It was a satisfied, evil smile. Obviously, Rock had already figured out their goal was to assassinate Morgan. "I'll see what I can do, but it's going to take a while. I'm leaving for a mission tomorrow. I'll be gone about a week. What are you looking for in Onyx?"

"Use your judgment. Of course, the obvious, weapons, ammo, but anything you think might help, like binoculars or body armor. What I'd really like to get my hands on is a Taser. It'll take someone down silently and that's going to be priority if I'm going to infiltrate the Peacekeepers Compound."

In unison both men said, "That's not happening."

They looked at each other, eyebrows raised in surprise, and then looked to her.

"Rock, I have my own command. You don't tell me. I tell you."

Rock stared straight-faced for a pregnant moment. Then, his lips twitched. "Yes ma'am. Who are you answering to?"

She looked at Patrick, wondering if she should reveal the name but decided it wasn't that big a secret since Shane knew the information already. "Xander. And Rush is heading up the whole operation."

"I should have supplies for you by the time the tunnel is done." He looked to Patrick. "I'll be back from my mission in a week. I'll leave an update here on what I've collected when I get back. I'll start working on Morgan's routine." He squeezed Jordan's hand again. "How's Journey?"

"She's doing good. Xander keeps a close eye on her. She's his assistant or runner or whatever you call it. The work has been good for her. She's busy and meets a lot of people doing resistance errands for him in Circle City. She just got a new roommate. It seems like that's going well for her, too." She smiled a wry smile. "I suspect that Xander had a word with the man."

He nodded and took a deep breath. "Good. Tell her I think about her every day." Then before anyone could say anything else, Rock let go of Jordan's hand and scooted his chair away from the table. "I've got to go. Being around me is generally not safe." He stood next to the table looking down at her. His fists clenched at his sides. Jordan wanted to hug him, hold him. He was obviously in pain and alone.

It was hard to see him this way. She knew what the isolation felt like, what it did to a person. It was a pitiful existence. Tears began to pool in her eyes.

"Don't, Jordan. We all have our lots in life. This is mine." Then he walked away with his steely mask securely in place.

After Rock left, Patrick looked at Jordan and took her hand. "Come on. Let's get out of here."

She swallowed the lump in her throat and let him lead her out the heavy wood doors into the gorgeous fall morning. It was the perfect temperature, and the endless blue sky was absolutely pristine with the absolute absence of clouds.

Jordan was quiet during the drive to their next destination. She felt Patrick looking over at her several times, but he must have sensed she needed the quiet time.

He waited several minutes before finally asking, "So what's his story?"

"He was a cop in Amber, like me. The Gov killed his girlfriend then transferred him to Emerald because of his"--she air quoted--"'heroism' in catching a nonexistent serial killer." Her tone was angry and sarcastic, but she couldn't help herself. "It was the Gov's way of separating him from everybody."

"From the way he talked it sounded like Journey was his girlfriend."

"No. Journey was his roommate."

Patrick fell silent. "Roommate relationships are that intense?"

"Yeah. Roommates are family. They come before boyfriends and girlfriends. The men consider caring for the woman assigned to them as a serious responsibility."

Patrick pulled into the small lot of an upscale apartment building and parked. "Home away from home," he said to her before coming around the outside of the car and opening the passenger door. He held his hand out and smiled. "This is my apartment building."

She walked hand in hand with him into the building's elevator and looked at her reflection in the stainless steel doors during the silent ride. The doors opened to an empty corridor, and an eerie dread tickled down her spine. It didn't feel right. There were no hordes of people gathered everywhere like in Circle City. She hadn't seen a person since they'd turned down his street. It was creepy.

Patrick gave her hand a quick squeeze. She looked up at his scary blue eyes and back down the empty corridor they walked, and doubt crossed her mind.

They stopped at a door and he scanned his hand to unlock it. Jordan took Patrick's left hand and looked into his palm. "I assumed your code was for work things only."

"It's for Guard. For everyone else in Sapphire there's no code, at least not yet, but Morgan pushed for all Gov employees to have a code." He walked into the apartment and held the door for her.

She peered in. Just a living room. No Guard torture chamber or underground prison. She took in the serenity of the apartment as she entered the room. It felt unoccupied, just a space, not a home. "Do you have a roommate?"

"No. And I don't spend much time here."

She looked over her shoulder at him. "No? Where do you sleep?"

"My parent's house, mostly."

"You're close with them?"

"Yeah. My mom, she's all about family. What about your parents?"

Jordan turned away from Patrick's gaze. "My parents are dead. Now that Dennis is gone, I don't really have any family at all."

Patrick stood silent behind her, and she quickly changed the subject. "It's so..." She shook her head and turned in a circle to take in the entire room. "Is that your bedroom?" She pointed up at the railing skirting the open end of an upper room.

"Yeah."

"It's so cozy." She looked around and then down at the floor. "It's the carpet and the colored walls, I think."

He walked farther into the room. "Come on, sit down." He motioned to the couch and sat down at one end, angling himself toward the middle. She did the same on the other side.

The couch was the color of dark honey, the walls the color of sand. She ran her hand over the ultra soft upholstery of the couch and then nuzzled her cheek to it. "Jeez, it's so soft."

Jordan looked into his deep blue eyes and immediately felt a shift in the space between them. They were alone and free of other, more immediate, issues.

"Do you think I could take a shower? They've restricted our water supply in Amber for the last few days. We're getting just enough to keep us alive, not enough to bathe with."

A few beats passed, and then Patrick cocked his head. "Are you scared of me, Jo?"

She shook her head. "No. I'm sorry, bad timing but seeing Rock threw me. I need to take a shower and pull it together. Is that okay?"

"Sure." His expression turned her insides upside down. It was... interested. When he looked at her, she felt as if he actually *saw* her instead of skipping his gaze over her, placing her within whatever crowd she was in.

"Let me show you."

She followed him up the twisting metal stairs to the upper room. The decor was the same palette of neutral tans, off-white and browns as on the first level. "My mom borrowed some clothes for you from one of her friends so you wouldn't have to stay in the same outfit for two days."

Jordan glanced at the long, flowing skirt and peasant blouse draped on the bed. There were also pajamas, yoga pants and a t-shirt. He turned on the light in the adjoining bathroom. "The towels are clean." He leaned against the doorjamb and peered at her with slightly hooded gaze. They roamed up her form. His inspection trailed up her thighs to the apex between her legs, then moved up to her breasts. Her breathing accelerated when their gazes met. He licked his lips and smiled like the devil on vacation. Several more seconds passed.

"I like you, Jordan. So much that you're just about all I think of lately."

"You don't really know me, Patrick."

He took a step forward. "Isn't that why you're here? So I can get to know you?"

She looked down and stared at the plush, chocolate-colored carpeting, wondering what, exactly, he saw in her. "I guess it is."

He took two more steps, landing him only a foot away. With immense effort, Jordan yanked her gaze from her feet and lifted her chin. He looked down at her with blue flames sparking in his eyes. She held her breath eager to feel his skin touch hers. A rush of anticipation swam through her veins.

He hooked out a hand and circled it around the nape of her neck, gently pulling her the last few inches toward him. Gingerly, as if she was a skittish animal, he leaned in and touched his lips to hers. His kiss was gentle and sweet, and he groaned as soon as their tongues touched. Like dancers dressed in steamy velvet, their tongues rubbed, circled slowly one against the other.

He firmly held the back of her neck and wrapped an arm around her waist, pinning her to him. Her head tilted all the way back and her body bowed from his aggressive, seeking lip-lock while his large hand cradled her ass, pressing her closer to him. It was the first romantic kiss she ever received and a flash of fear about what they were starting nearly immobilized her.

When Patrick broke the kiss and looked down at her with need, his breathing was labored and his cock was hard against her belly.

"I need a shower," she whispered.

"Okay," he breathed back, releasing her and stepping away. The look on his face reflected how difficult that single step had been for him. "I'll be downstairs. Take your time." He didn't leave, though. He just stood, chest heaving and eyes flashing hot promises as Jordan closed the bathroom door behind her.

She twisted the spray on in the shower, immediately appreciating the strong current of water shooting from the nozzle. She stripped off her clothes and stepped inside the glass-enclosed stall. Steam already started to billow and swirl and the hot, pounding of water on her bare skin was bliss.

While her body steeped in the comfort of the water, her brain delved deeper into the dynamics of her situation. She wasn't sure how to react to the desire Patrick had for her. He wanted more than sex, she was sure. Nobody would risk all they had, home, family and freedom for a piece of ass, no matter how sexually repressed Sapphires were. But she still had a hard time accepting his feelings at face value.

Unlike most women in Amber who'd been treated like treasures since the day they were born, she was not accustomed to an expression of affection being pointed in her direction. Most Ambers went from the doting unconditional acceptance of their childhood home to the protection of their roommate when they reached adulthood. She wasn't those women.

She was neither pretty nor delicate. And she just couldn't figure out what was really going on with him, why he liked her so much. She was a person who couldn't even draw the love of her own parents let alone anyone else's.

She was sticking her toe into an ocean she'd never swam in before and the thought kicked up her heart rate. She'd never had sex with someone she had feelings for or who had feelings for her. Sex in Amber definitely did not carry the same weight as it did in Sapphire. Here, sex meant something more, it was indicative of feelings. It was a precursor to love.

Men wanted pretty, delicate women. They wanted flowers that needed to be constantly cared for and doted upon to thrive. She was more of a weed, wild and tough. One that had been plucked until there was practically nothing left and still survived, coming back stronger, but uglier too. Uglier in ways she didn't think she could ever share with Patrick. He wouldn't understand. She didn't want to set herself up for the hurt that would follow when he found out she had issues.

She'd never be able to pass for normal, so she hadn't ever tried before.

"Fuck. What am I doing?" She cursed under her breath and turned so the hot spray hit her face.

This addiction was going to be the end of her. She already felt the need coiling. She'd been fighting it for the last few days. But what started as a subtle surge of emotions pressing against her insides was now clamoring to be released.

"Oh, Dennis," she whispered into the steamy air of the bathroom, swallowing a sob and chastising herself for being so weak. With Dennis gone, she'd have to find a way to deal with her addiction, but Patrick wasn't the answer. He'd be disgusted with her if he knew. She didn't think she could face that kind of judgment from the first man who wanted to have something more than a meaningless biological release with her.

Jordan pushed herself out of her melancholy introspection and picked up the soap. Now was not the time. She couldn't lose focus and forget the true reason she was there. She had a mission objective. She was a soldier. The rest had to be secondary.

She finished showering, dressed in the flowing bohemian skirt and blouse, then finger combed her short, brown hair behind her ears. Pixie-sized, Shane had said. She smiled at herself in the mirror. It was not the first time someone had used the word pixie to describe her, but the other time they'd been referring to her haircut. She straightened her spine and took a deep breath.

Jordan met Patrick in the kitchen. He was preparing breakfast.

She nearly gasped out loud when she saw him crack a real egg into a bowl. She peered around his shoulder as the last one plopped into a bowl with three others. "I've never seen a raw egg before. They look weird." The floating yellow bubbles in the viscous fluid were not what she thought raw eggs would look like.

He raised an eyebrow. "No eggs in Amber?"

"Only powdered."

"You're in for a treat. Could you grab a couple of plates and some silverware?" He pointed to a cupboard. "I'm almost done here," he said as he pressed the lever on the toaster, sending two pieces of bread into its depths. She set two place settings at the round table and then sat at one of them.

He peered over his shoulder at her while he still worked on swirling the cooking eggs. "Are you tired?"

"No, not really."

He smiled. "Good. We've got a big day ahead of us."

Chapter 8

Jordan spotted Patrick's hesitation as he looked at her surreptitiously. She knew that look. It was an apology before the fact. To her, it signified that whatever he was about to say was not something she wanted to hear.

"My mom wants to meet you."

"Uh." Jordan felt the blood drain from her face. "She does?"

He nodded.

"Why?"

He cocked his head and raised his eyebrows. "Really?" He stepped toward her. "You don't know the answer to that question?" Another step. "Because I haven't made my feelings about you a secret to anybody." He pointed at her and then poked her in the center of her chest with his index finger. "Including you," he whispered. They were close together, face-to-face, with his finger tracing lazily over her chest. The heated moment held electricity, and the hairs on the back of her neck stood at attention.

Abruptly, he turned, dispelling the moment. Disappointment dashed her secret hopes as he placed two plates on the table and sat down with her. "Now eat. You're going to need the fuel to withstand the whirlwind that *is* my mother." He smiled. It was a devilish expression meant to relax her. But Jordan's insides still clenched with anxiety. "I got the impression from Shane that she wasn't going to be my biggest fan."

"Don't worry. That's been handled. However, she is an inescapable component of this visit." He chuckled. "You'll see why."

Jordan pricked the yellow part of the egg and watched it drain over the white before she cut a piece and put it in her mouth. Her eyes fell closed. "Mmm. This is so good." It tasted nothing like the add-water-and-cook eggs she'd eaten her whole life. "No wonder Shane's so much thinner than you. If I had food like this to choose from, I'd be a few pounds heavier, too."

"This?" Patrick snorted. "It's not too hard to mess up. Wait until you taste my ma's food. You're going to think you died and went to heaven."

She smiled before shoving another forkful of egg into her mouth. Maybe a meeting with his mother would have some redeeming qualities. They ate together in silence, with only the clinking of flatware on the plates passing between them. When Patrick was done, he leaned back in the chair, watching her until her food was gone too.

"Since I didn't get yelled at for sending Shane over, I assume he's helped you adjust a little easier to your roommate being gone?"

"I thought he was you at first." She laughed. "I yanked him into the apartment so fast I'm surprised he didn't get whiplash."

He met her gaze. "He's the next best thing to having me lying next to you." There were sparks in the deep blue eyes regarding her. The charge in the air was undeniable.

"Patrick," she whispered. "I'm flattered--"

He abruptly stood, scraping his chair against the wood floor. "Stop right there. I don't want to hear the rest of that sentence." He gathered up the plates and stowed them in the kitchen sink, then returned, holding a hand out to her. "Come on. Let's get going."

The sexual tension in the air dissipated and was replaced by his good-natured aura. She nodded and stood.

Jordan searched the streets during the five-minute ride to Patrick's parents' house. The few people walking on the sidewalks carried the physical characteristics of Sapphires. It struck her as odd that their expressions were somber. They should look happier than the people living in Amber.

"You grew up here?" she asked when he pulled into a driveway.

"Yep."

Jordan didn't move to get out of the car after he turned the key to shut off the motor. The brick house was cute, with a riot of flowers growing in the front beds and a tiny sculpture of a leprechaun next to the front entryway.

"It's so…" Normal was the word she wanted to use. The car, the house, the scented soap in his shower, the real eggs, it was all so surreal to her.

Suddenly, Jordan was very aware of how much she didn't belong there.

She was so deep inside her own head that she hadn't noticed Patrick walk around the car until she heard the sound of him opening the door beside her. She looked up at him, debating with herself whether she was going to get out, when the front door of the house opened.

Patrick's mother stood outside on the porch before Jordan could voice her misgivings. She was red-haired and rosy-cheeked, smiling from ear to ear. Jordan's muscles relaxed when she felt the woman's good-natured demeanor from her seat in the car. Patrick pulled Jordan from the passenger seat and guided her toward his mother.

"Jordan Ford, this is my mother, Kate O'Connor."

"Jordan." Patrick's mother grabbed Jordan and hugged her breathless. "It's so good to meet you, lass. Just call me Ma. Everybody else does." The woman let her go from the embrace, but still held Jordan in front of her, grasping the sides of her arms and examining her closely. "I have to get a good look at the woman who's got my Patrick in such a state."

"Alright. Leave the poor woman alone, Ma. You're goin' to scare her right back to the Amber Zone."

"I wasn't sure if Patrick told you I was an Amber."

"She knows everything, Jo," Patrick piped in. Her expression must have transformed, revealing the trepidation she felt about more people knowing about her presence in Sapphire.

"Don't worry. Your secret is safe with me." Kate hooked an arm through Jordan's. "Come on inside. We've got a lot to talk about."

Jordan looked behind her to make sure Patrick was coming, too. He winked at her when their gazes met.

They walked through the front door and headed toward the back of the house into the kitchen. "Sit. Sit down," Kate said, pulling out a chair for her. "Would you like something to drink?"

"No thanks."

"So tell me how Shane is doing. Give it to me straight now. I'll have no fibbing from you to soften the blow."

"I've only known him for a couple of days, but he seems to be doing well. He's thinner than Patrick."

Kate frowned. "Is he now?"

"He says he misses your cooking."

Kate's face lit up. "Of course he does. No girlfriend?"

"Not that I've seen."

"Shane's moved in with Jordan. She lost her roommate in the massacre last week."

The woman turned then and met Patrick's gaze. "Really? How did that come about?"

"I asked him. He's joined the Amber Resistance, too."

"I just thank God he wasn't killed. I know it's selfish of me. So many other young people died, but…" She swallowed hard and Jordan saw pain darkening her eyes. "I miss my boy."

She turned away from the table where Patrick and Jordan sat and busied herself putting together a small plate of sweets and a kettle on to boil. "I'm sure I don't miss him half as much as Patrick does." She glanced at her son lovingly. "Those boys never had more than a few feet between them for their entire lives. Peas in a pod, those two."

Kate O'Connor looked terribly sad at that moment. She knew it, too, because she turned away from them again even though her busy work at the counter was done. "Right, boy?"

"Right, Ma."

Kate O'Connor promptly set the food on the table and then began a stroll down memory lane, dragging Jordan with her. She was regaled with sweet stories of Shane and Patrick's mischief and the uncanny connection they shared during their very traditional childhood.

The stories and the obvious love Kate had for her boys made Jordan's heart ache. Her whole life she'd secretly wished to have a mom like this one. Love saturated the air and filled the whole house. She was sure neither one of those boys had ever wondered if they were loved. Jordan's throat squeezed shut at the thought, and she was close to spilling tears when Kate's eyes began to water, too. The woman's separation from Shane was obviously traumatic, though she was sure Kate tried to hide it.

"Alright Ma, much as I'd love to sit here all day, fully knowing that at some point you're going to pull out the naked baby pictures, we've got to leave soon and I haven't filled Jordan in on the meeting we have scheduled."

"You haven't?"

"No."

"You better get to it. I'm going to go freshen up." She patted Jordan's arm. "I'll see you in a little while."

Jordan looked to Patrick. "What's going on?"

"Tonight is the first meeting of the Sapphire resistance."

"You formed a resistance in two days?"

He scooted his chair right next to her, slung an arm around her shoulder and leaned in close. "I did."

"How many?"

"About a hundred."

She turned her head to look him in the eyes as alarm rose within her. "That can't be right. How do you know each one of them is trustworthy? Numbers aren't worth anything if someone turns us in to the Gov."

"It's hard to believe, I know, but what's even harder to believe is we sat here talking with my mother and she didn't mention she's founder and president of the Irish Heritage Club. She holds court with the women of every Irish family in Sapphire. She's godmother to damn near every Irish child born here in the last quarter century. She trusts every person she's talked to. Promise."

He whispered the last word into her ear and the hot air from the whisper sent a shiver down her spine.

"Okay." She nodded. "It makes sense that a club would be spearheading the Sapphire resistance. I've always thought it was to the Gov's advantage that the entire population of New Atlanta were strangers to each other. Even now, twenty-five years after the pandemic, the number of family members a person has, even in Sapphire, is limited. It's hard to know who to trust when practically everyone is a stranger."

"Her club will be our cover for meetings. The Guard aren't going to be bothering a bunch of tittering women gossiping and doing crafts." He sobered quickly when he saw she wasn't smiling back.

She was in shock. "A hundred people." She shook her head. "It's more than I could ever have imagined."

Patrick scooted away from the table and pulled Jordan's chair toward him. He framed her head with his hand and looked directly into her eyes. "You doubted me," he whispered. "I told you I'm optimistic. If overthrowing a dictatorship is the only thing standing between you and me…" He leaned in and brushed his lips against hers for barely a second. "Then I'm going to get it done as quickly as possible."

Jordan took in a quick breath of air and held it while his lips moved, light as a butterfly's wings against the exposed skin of her face, her neck, her ear lobe. She was, literally, breathless while the warm wafts of his breathing floated over her skin, raising goose bumps on her arms and sending a tickle down her back. He raked his fingers up her nape and through her short cropped hair, grazing her scalp with this nails. Then, with a nudge of his finger under her chin, he angled her face toward his.

Those magnificent cobalt eyes focused on her lips and an unconscious whimper escaped the back of her throat. It was a groan and plea combined and obscene in the way it betrayed her need. She sat frozen as he dipped his head to kiss her.

When their lips met again, the back door of the kitchen opened and the sound of a man clearing his throat broke the thrall. Patrick leaned back in his chair and then gave her a long, sexy look of promise before he turned his attention to the slightly older version of Patrick and Shane standing by the back door. "Aaron O'Connor, this is Jordan Ford."

Mr. O'Connor smiled warmly. "It's nice to meet you, Jordan," he said as his eyes darted to the Amber band around her wrist and then back and forth between the two of them. "I'm sorry to run off, but I have a meeting to attend tonight. We'll talk later." He walked through the kitchen in the same direction his wife had gone before him. "Carry on," he said as he left the room. Almost immediately Patrick leaned in to kiss her again. But Jordan leaned away and started to giggle.

"I have to listen to my da, Jo," he said with a wicked, wicked smile.

"My name is Jordan," she reminded him.

More of the wicked smile. "I know."

"Jo is a boy's name."

Only one side of his mouth quirked up as if he was trying to be serious but couldn't. He nodded. "I don't think anyone is going to mistake you for a boy." He waggled his eyebrows. "Besides, I'm planning on staying close to you so everybody knows you're my girl. If someone's not sure you're a girl after lookin' at you, which I can't imagine by the way."--he looked her up and down and then met her gaze with sparkling eyes-- "I'll be there to set them straight."

Patrick leaned in. "Just one little kiss to hold me over until later?" Jordan didn't have the willpower to turn him down. She'd really only spent a handful of hours with this man, but he was irresistible. The way he treated her was a new experience. Being the focus of his attention exhilarated her and his sweet words softened her sharp edges.

Jordan leaned in the last few inches until their lips met. She was fascinated by the difference between a kiss that meant nothing, like when she engaged in sexual foreplay with a benefriend in Amber, and a kiss from someone who wanted her to be his. It was like the difference between a spark and an inferno.

A few minutes later, Kate and Aaron rejoined them in the kitchen. In a whirlwind of activity, they all transferred the food and drink Kate had made for the meeting into the car and left the O'Connor home.

Tense silence filled the car while Patrick sat next to her, holding her hand. Thankfully, the ride was short.

The meeting room in the basement of the Sapphire Zone Community Center was filled with the white noise of a hundred softly spoken conversations. The vast majority of the people gathered were women and when they saw Kate O'Connor leading their little group to the table at the front of the room, they quieted noticeably.

Kate took charge quickly, yelling, "Take your chairs, please."

A minute later, everybody was seated in the rows of metal chairs and it was quiet enough to speak over the noise.

Kate spoke again. "Alright ladies," she paused and noted the group of men standing in the rear. "And gentlemen, welcome. I've done a lot of talking with all of you over the past two days, so I'm keeping it very brief."

"Mother of God, Kate O'Connor is going to be brief," an anonymous voice rose from the crowd.

"Yeah. Ask her what time it is and she'll tell you how to build a clock."

The laughter that followed broke the tension in the room. She held up a hand with notebook in it. "Once we get down to business, I'm going to pass this around. If you're committing to join we need your name, com and current place of employment. If you have any special skills you think may be helpful write that down, too. I'm giving the floor to Jo. She'll fill us in on what is really going on in the Amber Zone, and help us do some preliminary organization. Jo…"

All gazes turned with Kate's to look at her. Jordan stood and walked around the table she'd been sitting behind and leaned against it, scanning the crowd.

She waffled for a second, not knowing exactly where to start.

"It doesn't really matter how bad it is for us in Amber. Suffice it to say the Gov has just started increasing their brutality against a group of already defeated people, and I pray the Sapphire Zone never has to withstand the persecution the people of Amber do. The point to this meeting, to all of what the resistance has done and will do in the future is freedom. It's been over a quarter of a century since the Gov passed the Repopulation Laws. There is no more need to worry about the eminent extinction of the genetic traits that propagate blond hair and blue or green eyes. The Laws simply aren't needed anymore. The Gov has made the people of the Amber Zone a minority in New Atlanta, giving us labels like diseased and retarded to keep the people in the other Zones scared of us." She paused and shook her head. "Most people are designated Amber simply because they have brown hair and brown eyes. What gives the Gov the right to condemn Kate's son, Shane, whom I'm sure many of you know, to spend the rest of his life away from his family?" She caught Patrick's eye for a second before moving on to scan the rest of the crowd. "My best friend grew up in the Sapphire Zone until she was ripped away from everything she knew and forcibly sterilized. Her story could just as easily have been yours or someone you know, just because of a gene the Gov doesn't like.

"That's it. That's all it takes. Yes, there are some really dumb people in the Amber Zone, as I'm sure there are in Sapphire." A short burst of laughter erupted from the crowd and Jordan waited for it to quiet down before she spoke again. "But the reality is that the education of our children is substandard. This fact ensures that very few men and women born and raised in the Amber Zone will be able to escape to a better designation at the time of their testing. We have no medical care, no money and now the Gov shows no compunction about slaughtering innocent people to send a message, to intimidate those who are willing to fight to change things.

"Tonight, I want all of you to think about the United States of America. Imagine how it used to be fifty years ago, before the pandemic. For almost three hundred years being an American was synonymous with being free. During that time, millions of people, our ancestors, fought and gave their lives so that every person in this country could live and work where they pleased. So we could have as many babies as we wanted. To assure the right to vote for our leaders and the right to own a firearm for protection. They had the freedom to assemble like we're doing now and say anything they wanted to say without having to hide it, without having to be afraid.

"Back then, the Gov didn't write the daily news reported on the video feeds. Those Americans were not afraid to report the truths of their world or fight for what they believed in." She looked around the room at the solemn faces pointed at her. "This is the same country. Though I'm not sure many of our grandparents would recognize it anymore.

"The resistance in the Amber Zone is armed. We are organized and resolute. This will be hard. Once it becomes clear to the Gov that there is a real threat, Morgan will try to teach us all a lesson. He will punish everybody for the resistance's disobedience. It's happened already in Amber with the massacre of innocent people who were not even aware that a resistance existed. Now, they've also restricted our water supply. They will do similar things here. Some of us may die in the fight. So please, think carefully before you put your information down on the paper that's being passed around. There is no shame in thinking about it. I know many of you have small children and other responsibilities that would make joining the resistance difficult. No one will judge if you choose to walk away." She paused. "For those who stay tonight, please know you may be asked to kill for this cause. You may also be asked to do something that scares the hell out of you. And there's a good chance you may never be asked to do anything at all. I can't tell you right now which category you'll fall into. Please, if you have any doubt, I'm asking you to walk away." She shrugged. "That's it, I guess."

Jordan stepped down into the crowd and spent several hours talking with the women. During that time, she saw a few groups hotly debating but she'd not gotten a gist what topic they were debating about. She hadn't seen anybody leave, but she hadn't been looking either.

Finally Kate's voice rose over the crowd. "Come on, get in close. Let's close with an Irish blessing." The room quieted and bodies bunched together until Kate was surrounded by a circle of women. Most of them held hands with the person next to them.

"May God Give you…
For every storm, a rainbow,
For every tear, a smile,
For every care, a promise,
And a blessing in each trial,
For every problem life sends,
A faithful friend to share,
For every sigh, a sweet song,
And an answer for each prayer."

She paused for a few seconds before she looked up at the crowd. "I'll be developing the communication tree within the next twenty-four hours so we'll be able to get information out quickly. Thank you for coming."

Jordan leaned in to whisper in Patrick's ear. "What's a communication tree?"

"My ma visits two people and they visit two people and so on. It's fairly common at least for what I've seen. Everybody in Sapphire limits the use of their coms for social and apparently subversive conversations. You have to assume the Gov is always listening."

"Smart. You guys seem to have your own Gov problems to deal with. I think a lot of people in Amber would be surprised to know that."

Eventually, they were ready to leave. Patrick's parents begged off, saying they'd catch a ride with friends. Jordan and Patrick left shortly after.

Jordan could hardly wait for Patrick to slide into the driver's seat before she began talking. "I can't believe all those women stayed. Why weren't their husbands there too?"

"The Irish, at least at this point in history, are more of a matriarchal type of clan. The women carry much of the responsibility and the men, well, most drink a little too much and do what their wives tell them. It seems to work for all parties involved."

Jordan laughed despite the fact that Patrick wasn't trying to be funny. "So the men who were there?"

"They're the exceptions to the rule."

"And which side of the coin do you fall on?"

It was Patrick's turn to laugh. "I haven't decided yet."

They arrived back to his apartment complex after midnight, and he held her hand as they walked through the moonlit parking lot. The quiet of the night was stark and kind of creepy.

Jordan found herself looking down at her feet when she stepped over the threshold and felt the subtle give of the floor. She wasn't sure she'd ever get used to that small sinking feeling of walking on carpeting.

Without a word, Patrick took her hand and led her up the circle of stairs to the loft bedroom. When they entered, Jordan was softened by the mood of the room. The warm earth tones along with the comforting glow of a small bedside lamp made the area inviting and rich. Her life in Amber seemed black-and-white compared to this colorful day filled to overflowing with new tastes, new friends, she looked to Patrick, new lover. She felt like she was in a dream.

Patrick pulled her into his arms, and her cheek came to rest on his chest. He was an average height for a man, but still towered over her small frame. He bent slightly and spoke next to her ear. "My ma brought some nightclothes for you to wear but I'm hoping we won't need them." The throaty rumble of his words vibrated under her cheek. She arched her body and looked up at him. In the low light of the room his eyes were the deepest shade of midnight blue.

"I won't need them."

The white of his smile flashed, and his expression turned devilish. This man was spectacular. He unbuttoned the top button of the flowing blouse she wore and advanced on her, walking her backward while he leaned in and licked the hollow of her throat. She giggled and attempted to squirm away from the tongue trying to hunt down the spot again. The back of her legs hit the side of the bed, and she struggled to remain standing as he leaned closer and unbuttoned the next button of her blouse. She watched his hands while they unbuttoned the blouse one small button at a time. The backs of his hands brushed the skin between her breasts and then lower on her abdomen as he worked each button. She sucked in and held a breath when he knelt in front of her and unfastened her skirt, letting it pool on the cushy brown carpet.

He trailed his heated gaze up her body until it locked with hers. His expression was carnal. Slowly, he rose to his feet and leaned in toward her but stopped short at the last second. They were nose to nose. She stilled, waiting for what came next.

"I know sex is freer in Amber," he whispered and then hesitated, looking like he was in the process of finding the right words. "This, tonight, means something to me, Jordan. It's not just sex. To me, this is the beginning of us, and there *will* be an us. I won't ask if you feel it, too. I know you do."

"You hardly know me, Patrick."

"My heart knows."

"How?" She couldn't understand how he was so confident about his feelings for her. He made her feel like he'd never give up attacking the barriers that kept them separated.

"I know because I'm already falling in love with you."

Jordan's world stopped with those words and a tumble of thoughts and feelings rushed her. God it felt amazing. She just wanted to absorb it, soak it up and store it so the memory of it would remain imprinted inside her forever. She nearly broke down from the potent combination of joy and fear his words brought. But the flash of fear occupied her brain for a few seconds longer than the joy. He didn't know all of her and fear that he wouldn't love her once he did stole the full impact of the moment. This gorgeous man deserved better than her.

As she stood there, more inside her own head than in the room with him, he pushed on her shoulders, and she began to fall backward to the bed, surprised. A sound that closely resembled a squeal erupted from her mouth, and she shot a hand up to cover her mouth, startled at the unfamiliar noise as she landed softly on the bed and spread out, like a feast, before him.

"Now that's a beautiful sight." His eyes fixed on her as he stripped to his boxers. The scene was familiar and her thoughts flashed to Shane for a moment. Visually, it was hard to separate the two in her mind sometimes.

Patrick crawled onto the bed next to her and she scooted around to join him until they were face to face with their bodies close and their legs entwined.

Jordan placed her hand in the middle of Patrick's chest and held him at arm's length when he leaned in to kiss her. "I'm nervous. I've never…" She shook her head and looked away from his confused gaze.

He leaned away, eyebrows raised. "Never had sex?"

"Hardly." She smiled then. "Never had sex with someone who had feelings for me. It's a little nerve-racking. I've never cared before." She shook her head. "That doesn't sound right. I mean it didn't matter to me whether I was sexy enough or pretty enough.

Patrick's navy blue eyes bored into her. "And you think I'd risk my life for a woman I didn't think was spectacularly sexy, and thoroughly gorgeous?" His voice was deep, rough. He leaned closer despite the fact she was trying to hold him away from her. "Don't you think I know exactly what I want, Jordan?" he growled as he ignored her hand and used his weight and strength to position himself closer.

Jordan wanted to hide. The intensity of the feelings this man stirred inside scared her. Trying to avoid his gaze, she switched her focus to his lips.

"You're sexier than any woman I've ever met."

Her body reacted to his words, softening, relaxing.

He shook his head. "God, I'm stupid with what you've done to me. When we're apart, I can't go more than five minutes before my mind wanders back to you. I'm constantly wondering where you are and what you're doing." He raked his hand through the brush of his coffee colored hair. "Can't you feel the chemistry between us? It's so heavy in the air I feel like I'm drowning in it."

"I--" She nodded. "Yes."

"Don't be nervous. I don't think there is anything you could do or say that would make me less attracted to you." He grasped her wrist and removed her now-limp hand from his chest. "Let my actions express how I feel. It will be better than any words I could string together." He hesitated. "Do you trust me?"

"Yes," she breathed. "I trust you."

"Good. Now"-- he lifted himself up and twirled a finger-- "lay on your belly."

Moving away, he opened a drawer at the bedside table. She watched him pull out a small bottle of liquid while she followed his directions, laying herself out on her stomach in the center of the bed.

She sighed. Everything seemed better in the Sapphire Zone. Even the rich, cream-colored sheets felt softer on her cheek when she laid her head on the pillow.

Jordan absorbed every inch of his exposed skin. He glanced at her as though waiting for her protest as he slid the material of his boxers down over the curve of his rear end and thighs. He was semierect and she got a sense that he was less comfortable being nude than she was. It had been almost ten years since she moved into Circle City, and during that time, she'd finally learned and adapted the best she could to the relaxed attitudes about sex and nudity. She was a decade behind her peers, but she'd learned. It was ironic that, with Patrick, she hadn't needed to learn or change anything. Sex was different there in Sapphire.

Jordan was reminded of a conversation she'd had with Jaci earlier that year. The core message of it was that Sapphire men weren't good in bed. She found that, at that moment, she didn't care. That could be fixed, if necessary, though it would probably be humiliating for him if she tried to teach him. She hoped she wouldn't have to.

Patrick climbed into bed and straddled her rear end, bringing her contemplation to an end. The sound of his hands rubbing together preceded the warm, slippery skin of his palms traveling from the small of her waist up to her shoulders and back down again, spreading massage oil over her exposed skin. The spicy smell of cinnamon and cloves infused the air, adding to the erotic atmosphere in the room. During the next pass of his hands, her body melted, releasing more of the tension her muscles carried.

She sighed.

"Tell me if it's too hard."

"Mmm. Unlikely."

Patrick dug his thumbs into the knots behind her shoulder blades and then worked strong digits up her neck and into her scalp. She pressed her forehead into the mattress to stretch stiff straps of muscle at her nape.

Jordan moaned in pleasure at the relief his intuitive thumbs provided to muscles that had, only moments before, been locked up and hard as rocks. The repetitive press and release of the pads of his fingers traveling over her did exactly what he'd set out to do. She couldn't help but let her reservations go and enjoy the undivided attention this man gave her body.

He took his time with movements that were slow, meticulous, and he lingered long after her muscles softened and warmed. Then, after several minutes of undivided attention to her neck and shoulders, his magic hands traveled lower, slithering over the smooth curves and slope of her back. She was thin and knew her ribs were visible under the skin of her back. Dennis had told her once it was like rubbing his hands over corrugated cardboard. Briefly, she wondered if Patrick thought the same thing about the skin underneath his slick palms

She pushed the distracting thoughts out of her mind and focused once again on the hands creating what could only be described as a gluttony of the senses, warmth, the slight pain that came before the release of tension in the hard muscles, pleasure, arousal.

When his hands traveled to give attention to a new spot, it only took moments for her flesh to change from cold and hard to heated and pliant, like mush. She groaned again as warm drops of oil landed on the small of her back and then reveled in the sensations from the silky glide of skin on skin.

She'd never before noticed the sighing hiss resulting from the friction of hands running over her skin. It was never quiet enough in Amber to hear the subtle sound. He smoothed his hands tenderly over her curves right up to the crack of her ass. When he scooted lower toward her feet and kneaded the flesh of her ass and thighs, she groaned again.

"I could lay here forever like this," she whispered.

"Good. Because I could spend forever doing it."

"You're a sweet talker, Patrick O'Connor," she murmured.

He chuckled. "Is it working for me?"

"Oh yeah." Jordan groaned again while Patrick worked diligently. His strong hands delivered unbelievable pleasure all the way down her body to the soles of her feet.

"Roll over."

She followed his direction, keeping her eyes closed. He straddled her again and then she felt more warm oil drip between her breasts.

However, his hands didn't immediately go for her breasts, and she smiled to herself. In Amber, there was never this much foreplay. Sex was a means to an end, much more like a function that had to be completed than a connection being established.

With Patrick, everything was different. Their coming together was a process. He built her need with his touch and with his avoidance of her pleasure centers.

Leaning into her, he spread her arms out wide, and then began long strokes at her shoulders, continuing outward toward the wrists of her widespread arms.

At the end of each stroke, when his hands passed her wrists and slid to briefly lace his fingers with hers, their faces were close. His eyes glittered. Their heated breaths mingled. His cock lay hard and heavy on her belly.

So far, only the slightest brushes of his hands had touched her erogenous zones and she was going to die from it. She found herself subtly arching her body up off the mattress, seeking more than he gave her.

He worked his way down the front of her torso. Her breasts got no more or less attention than any other part of her exposed skin. She moaned her complaint as he scooted down toward her feet and began kneading the tops of her thighs.

"Patrick," she rasped as his thumbs slid for only a moment, exploring part of her labia before he moved again, manipulating the muscles of her legs. "No. I need more of that."

"Not feeling shy anymore?"

"No. Not anymore."

Jordan opened her eyes and found his heavy-lidded gaze focusing on her, searching out the curves and shadows of her face as if trying to commit every last detail to memory. It was clear he'd relaxed as well. Even the blinking of his eyes seemed slower. He nudged her legs apart with his knee and shifted himself so he knelt in between.

He leaned in, bracing a forearm on either side of her head. The normally animated Patrick she'd become accustomed to, had slowed. His movements were lazy, his breaths, long. He kissed her softly, and as his lips touched hers, the blunt end of his cock butted up against the slick opening of her pussy. He pulled away, ending the kiss.

She opened her eyes and found him staring into them. It seemed like the eye contact was what he waited for before thrusting his hips forward, penetrating her.

"Ah, Jo," he whispered. "A more beautiful feeling, I've never felt." His expression was intense as he stilled once fully buried inside her. They were locked together, eye to eye, their breathing synched. His heart beat hard against her chest as if knocking to be let in.

In that moment, it felt as if their souls moved closer to one another. His gaze held love and reverence, feelings as foreign to her as everything else in the Sapphire Zone. It was exhilarating.

She caught her breath as every cell in her body sang with the thrill of the moment. Five seconds, ten seconds, and then he moved, growling, "I can't wait any longer, Jo."

He curled his arms underneath her, resting his weight on his elbows and holding her as closely as he possibly could without crushing her.

The sweet relief of his cock filling the sensitive recesses of her body battled with the sensational pull of his mouth at the spot where her shoulder connected with her neck. He'd latched on, sucking forcefully on her flesh and pumping in and out of her at the same time.

She groaned her approval. Her entire being responded to this man as she wrapped her limbs tightly around him.

Her defenses dropped.

Her raw soul bared itself, and her lonely body received all of him without hesitation.

She held on as if her life depended on it.

Patrick rose to kneeling, holding her close until they were both vertical and she was straddling his kneeling form. Happy to take advantage of her position, she placed her feet flat on the bed and undulated her hips, grinding her clit into the place where their bodies met. Patrick's embrace loosened, and his large hands grabbed the cheeks of her ass. They rolled and swayed, against each other, and the pleasure rippled outward from where they were connected.

Patrick's finger rimmed her anus, and then he pushed it inside the puckered hole. She didn't break her rhythm or the perfect placement of her clit at the base of his cock. But a few surges of his finger pushing into her in time with his cock sent her over the edge. She held tight to his shoulders as she tumbled, mindless in her pleasure, her pussy spasming around the cock inside her. When Jordan stopped moving in the grip of her climax, Patrick took over, slamming up into her while the keening response to her orgasm filled the room.

Patrick's climax followed close behind. With a curse he flooded her with his hot seed, his cock jerking as it spurted inside her.

His movement slowed from thrusts, to waves, to a gentle rocking motion. They stayed, locked together in that beautiful embrace, like Renaissance statues, until they both were breathing normally again.

Patrick shifted to one side and then the other, settling himself cross-legged, with his cock still inside her, and her legs wrapped around behind him. They were cheek to cheek and his hands roamed over the oiled skin of her back.

He shook his head. "Jo," he whispered. "I don't think I can let you go back."

Chapter 9

The next afternoon, Patrick took Jordan out to discover the Sapphire Zone. He drove everywhere while she soaked up the lay of the land, and then eventually, he parked the car.

Her legs shook slightly as her feet touched the blacktop, and she lifted herself out of the passenger seat. They were right in the center of town. Shops with wide sidewalks lined the busy car filled street.

The Sapphire Zone was nothing like what she thought it would be. It was dreary, almost ugly, even on what was turning out to be a perfect, sunny day. There were no beautiful landscapes like in Circle City but that wasn't what gave the zone negative impressions in her mind. It was the vibe of the place. It was the people. They exuded the gloom. The Sapphires milling around, walking in and out of shops, doing their business seemed to project the dismal atmosphere.

In Circle City, they didn't have much, but they did have camaraderie. They shared the sense that they were all in it together. It unified them. That friendliness was absent here.

As she strolled through the center of town with Patrick, taking it all in, she noticed nobody looked directly at them as they passed. These people had a strange way of never meeting another person's gaze.

She was confused. Sapphires had privileges and rights the Ambers didn't. She couldn't understand why they were so meek.

As she and Patrick continued to walk, she realized the avoidance was directed at them specifically. As soon as someone caught sight of them, their expressions changed. They sobered or avoided making eye contact altogether.

"Why is everybody turning away from us?" she whispered.

"It's my Guard uniform. They're afraid of me."

"Why are you wearing it? You don't have to leave for work until tonight."

"Morgan requires all Guard to be in uniform outside of their homes. My guess is he wants a constant show of force intimidating the Sapphires as they go about their daily business."

The longer they walked, the more evident it became that the Sapphire population lived in greater fear than the Ambers did. Nobody on the other side of the border had a clue what it was like here, that the Sapphire population lived in fear every time they exited their homes.

So many Ambers longed for all the privileges they assumed the other classes had. But it seemed to Jordan like Sapphire's privileged status was an illusion. They may be able to have two children instead of one, they may have better food and housing, but the bottom line reality of it all was Sapphires' lives were ultimately little better than Ambers'.

The fear they lived with on a daily basis was significant. It hung tangibly in the air. The Amber Zone was an oasis, free from that kind of oppressive fear since the Guard stayed out, except for those occasions when they made a show of removing someone.

She began to understand the big picture, the dynamics of how Morgan kept everyone in line. He isolated the Amber Zone, pacifying them with self-policing just enough to keep them docile. But in the Sapphire Zone, he needed a different method of control-- fear. It was his friend. He used it like a tool, and apparently, he was good at it.

A mother and child approached them from the opposite direction on the sidewalk. The woman reached down and grasped the toddler's hand, quickly steering her around them and giving them a wide berth. Then she caught an older woman's gaze before it darted away as they passed.

Jordan cocked her head, trying to figure out--she gasped as the epiphany came. These people weren't a little intimidated. They *cowered* from Patrick, afraid of the consequences of gaining attention from a Guardsman. They were afraid his gaze would pick them out of a crowd, that their mere presence in his awareness was a danger.

It was ironic really. The people of Sapphire probably wished they had the bliss of being invisible to the Gov like the Ambers were.

Now she understood why all those women stayed to join the resistance.

She looked up at Patrick. The grave look on his face moved her. It was obvious that old women and small children cowering from him affected him deeply.

"I started noticing it about two years ago," he said when they were alone on the sidewalk.

She nodded her response to his statement, and they walked in absolute silence back toward the car. Jordan perceived the zone differently from the way she thought it was on the ride in.

After shutting themselves into the privacy of the car, Jordan whispered, "What is going on here that I'm not aware of?"

"In the past few years, young men coming of age have seen the direction Morgan's been leading us. Power-hungry elitists and bullies are drawn to the Guard now. They're like vultures, picking their own survival from the bones of others. They're trained differently, too. By the time they get assigned duties, it's clear they know they can do what they want, to whom they want with no ramifications. They're a street gang with the full backing of the Gov. People get beaten, raped or simply disappear. Just vanish into thin air, never to be seen or heard from again. There is no police force here. Just the Guard."

He pulled the car out into the street. "I've heard rumors Morgan keeps women in the underground prisons for his own personal use." He glanced over at her, taking his eyes off the road. He looked disgusted as he gritted out, "For sex."

They rode in the silence of the car for several minutes, and then Patrick started pointing out other places of interest.

They rolled past an ugly, squat building with no windows. "The church. It's the only one in the Zone and is used by all denominations."

She thought it looked more like a warehouse than a place to worship.

"Most people don't attend church anymore, even if they're religious. I'm not sure how the Gov keeps track, but people generally know that they're taking a risk by going there. Bad things happen to those who attend regularly."

"Sounds like Morgan doesn't want anyone usurping his authority, not even God."

Patrick pulled into the parking lot of a store. He turned the engine off and they sat in the silence of the car.

"I just want to grab some food and then we can head back to the apartment." He must have seen it in her eyes. She was still nervous getting out of the car, especially now that the risks were in sharper focus. "There's nothing to worry about. Your wrist is covered by your sleeve. Just keep your left palm covered and you'll be okay." Jordan nodded her response, and Patrick got out of the car, slamming his door. In the few seconds it took for him to walk around the car, Jordan took a deep breath and attempted to relax. Then, he opened her door and held out a hand. "Come on, Jo."

Sylvia Ryan

They walked hand in hand through the parking lot directly toward a glass door at a pace that told her she was going to walk right into the thing. Jordan stopped in her tracks just as the door slid open on its own in front of her.

"What the hell?" She tried to turn to figure out how it worked, but Patrick grabbed her hand and continued walking as if nothing happened, taking her with him.

"You can't do that. You'll draw attention to yourself."

But Jordan had already left all thoughts of the door behind. She took in the rest of the store while still trying to remain inconspicuous. Goose bumps rose on her arms and she looked up at Patrick. "It's cold in here."

"Some of the public buildings have air-conditioning. The foods store and Gov offices."

Jordan barely heard Patrick's answer as she tried to absorb the information her brain took in. They had milk. Real milk and real eggs packaged into little four-packs. There had to be almost a hundred of them. She walked along the case that kept the fresh meat cold, glancing down at the labels. Chicken. The only chicken she'd ever seen had been white, and she'd assumed it would be white when it was raw, as well. But it wasn't.

"What is that?" She pointed to an ugly black thing.

Patrick looked and smiled. "It's an avocado." He picked one up and held it in his hand for a moment before putting it in his basket. "It's ready to eat."

"Eat? It doesn't look like it tastes very good."

"Sometimes what you see is not always what you get."

He was right, of course. Wasn't that the point of this whole tour he gave her today?

Patrick was efficient in his route around the store, and Jordan felt like a wide-eyed child taking in the piles of colorful food. The sheer abundance of it all was mind-boggling.

Moments later, they were standing in line to pay. Patrick pulled several silver coins out of his pocket and Jordan couldn't take her eyes off them. She'd only seen pictures of the coins he held. The Amber Zone worked on credits and it was illegal to possess money there. The coins were smaller than she thought they would be. Patrick gave her a few to look at. She studied both sides of each, turning them over in her palm.

"First time?" Patrick whispered.

She nodded. She shouldn't have been so impressed by the tiny rounds of metal. She'd learned about money in school, seen the pictures of the long-gone paper currency used before the pandemic. Paper couldn't be soaked in disinfectant like coins so its use was outlawed at the height of the pandemic. They burned it in great bonfires in an effort to stop the spread of the virus. "The small one is a dime. It's worth ten dollars. The larger one is a nickel, worth five." He said, pointing them out to her.

"It doesn't make sense. You'd think the larger coin would be worth more than the smaller one."

"The twenty-five dollar coin is bigger than them both and the fifty dollar coin is even larger than that. It's just the small denominations that are mixed up size-wise."

She offered the coins back to him. He took the nickel and closed her fingers over the dime. "Keep this one in your pocket. Something to remember me by when we're apart."

Her stomach lurched. With his words, she remembered she had to leave him in a few hours. She didn't want to.

She looked up into Patrick's deep blue eyes and fell in. Her belly dipped wildly and that giddy need to scream out her joy rose at the back of her throat. She liked it here. She liked being with him in a way she'd never felt before.

He stepped forward in line and paid for the items while the shock of her feelings sank in. These two days in Sapphire had been the best days of her life. This had been a once-in-a-lifetime experience on many levels. She'd left her past in the Amber Zone, on the other side of the border guard station. The hurts of her history were so far removed from this time with Patrick, that her life in Amber rarely crossed her mind. And that was a beautiful gift beyond measure.

When the car came to a stop in the parking lot of the apartment, she got out and gathered up one of the bags. Patrick grabbed the other.

Drawn by the sound of a child's laugh to their right, Jordan looked that way. A blond-headed man was twirling a sweet blond-headed girl by her arms until her feet left the ground. She flew around and around in a circle, squealing and laughing as her body stretched out almost horizontal to the ground.

"Did your dad do that with you when you were small?"

She was smiling as she turned to look from the sweet scene to Patrick. When his question sank in, she met his gaze and her smile disappeared. "No."

He stopped, put down his bag and relieved her of hers as well.

"Then let me be the first," he said, advancing on her.

Jordan stepped back. "Oh no."

"Come on, Jo. Let me make you fly." He took her hand and stepped off the pavement into the grass.

"I am not going to let you twirl me around in a circle." She tugged her hand. "Give me my hand back."

He didn't. He just flashed her a wicked smile.

She laughed as he tried to get hold of her free hand while she attempted to twist away. He countered her moves perfectly until both of her hands were firmly clasped in his.

"Are you ready?" His eyes were blue jolts of anticipation and she caught her breath.

She looked up at the sky. "Oh God." Then she looked him in the eyes. "Okay, yes."

An instant later he had her rotating so fast her feet fell out behind her. Air rushed past her ears and a scream stayed barely contained at the back of her throat. He spun her around in tight circles. The world outside of their whirlwind blurred.

She was flying.

In the space of twenty seconds it was over. Jordan's feet landed back on the ground, and Patrick held her while she laughed in his arms. They both were breathless.

He kissed her hard, then grabbed her hand. "Come on." He plucked up the bags of food from the ground and headed to the apartment.

They spent the evening cooking together. She thrilled in the way he touched her absently as he moved around the kitchen. While she cubed tomatoes for a salad, she watched him in her peripheral vision. He was confident with his cooking skills, seeming like he knew what he was doing, and it was sexy as hell. He caught her looking at him and threw her a cobalt wink. She felt a little weird in the pit of her stomach from the casual gesture. It would be so easy to feel like she belonged there with him.

"You got awfully quiet all of a sudden."

She'd been so heavily in thought that he'd been able to step up behind her without notice. Something no one else has ever been able to do since she was small. He placed his hands on her waist. "We're all set if you're done with the salad."

Jordan threw in the tomatoes hurriedly and followed him to the round table set for two. She eyed that awful black thing in his hand with disgust as he carved it carefully and pulled it apart. "Yuck, it's green. I am not putting that in my mouth."

He smiled at her mischievously. "It tastes good. I promise."

"I've heard those exact same words before and they were a lie." She pressed her lips together as he scooped a bit onto a spoon.

"Here, taste." He held the spoon close to her lips, his eyes dancing with amusement. She shook her head wildly back and forth as he tried to touch the spoon to her lips. "Come on, Jo. You're not chicken, are ya?"

Her shoulders slumped and then she rolled her eyes. "I think it was those exact words that got me here in Sapphire two days ago."

Patrick lifted the spoon to her lips and fed her the green piece of mystery food. She braced herself for the taste of it because she knew something so ugly did not taste good. The creamy texture melted on her tongue, and the mild taste surprised her. "Mmm. Not bad."

"Told you. They're good on salads," he said as he carved up the rest of the green part and dumped it into the salad she'd made.

They sat at his table together with the feast laid out before them, and Patrick's gaze didn't leave her. He didn't so much as glance at the food, just stared at her in the utter silence, mesmerized.

Without warning, the enormity of the past two days hit her.

Instantly she knew what Patrick had said to her earlier in the weekend was true. This visit to the Sapphire Zone was the beginning of their us.

Chapter 10

Xander was furious. Jordan could tell the extent of his anger by the jaw-clenching muscles that twitched at the side of his face and the glare he pointed at her. A very silent Shane looked on from the back of the room at the Wellness Center. She'd briefed them both on the last forty-eight hours, minus the sex.

Everything had gone well. She couldn't understand why he looked like steam should be coming out of his ears.

She shook her head. "Am I missing something? This is better than we hoped."

Xander closed his eyes and swallowed. The action opened a pit in her stomach, and his inability to say what he needed to, began to fill the pit with dread.

"What?" she croaked through her suddenly dry throat.

"Rush was shot while he was walking home last night." He paused and glanced at her.

Oh, God, it was bad. She took in a breath and held it as this rarely demonstrative man visibly softened and looked at her with compassion She held her breath and internally steeled herself before she heard the rest. "It was Guard."

The silence lengthened while her vision tunneled.

"He's dead, Jordan."

The words sliced through the haze. She shook her head. "Oh, no. No. No Xander, please don't say that." Jordan slumped in her chair and covered her face with her hands, hiding her agony and shielding herself from the inspection of the two stoic men focused solely on her. She was good at that, lots of practice. The cries she kept prisoner inside her own head bounced and ricocheted within her cranium.

She loved that man. Captain Rush and Dennis were the only two people who knew her, knew what she came from. They both were dead.

Arms encircled her and pulled her out of her chair. The soothing expanse of a man's chest landed under her cheek. "I know you two were close. I'm sorry," Xander murmured. "This is why I'm so damn mad at you. I didn't know where you were, or if you were safe." After a minute, he released her and stepped away.

She felt his gaze inspecting her silently. If he was looking for tears, he'd be disappointed. She did an excellent job preventing herself from coming unglued. She still maintained that skill even after so many years of not having to use it. Straightening her spine, she looked up at Xander. "Is there anything else?"

He cleared his throat and narrowed his eyes at her. It was going to be a long day of him trying to figure her out, and her not giving anything away.

"It looks like the Sapphire resistance is going to need some leadership and someone who can coordinate with Amber. You interested?"

Jordan nodded. "Very." She looked down at the bag next to her. "Patrick gave me this." She handed Xander the bag that held the tattoo gun and ink.

His mouth dropped open as he examined the contents, "Holy hell." He looked to Jordan, smiling. "Nice. We'll cover your amber band with the dark blue. That way, you won't have to worry about moving around when you're in Sapphire. Having a blue band here in Amber will be less dangerous than having an amber band in Sapphire."

"I won't be spending much time here in the Amber Zone if I'm organizing and coordinating the Sapphire resistance."

"You'll have to make regular trips back. The Gov tracks our codes. They'll be alerted if you suddenly stopped going to the commissary for groceries or scanning your hand to get into your apartment. I think half time there and half here would be best for the time being."

She nodded.

"Once you figure out your schedule, I want a copy a month in advance. Make sure Shane has one, too. Shane will take over your role as messenger between Amber and Sapphire on days you're on the other side of the border." He looked at Shane. "That will give you a chance to see your brother regularly."

Shane nodded. "Thank you."

Then, Xander dismissed Shane, and the two of them spent several hours reviewing the list of Sapphire resistance members, their jobs and skills. They developed a preliminary plan and identified Jordan's first course of action when she returned to Sapphire.

When they were done, Jordan was exhausted. She'd been up all night, and her head was full of all the details they'd mapped out. She trudged slowly out of the Wellness Center into the early afternoon sun and brisk autumn air, turning in the direction of her building.

She braced herself against the drastic shift in the weather, while she walked against autumn wind that blasted her face with frigid gusts. It was cold on the inner courtyard path shaded by the buildings. She drew her jacket closed with her hands.

She'd expected Shane to be there when she arrived home, but he wasn't. She kicked off her shoes and looked around her stark apartment.

She sighed. Back to her black-and-white life for a while longer. She set the bag with the tattoo gun down on the kitchen counter and looked into the rest of the apartment, making sure she was alone.

It seemed like solitude was all her subconscious mind had been waiting for, because feelings of loss descended on her brutally fast.

First Dennis, now Rush--dead. Her resolve fell away, and emotions jumped to the foreground.

Rush was a young man the first time she'd seen him in his uniform standing at the front door of the house she grew up in. He'd smiled at her, and the small kindness almost made her cry more than the physical injuries her parents had inflicted upon her. She'd seen him many, many times after that, always at the door, admonishing her parents and smiling at her with tenderness. Rush was the reason she was a cop. The reason she had self-esteem. He believed in her when she didn't even believe in herself.

She loved him like a dad. He'd been more of a dad to her than her own blood.

Jordan neared her breaking point. God, she needed Dennis.

Overcome by emotions, drowning in the sudden deluge of grief and anger, Jordan lost the battle with herself as thoughts she hadn't had in years resurfaced. They inundated her as if there'd been no intermission at all from the depression. It was amazing how easy it was to fall back into her misery.

She had been doing so well. Dennis was weaning her slowly from her addiction. She was down to once or twice on a good month. But this wasn't a good month and she needed. Oh, God, she needed.

In the kitchen, she reached for a glass in a cabinet, and her trembling hand betrayed the edge she teetered on. It shook with small, uncontrollable tremors while she held a glass under the slow trickle of the kitchen faucet.

The longer she waited for the meager trickle to fill the glass, the more she wanted to scream. Until finally, she did.

Jordan let go of her tenuous grip on her emotions, screaming all the air out of her lungs. She slammed the partially filled glass down on the counter, and it shattered within the confines of her hand. She stared at the shards, glistening with her blood, and then threw the whole mess across the room. The glass made a paltry clinking noise as they hit the wall and tile. It was a discordant sound in relation to the rage inside her. She pulled a large piece of glass from her palm and watched her blood pool, then drip.

Why did she even try to get close to people? Ultimately she was always alone in the end.

"Whyyy!" she screamed as long and hard as she could and then swept her arm across the counter. A day's worth of Shane's dishes and glasses crashed to the floor into the living space. The loud sound was satisfying.

Jordan left the kitchen poised on the fine line between rage and agony as she walked around the counter into the living space.

Her mind raced.

The vague sense she was losing it hovered in her head for just an instant.

Spotting the mess she'd made, the ever-present anger and contempt she held for herself detonated. Without Dennis to help her work though it, the loose containment she'd had on her feelings finally ruptured and the inevitable explosion consumed her.

She stepped on the broken dishes and glasses, making her way to the dinette table.

Another yell of anguish shattered the silence of the room, expelling out of her so powerfully her body curved from the forceful release of breath while her hands fisted at her sides. She had to release all the feelings of responsibility, anger and loss.

She picked the bedside lamp up by the shade and awkwardly threw it across the room, screaming along with its flight. The crash if it hitting the wall and falling to the floor was loud and fulfilled her craving for release.

She tread another pass over the shards of glass and dinnerware to the dinette and gripped the back of a chair with both hands. She picked it up and slammed it against the wall over and over again, painting the clean white canvas with her rage, five, ten, fifteen times.

Wailing along with the crashing thud and hail of dust from the wall's destruction, she attempted to deplete her abundance of unwanted feelings.

She always knew it would come to this, that in the end she was destined to be crazy and alone. It was her ultimate fear.

She screamed again even louder and used all of her strength for one final slam before she dropped the chair and fell to her hands and knees, sobbing.

Without Rush and Dennis, her anchors, she was adrift, lost and wrecked.

"Broken," she cried out loud. She was broken.

Her howls echoed in the bleak space as she crawled out of the shattered glass and pieces of drywall, watching her tears splash onto the tiles until finally she crumpled to the floor. She lay there crying and exhausted while her mind struggled to fight its way out of the murky, sucking hopelessness it wallowed in.

Once the din had mellowed to quiet sobbing, Jordan registered the frantic pounding at the apartment door. She didn't move to answer it. She didn't care who it was.

Closing her eyes, she caved in on herself like she did when she was a little girl. She tucked into a small ball of human with her arms protecting her head. Then, she cried and cried, her sobs creating a weird rhythm when combined with the pounding and yelling at the door.

A few minutes later, she heard, "Jordan? You guys wait for me outside." It was Xander. She felt him beside her. "Jordan?" He touched her shoulder. "Hey, look at me."

She shook her head in the tight little space her arms created. She kept her eyes closed to him. "No. Get out," she yelled. "Just leave me alone."

"Fuck that." He sounded angry. "You're going to tell me what the fuck is going on, and you're going to tell me now." He took her hand and pulled it away from her head.

She refused to look at him.

"Here." He grabbed the chair from the dinette set that remained intact and sat it in front of the window, away from the glass on the floor. Then, he picked her up and sat her in it. "Stay there."

Xander disappeared into the bathroom and came back with a damp hand towel and bandages. He knelt in front of her and met her gaze before he grabbed a hand and examined both sides.

Talk," he said when he began cleaning the cuts in her palm.

Jordan shook her head and looked out the window.

"Dammit, Jordan!"

His booming curse startled her and her body instinctively shrunk away. "I'm not leaving until I have an explanation for all of this."

She remained silent as he reached for the bandages, but she knew she'd have to pacify him with something before he'd leave her alone.

"I'm just upset. Rush was like a father to me. And Dennis"-- she hesitated and shifted her gaze toward the window again-- "he helped me when I was feeling like this. But he's gone too."

He wrapped gauze around her hand. "Helped you how?"

She gulped and then sighed. "Like how you help Jaci."

He looked up at her and shook his head. His dark eyebrows furrowed. "I don't understand. I saw your disapproval when you saw I was using CALM with Jaci."

"I didn't approve because CALM therapy is addictive. I didn't want this for her, to be dependent on someone else just to feel normal."

She turned to look at him then. "I'm addicted." Her tone was flat, unfeeling. "I can't seem to totally stop. Things build up, and lately, a lot of things in a really short period of time. I just lost it, I guess."

"Dennis was your dominant?"

She nodded, and then her attention was drawn to a quick movement by the apartment's door. Shane stood there, his cobalt eyes flashing like lightning.

She saw the two men's gazes meet and their silent exchange.

Xander stood. "I'll let Shane finish up your other hand."

Without another word, he walked out the door, closing it behind him. She heard him disband the people out in the hall, and then there was only the two of them.

* * * *

Shane stood silently looking at the dazed woman sitting across the room. He'd been waiting years for the opportunity sitting before him. Now he knew for certain God was cruel and fate was a bitch. This woman who needed him, needed what he could give her, was Patrick's.

He was frozen with indecision. Jordan had clearly fallen to pieces and needed something he could give her. He was trained. But he didn't know if his brother would want him to. Patrick wasn't aware such a thing as CALM therapy existed. What would his twin know of being so rock bottom, of being compelled to seek out relief only pain and pleasure could achieve?

Life had never been that bad for Patrick. Not like it had been for him, and apparently, not like Jordan either.

He knew what it felt like to be in the headspace where Jordan currently existed. He'd been filled with rage during his first couple of years as an Amber. When someone gave him information about CALM therapy and the contact information of someone who could help him, he thought the dude was nuts and didn't see how this practice could possibly rectify his issues.

Shane went on suffering because of the separation from his twin and everything he'd ever known. He was angry and unstable until finally, he sought her out. He spent the next year seeking relief from the unrelenting hands of a dominant female. She gave him oblivion.

It was a gift from God.

When he was done purging the pain, he felt compelled to be in control. To him, being in control of his environment was a confirmation of the power he had over his own life. He could not stop himself from taking what, to him, was the logical next step in the CALM therapy and trained in the discipline.

Patrick would have a difficult time understanding how pain could take away pain. But Shane also knew Patrick wouldn't want Jordan to be hurting this way. Shit, he didn't want her hurting this way either.

Shane strode over to Jordan and began tending her wounds.

"I don't understand why he just left like that." Jordan's eyes were pointed at him, but they were unfocused. She seemed a million miles away.

"How long were you under Dennis's control?"

He looked at her until she finally focused and glanced toward where he knelt on the floor in front of her. She was surprised. "How did you know that's what I was talking about?"

"Xander and I trained in the same CALM therapy class."

She remained silent and he let her mind work over the information. "That's why he left. He knows you're in a better position to help me than he is."

"I suppose that's true if he already has someone he's caring for."

She nodded and turned her face away from him, pretending to gaze out the window. But it was obvious she was almost completely submerged into her own headspace. What she saw was probably completely overwhelmed by her internal processes.

"I'm an addict, Shane. I can't stop." Her face was expressionless, her voice flat. "Patrick won't understand."

Her eyes darted to his. It seemed as if she looked at him with hope. Hope that he would contradict her, tell her everything would be fine with Patrick. But he couldn't.

Shane finished cleaning debris from her other hand and lifted her right foot. He examined the bottom and pulled a few shards from the insole.

"I need it to free me from my life," she said softly.

He repeated the procedure on the other foot without comment.

When he was done, he lifted her in his arms and carried her to the bathroom, setting her down on the counter next to the sink. He plugged the tub and started a bath. The water came superslow, but it came.

Then, sitting on the edge of the tub, he turned his attention to her. From his lower position relative to hers, he looked up at Jordan's slightly slumped form. The height disparity was done on purpose. She would not open to him if he took an aggressive approach now.

"Tell me, specifically, what Dennis did for you."

She shook her head with pursed lips and furrowed brow. It was an expression of determination. He imagined this look was one that graced her face often.

His stomach twisted as he gazed at her, and in a way, saw her for the first time. Her tiny feminine body and enormous eyes were usually overshadowed by the alpha-female personality--short hair, and the asexual clothing she wore.

"It's nice of you to take an interest, but this is very personal. If any of this got out, my leadership in the resistance could be questioned. Most people, even in Amber, don't understand this therapy very well. I can't just run to the first man that can give me what I need." She looked away from him, over his shoulder. Her voice softened. "There's a lot of issues connected to this."

"Patrick is one of those issues and if you think he's going to endorse someone other than me controlling you, giving you relief, you're mistaken."

"After he finds out, I doubt he'll care about me anymore."

Shane rubbed a hand over his face and sighed. "I'm not sure he would understand any part of this. I'd never heard of it prior to being designated Amber. But Patrick is a smart, kind man"

He shook his head. "If you want me to help you, it wouldn't be your responsibility to explain it to him. It would be mine." He stared at her without speaking then. There was nothing else to say. She had to agree to try the arrangement and submit herself without pressure. He watched her as the silence stretched, with only the trickling sound of water as it pooled in the tub.

Her gaze was far away. Her body was in the bathroom with him but her mind had her somewhere else completely.

"Do you think I'll lose him because of this?" she finally whispered.

"If you do, then he wasn't the right man for you."

Her eyes widened for a moment and then she nodded. "You're right."
She sat up, straightening her spine. "Will you be able to follow my
orders outside this apartment?"

"If you go to the Sapphire resistance and I'm staying in Amber, I doubt
you'll be giving me many orders. But yes, I would be able to follow your
orders outside these walls. I wouldn't betray your trust or undermine your
authority in that way."

"You won't tell anyone, except Patrick?"

"No."

Moments later, she nodded.

With her motion of agreement, he became fully aware that he'd just
taken on a long-term responsibility. He silently prayed that Patrick would
understand.

"Now, what did Dennis do for you?"

Jordan's gaze darted to the small puddle of water in the tub behind
him. He smiled. She was looking for a way to put off the rest of this
conversation. But, with less than two inches accumulated in the tub, they
had plenty of time to hash this out.

"I was down to only twice a month for needing pain." A tone of pride
was laced through the words.

"How often when you started?"

"Every three days, maybe four if they were uneventful. When we were
home together, he directed me in everything. It's hard to explain what we
had in words. In many ways, he was like a parent to me. I'd improved
so much, he was in the process of releasing me. He would have been so
disappointed in that."

She bobbed her head toward the disaster in the next room.

"Home with Dennis was the complete opposite of my life outside the
apartment. Here I could show the secret part of me. The part I keep inside
because I know it's fucked-up. The part I don't want other people to see
and judge me because of it."

He nodded his understanding. He knew exactly what she was talking
about.

Jordan continued. "It seemed like he knew every single destructive
thought I had. He always knew exactly how close I was to losing it, and
invariably knew when I needed a session. He ruled me, and I gratefully
let him." She shook her head and covered her face with her hands. "Oh
God, that sounds so…"

"Stop worrying about how it sounds, Jordan. Keep going. I need to get
a feel of the dynamic so I can give you exactly what you need."

She sighed. "I enjoyed having a home where I wasn't expected to call the shots. I didn't have to act like I was tough when I wasn't feeling that way." She paused and looked down at her hands. "I have depression." She shrugged. "It's not as bad as it used to be. It comes and goes now. But when I was with him I was able to hurt if I needed to," she mumbled. "For me, that is the true gift of submission, feeling safe to be who I truly am instead of having to be a revised version of myself."

"So Jordan the cop and Jordan the resistance leader is not the real you?"

"It is, but not all the time. Sometimes I feel explosive or hopeless or lonely. Dennis was very good at helping me regulate my emotions. Without it I came undone. I've come a long way in the years he was my roommate. I felt unsavable when I got here. I was so damaged. But he saved me. Him and Rush. Now they're both gone." She shook her head. "Fuck. I'm lost."

Shane redirected her attention. "Did you have sex with Dennis, too?"

She glanced at him and then looked away. "He never fucked me with his dick, if that's what you mean."

"But he fucked you with other things?"

She nodded.

"Where's his equipment?"

"Top drawer of the dresser."

"Did he use restraints?"

"Always. He said it forced me to give up all of my control." She paused. "Do you think you can make Patrick understand?"

"I don't know, but I'll find out tonight. I'll meet him in your place." He lifted up one of her feet and looked at the bottom again. "I don't think you'll be walking anywhere."

Shane stood. "Take your bath." He looked over his shoulder and then turned back to Jordan. "Look, you actually have about four inches of water, now." He made an attempt to smile reassuringly at her. "Take your time."

He left shutting the door behind him.

While Jordan took her bath, Shane cleaned up the shattered glass and shards of broken lamp strewn over the white tile floor of the apartment. He was immersed in his own thoughts and barely saw his actions. He was ready for this. He'd kept his skills up to par, joining in sessions often in the spontaneous sexual atmosphere of Amber. He wasn't worried about his ability to help Jordan. He knew he could, and he wanted to, as well. Hell, his protective instincts had already kicked in.

His worry, he realized was his personal knowledge about the dynamics of the relationship they were entering into. He was going to fall in love with her. It was the nature of the therapy and a necessary component for the dominant in order to do it correctly. He was sure it was impossible to have a person bare their soul, open up so honestly and trust so completely as was necessary for this therapy and not fall in love with the person who was laying all she was before him.

Patrick loved her. Shane would love her too. He'd do his best to help Jordan get through this so she could be the woman she wanted to be for his brother.

When Jordan finally exited the bathroom wrapped in a towel, her head was bowed and she looked at the floor waiting for his direction. "Get your pajamas on. You're not going anywhere else tonight," he said calmly, softly.

Jordan followed his instructions, crossing the room to her dresser and pulled an oversize t-shirt over her head, then let the towel fall. She disappeared into the bathroom, presumably to hang her towel and then returned to the room. She stood waiting again.

"Sit on the bed. I want to dress your hands and feet."

"I'm supposed to meet Patrick tonight, to fill him in on today's briefing and our plan of action. I need to tell him I'm being transferred to help lead the group he's gathered in Sapphire."

He lifted a foot to inspect the bottom then looked at the other one. "I'll go. We have some other things to discuss as well."

Jordan's worried gaze locked with his. He shook his head. "There's no need for you to worry. This issue is no longer your problem. I will take care of everything."

Chapter 11

Shane hugged Patrick with a big squeeze and heavy claps on his back. "Do you have time? There's a lot of info I need to download."

Patrick nodded. "Where's Jordan?"

"That's one of the things I've got to get to. Let me get through the resistance stuff first."

"Okay."

"The resistance leader was assassinated while Jordan was with you in Sapphire. She hasn't said as much, but I think she's second in command now. They've pored through the information gathered from the first meeting in Sapphire, organizing and planning. She's been transferred to your group, primarily to help you organize and coordinate missions with Amber. She'll alternate forty-eight hours in Amber, forty-eight in Sapphire."

Shane glimpsed Patrick's white teeth gleaming through the darkness and stopped himself short. "Look at you. You're grinning like an idiot."

"Jesus, Shane, I don't think I've ever wanted anything more than that woman."

"You've got to get ready for her on your side. She didn't tell me when she'd be crossing over again but I can't imagine it would be more than a day or two. I'm your new Amber Resistance contact while she's staying with you in Sapphire."

Patrick grabbed Shane again and clutched him in a bear hug. "We'll be seeing each other all the time. Things couldn't be going any better." He finally released Shane from the clutch. "Ma's going to be so happy we'll be seeing each other regularly. She misses you, brother."

Shane closed his eyes, soaking in Patrick's sentiment. "Tell her I miss her, too."

"Maybe we can arrange to sneak you over to see her."

"I'm not sure how much you're going to be wantin' to see me after tonight."

Patrick straightened. "Why would you say that?"

Shane looked at his shoes. It was a reflex picked up after years of Kate O'Connor's lectures whenever he was in trouble.

"This is about Jordan isn't it? Why she's not here. What happened?"

"Jordan had a kind of breakdown this afternoon after she found out the resistance leader was killed. Apparently they were close. In the past week she's lost two people she cared for, depended on. She just lost it. When I got back to the apartment, it was destroyed. Glass was everywhere." He shook his head. "She was bloody and out of it."

"She hurt herself?"

"Patrick." He paused, worried about his word choice. "I don't think she tried to hurt herself, but I do think she's depressed and has lost her primary coping mechanism. She doesn't know how to deal with her grief."

"Are you trying to tell me she's crazy, Shane? Because I don't believe it."

"No, she's not crazy. I think she's afraid more than anything else you'll think she *is* crazy. She's afraid you won't want her anymore after I tell you what I have to say."

Patrick's face turned stony. "You fucking slept with her, didn't you?"

"Just hear me out and reserve judgment until I'm through talking. Okay?"

Patrick didn't answer. He stood stock-still, waiting with a slightly guarded expression on his face.

"She participates in a somewhat unusual practice. It's called CALM Therapy. It's one of the ways the women, and sometimes men, cope with the buildup of crap in their lives. I'm familiar with it. Now that Dennis is gone, I've agreed to help her with the therapy." He fished a wad of folded up papers from his back pocket and handed them to Patrick. "These are from the class I took. They'll explain how it works in better detail."

"How what works? I have no idea what you're talking about right now."

"I know. It's just…" Shane raked a hand through his hair and turned slightly away from his brother. "It's hard to say out loud because it sounds…wrong."

Patrick put his hands on his hips. "Shane."

He looked back at Patrick's nonverbal communication. It screamed aggression. Patrick wanted to kick his ass, and for a moment he wondered why he'd taken Jordan on.

He had already died a thousand momentary deaths since being designated Amber. He would literally shrivel into a corpse if Patrick no longer accepted him. If that happened, and he had to see his brother regularly due to resistance business, it would be like rubbing salt into an open wound.

"You have to trust me too, brother." Shane snapped out of his mind's inner machinations at Patrick's statement. He nodded in agreement.

"Can you read the papers and meet me again later in your shift?"

Patrick lowered his arms and nodded. "You'll be here until I come back?"

"I'll be here."

A moment later, Shane was alone in the alley. He walked a bit farther into the darkness and then sat against the wall of one of the buildings.

* * * *

"What the fuck?" Patrick was stunned after reading the introductory paragraph for the class entitled "Chemical and Limits Manipulation, CALM Therapy. Using the body's own chemicals in conjunction with providing a safe and controlled routine to successfully combat the negative symptoms of depression, PTSD and chronic stress."

He sat back in his chair and the grating squeak from the shift of his weight filled the silent and starkly barren interior of the border station.

He stopped reading after the summary of the class. It was a lot to take in. Jordan needed this? She seemed like the most stable, capable woman he'd ever met. It didn't make sense. But he reserved judgment and picked up the rest of the sheaf of papers and continued reading until he'd read every last word, studied every diagram and felt like he had a good understanding of this CALM Therapy.

Theoretically the home dynamic allowed her to shed her responsibilities, her burdens, and just be, without judgment, without stress and without having to be responsible for anything except doing what she was told. Then, occasionally, she needed the escape and release the sessions provided.

The structured home environment of the therapy was similar to parenting. Jordan told his mother her parents were dead. At the time, he knew that was a lie. Her parents were still alive, but he didn't challenge her. Then later, he'd forgotten to ask about it. He leaned forward and called up the contact information for Jordan's parents on his compad, wrote it down on a tiny piece of paper and then stuffed it in his front pocket. He'd have Shane check these people out.

So all these years this Dennis guy had been hitting her and bossing her around, and she wanted him to do it. He'd been helping her by doing it.

Patrick understood why Shane currently sat in a dark alley waiting for him to return. But after reading about the brain-chemical science and the cathartic properties of the sessions as well as the dramatic statistical increase in reports of feelings of wellbeing, it made sense. Shane was right. It would have sounded much more deviant if he'd tried to explain in a sentence or two.

Jordan had suffered a break down so severe she either didn't know, or she didn't care, if she was hurting herself. She'd lost it because she didn't have the structure and the sessions.

Sessions she'd needed badly due to the deaths of her two friends.

She'd probably been living this way since she was twenty-one. He shook his head. Five years.

He looked back over the papers. There was almost always a sexual component to the sessions. Those hormones rushing during climax would meet up with endorphins from the pain, and the adrenaline to boot, essentially creating a perfect storm.

Yet she'd told him she'd never had sex with Dennis. He supposed sexual stimulation, orgasms, did not necessarily mean fucking.

Now, Shane would be doing this for her. Patrick propped his elbows on the desk and put his head in his hands.

It had never occurred to him Shane might develop feelings for Jordan. And he had to be. There was no other reason to agree to help her this way, knowing he was putting their intense twin bond on the line, not unless he had feelings for her.

Patrick sat for an hour, thinking all the variables through to their conclusion. There was only one acceptable response for him. Everything else ended in a way he didn't think he'd be able to bear.

He rose from his seat and jogged out to the alley. He heard the rustle of Shane's clothes as he stood some feet away.

"Why did you take this bizarre class in the first place?"

Shane stilled. "Because I underwent the therapy for two years after I was designated Amber. When I had progressed as far as I was going to, I took the class. I wanted to know how it worked and maybe find someone I could help."

Patrick was shocked. He didn't know how to respond. They'd all hurt those first few years, no one more than Shane, of course. "And does it? Help, I mean?"

Shane shrugged. "Yeah, brother, can't you tell? I'm a bundle of fucking joy now."

He laughed.

Shane didn't.

"I don't want you to fuck her, Shane."

His brother didn't respond. He just looked at Patrick straight-faced, unblinking.

"Can we figure a way for me to be there when you do these sessions?"

"I'll let you know. It's going to take us a while to build trust and feel each other out so to speak. But yes, eventually, you'd be welcomed."

"Do you love her?" Patrick honestly didn't know if he wanted his brother to answer that question. Neither of the two possible responses seemed acceptable at the moment.

"I think after a period of time it will be very hard for me not to, but I'll try to curb those feelings. For you, I'll try. But Patrick, I'm not so sure she's able to return feelings of love to either one of us."

"Why not?"

"I've met a lot of women in Amber, and there's definitely a small percentage that have gone though enough suffering that they need this therapy. All the ones I've met have a tight grip on their own hearts. They're on guard and wrap themselves tight in their defenses. "I doubt she knows what it is to love, what it feels like to have someone care about her despite all the flaws. I'm betting she's never experienced it before and may not recognize it's for what it is. We may have to teach her how it feels, what it looks like, how to give it and receive it. How to trust it."

Patrick nodded once and released a long breath. "Okay."

"Oh." Patrick said, pulling paper from his pocket. "You've got to get to the bottom of this for me." He handed the paper to Shane. "It's her parents' address. I want to know why the fuck she needs this therapy in the first place and why she says her parents are dead when they aren't."

Surprise flashed in Shane's eyes. "Her parents aren't dead?"

"No."

Shane tucked the address in his front pocket. "First thing. I promise."

"Listen, Shane. Maybe I should back off. I can't do for her what you can."

"No." Shane's face softened. "Don't you get it? At this moment, she's sitting at home waiting to hear how horrible you think she is. How crazy you think she is. You can't do that to her."

"You know that's not how I feel."

"I could tell her as much, but it won't carry a lot of weight. She knows what the other zones think about Ambers. They grow up knowing that they're considered inferior by all the other people in New Atlanta. The prejudices reach them, affect them even in their zone."

"I don't have any prejudices."

"I know that, but right now, she doesn't. Trust me. I'm an expert on this topic. Since the day I arrived in Amber, every woman I dated started to act funny around me when she found out I grew up in Sapphire. I don't tell people anymore. It's just too much of a hassle trying to convince people I'm not an asshole."

Patrick put his hands in his pockets and hung his head. The absolute silence of the night settled between them. "How long do you think she's going to need this?"

"Years."

"This is a dangerous road we're traveling. I'm afraid she'll eventually come between us."

"No." Shane looked up at him, shaking his head with a glint of determination in his eyes. "No worries. That will never happen."

He sighed. "So when she crosses over tomorrow I'm supposed to act like you and I never had this conversation?"

"It doesn't have to be that extreme. It makes things unnatural, awkward. If either of you needs to talk about it, the topic will come up. Just remember, she hasn't changed. She's the same woman. You just know more about her now. Let's take some time, see how everything meshes during this next visit."

Patrick nodded.

"Are we okay?" Shane asked.

"We'll always be okay."

Shane's shoulder's relaxed and Patrick noticed the sigh of relief his brother released. "Tomorrow then?"

"Yeah." Patrick nodded and pointed in warning toward his brother. "I'm expecting Jordan to be here."

"Don't worry. She will be."

Chapter 12

Pulling the paper Patrick had given him out of his pocket, Shane read Jordan's parents' address. He was going to get to the bottom of the parent thing right now. He needed to know her whole story and wasn't sure if she'd tell him this part, or if she did, whether she'd be one hundred percent forthcoming.

He followed the lovely voice of his com's directional app, instructing him where to go while he steeled himself, already knowing what he was going to find. Her parents had to be one kind of fucked-up or another. It was the only explanation for the fact that Jordan denied them. He just needed to find out the nature of the hurt they'd inflicted on her.

The neighborhood was pretty, parading identical monopoly houses on postage stamp lots, with only the color of the window shutters and the faded fall blooms in the flowerbeds differentiating one house from another.

As he turned the corner onto her street, he knew what house he was going to end up at as soon as his gaze landed on it. Halfway down on the right sat a squat eyesore. The house was dilapidated with dangling brown shutters and dirty white paint. The landscaping was overgrown with long, brown grass in the front yard, and the beds were choked with weeds tall enough to obstruct the view from the large front window. Random pieces of paper littered the jungle and an excess of garbage bags were piled in the driveway. Looking at it from down the street, showcased by the perfectly manicured lawns and tastefully painted houses of the properties skirting either side, the place had the odd effect of appearing in sepia tones. It was a dump.

When he approached it, he checked the address to confirm he was in the right place, and his hopes that maybe he'd been wrong were dashed as he matched up the numbers on the paper to the three nailed over the front door.

"Fuck." He scrubbed his hand over the crown of his head and then spat on the ground before facing Jordan's ugly secret. Shane stood in the street, trying to picture Jordan as a little girl running around in that cesspool of neglect. Then, somehow, he knew she never got the chance.

This was the kind of house average mothers on the street would have told their kids to stay away from. The kind of house that prompted the neighborhood kids to target any poor child that lived inside.

"Can I help you?" A woman startled him with her silent approach from behind. He turned to face a middle-aged female dressed sharply in a professional skirt and blouse.

"Do you live here?" He asked her pointing at the decrepit house.

She made a face. "God, no. I live across the street. Why do you ask?"

"What can you tell me about them?" He jerked his head toward the house and then looked her straight in the eye, ignoring her question altogether.

She eyed him for a pregnant moment and then snorted. "How long do you have?"

Shane walked closer to the lady until they stood side by side at the end of her driveway.

"Do you remember the daughter?"

"Yes, poor girl."

"Why 'poor girl'?"

"Well, look at the place. Their parenting skills are about equal to their aptitude for home maintenance."

"Tell me about them."

"The man? I don't know what he does. But the woman works in the elementary school cafeteria. Can you imagine? A school of all places."

She pursed her lips. "Those people are under the influence of something every time I have the displeasure of seeing them outside the house. The police are over there all the time. It's been that way for the twenty-five years I've lived across from them." She grimaced. "When the girl was there, the police took her away so many times."

"She couldn't get a break, drawing the brunt of people's judgment both inside and outside her house. It was sad, really, seeing all the neighborhood kids running around holding hands and learning how to accept and nurture one another." She shook her head. "She was always bruised and dirty, and it was obvious touching was not a good thing to her.

"That made her different from the other kids. Well you know how kids are. It was a terrible thing to watch. She finally escaped the parents for good, though. I haven't seen her in years. Now the two of them just beat on each other."

Shane clenched his fists and his heart pounded hard and fast. He was murderous after hearing the scathing indictment of Jordan's parents.

The woman touched her earbud. "Time." She paused. "Oh, jeez. I've got to go or I'm going to be late. If you're trying to find the girl, you're in the wrong place. I doubt she'll ever set foot in that house again."

Shane stepped to the side as the woman pulled her car out of her driveway. He was torn whether he should knock on the door, get some more information and maybe kick the father's ass before he returned to Circle City, or leave it alone.

He'd gotten the information he needed. There was no valid reason to continue invading her privacy. He turned toward the direction he'd come and forced himself to leave without laying eyes on the people who'd abused Jordan. After the information he received, if he saw the father, he would have beat the man, and he wasn't sure he'd be able to stop.

Rage simmered under his skin. It was a hot, roiling feeling that tensed his muscles and raised his blood pressure.

Random seemingly unrelated pieces of information seemed to come together and make sense now. She rarely kept her apartment door open as was the custom in Circle City. The closed door to the apartment was an excellent example of how much she still felt the disgusting feeling of being left out, of not belonging. She'd lived with this isolation her whole life.

A person could have a hundred so-called friends, but if they only know one side, a closely edited side at that, they don't really know the person at all.

Dennis knew her. And, he suspected, Rush, too. That old, married cop had probably been to her parent's house several times while Jordan was growing up. Everybody else in her life only knew the small part of her she let them see. It would not be that way between them. He would know everything.

Shane looked up and didn't immediately recognize where he was. He had been so wrapped up in assimilating the gossip bomb dropped on him, he'd unintentionally walked past the transport stop. Needing the time to process, he forged ahead, deciding to walk back to Circle City.

But there was one thing he didn't need to process ever again. It was a given, an unchanging fact. She was his now.

His to take care of.

His to do with as he chose.

His heart flipped at the thought of the gashes littering her hands, feet and knees. It was a visceral reaction, revealing his body had already made the distinction and shifted into a proprietary mode when he had thoughts of her. It was a powerful feeling to have another human relying so completely on him, following his every word, like a puppet, with the strings dangling from his fingertips.

A man could only have love for the woman who risked everything, trusting him completely. It was a serious responsibility made even more so by the involvement of his brother.

A tight knot of dread formed in the pit of his stomach. He was on a path that couldn't possibly end well for him. Not if he remained honorable and faithful to his bond with his brother.

He walked the entire way back to Circle City. Missing the transport turned out to be a good thing because the longer he exerted himself, the better he felt. By the time he reached building twelve, he'd worked out his aggression over what he'd found out about Jordan's childhood and mapped out his drastically changed life so he was cognizant of all his blessings and where the pitfalls were, as well.

It was midmorning by the time Shane finished his long walk back to Circle City. He entered the apartment quietly and found Jordan sleeping at the dinette. Her head rested on the table, cushioned by her arms.

He shook his head and sighed. Trying to stay up all night. That deficiency in REM sleep was a no-no. A lack of sleep could increase her stress levels, resulting in the need for more frequent sessions.

He stared at her, thinking. The importance of getting enough sleep shouldn't be a new concept to her. Dennis should have taught her this.

"Jordan." He touched her shoulder. "Wake up."

She flinched away from the contact for a split second before she seemed aware of her surroundings. Then, her entire posture relaxed. "Shane."

"How are you feeling?"

"Worried."

"About?"

She didn't answer for several long moments. "You know."

Shane nodded. "Trust is essential, Jordan. You know that."

"I know."

"I suspect there are a lot of things you know but aren't following through with. That is my oversight, so let me be clear of my basic expectations. "From this point forward, you sleep in the bed for a minimum of eight hours. You will not skip meals. You will not drink alcohol. If you're having anxiety or are upset in any way, you'll come to me immediately.

I don't expect to see another episode like yesterday. Ever." He looked at her as sternly. "You will follow these rules always, even when you're in Sapphire." He met her gaze. "Are we clear so far?"

"Yes."

"Good. Now, I'll take precautions prior to your border crossings to insure you won't need a session while you're over there, but that's not a guarantee. You're to cross back into Amber if you have any indication at all you might need a session. Normally, I would make that decision for you, but I won't always have access to you. Do you understand?"

"Yes."

None of what he said seemed to faze her at all. "Were your rules the same with Dennis?"

"Yes, pretty much."

"You haven't been following them since he died?"

Her gaze darted away from the eye contact he'd been holding with her, indicating she felt guilty. "No."

"Why not?"

She shrugged. "There was so much going on."

"The underlying message I'm receiving is you can't be trusted to take care of yourself unless someone is watching you."

"I hadn't been having many issues lately. I hoped I wouldn't need any of this anymore. Then, after Dennis died, everything else happened so fast."

"Let me identify your first misstep. You will always need sleep and food. Those things have nothing to do with the therapy and everything to do with being normal. What did Dennis use as redirection when you didn't listen?"

"Redirection?"

"Punishment, discipline."

Jordan swallowed and her pupils dilated. "It was always different. I don't know how he decided."

Shane crossed the room and looked out the window. The sun slanting through the glass heated his skin. The sky was pale blue and cloudless. He shook his head and sighed.

Despite the fact that the only thing he wanted to do was hold her and rock her in his arms, she had to learn she would not be able to disregard the basics without consequences.

"Today we'll start your training and have a session before you cross over to Sapphire."

When he turned around to look at her, her eyes were closed, still avoiding eye contact. "Okay."

"Okay, Sir," he corrected.

"Okay, Sir."

The words were formed on a breath that whispered warm contentment into his blood. He was her Sir. Overwhelming feelings swamped him without warning. She needed him. She needed him, trusted him and put herself in the palm of his hand to keep safe. God, he loved her already.

"How are you feeling?"

She attempted to look positive, but the half-assed smile she gave him wouldn't fool anybody, least of all him.

He walked over to the counter and retrieved the bag containing the tattoo gun and ink and then walked to the bathroom to get supplies for the cuts on her hands and feet.

"We need to get this done if you're planning on crossing to Sapphire tonight." He opened the bag with the tattoo gun and set it on the table.

She nodded. "Do you know how to use one of those things?"

"I think we can figure it out." He sat down next to her and took her hand. Turning it over, he examined the gash in her palm. "Looks good, clean. How are the feet?"

"Not bad. There's one slice on the arch." She lifted a foot to his lap to show him. He peeled the tape from the gauze covering the wound.

He held her delicate little foot, examining the damage she'd done to herself.

Slowly and deliberately, Shane treated each wound. The room was silent, and he knew she studied him intently as he meticulously completed his task.

When he plugged in the tattoo gun, she reacted. Her spine stiffened and tension radiated from her. He dipped the needle into the deep blue of the ink and tested the contraption on his inner arm. It seemed pretty straightforward. He set the gun down before scooting himself closer and positioning her arm to allow him maximum access to available light.

He turned on the tattoo gun, but didn't move to begin his job of permanently changing her designation. She seemed to understand his pause because she looked to him, met his gaze, and then gave him a nod, her consent to continue.

"Now, what would you like to ask me?" Shane asked as he turned his attention toward covering her amber tattoo with the official Sapphire Zone color.

"Does he understand?"

"He's starting to."

It remained quiet between them for several minutes with only the buzz of the tattoo gun vibrating the air around them. He was beginning to think she'd only had one question when she spoke again.

"Does he think less of me?"

"I don't think so. But I expect you'll be finding out soon." Shane caught the subtle stiffening of Jordan's body at his brutally honest answer. "Remember, if he thinks less of you, he's not the man for you."

She nodded. "True."

"Just be yourself. If he wants to talk about it, do your best to explain. But I doubt that he'll bring up the subject. The two of you have too many things to focus on as it is. He won't want to burden you more with an interrogation. If he does bring it up, I'd say it's an indication it may be bothering him."

He looked up to gauge her expression. She appeared resigned to whatever outcome awaited her.

"How long are you planning on staying in Sapphire?"

"Two days. Maybe less."

She was quiet, too quiet. "What is it?"

She shrugged. "I'm feeling scared about going back now. I'm not sure if I can face him. I feel so…I don't know…ashamed, embarrassed. If something bad happens, if Patrick doesn't want me like before, I don't know how I'd take it. I'm kind of afraid to find out."

He wanted to reassure her, comfort her. But he forced himself to withhold words of solace, knowing full well Patrick may do exactly what she feared. Instead he gave her a truth that would soothe her. "It's my responsibility to make sure you won't lose it in Sapphire. Rest assured, you'll be ready to handle anything by the time we go tonight. You'll go with confidence. "However, I want to be perfectly clear. If *ever* I misjudge, or if you feel near an emotional blow while you're in Sapphire, I don't expect you to stay there and try to deal with it yourself. If you're getting close to your tipping point, come back immediately. Do you understand me?"

"Yes."

He finished her tattoo and covered it with ointment and a surge pad to keep it clean and then his serious gaze met hers. "Are you sure about this?"

"Yes," she whispered.

"I'm not Dennis. *I've* been in your place in this kind of relationship. And because I've been where you are, I know the thought processes. I know how cathartic a session can be, and I know how far your limits need to be stretched to get the true relief that eases the soul. I'm not the kind of man who will provide you with a small burp of relief to ease the pressure. When we're done with a session, you will be who you want to be, at least for a while until the world starts to build up around you again. Do you understand that you'll have some new rules and expectations with me?

"Like?"

"When we're home alone, you will be naked—no exceptions. To me, it's a sign of submission, a constant reminder you are under my control. You will also call me Sir while we're here alone."

She nodded.

"When you're in Amber, you need my permission to come. While you're with Patrick, I will release you from that obligation, but you will keep a diary while you're away, recording how many times you've come while you were gone. I need day and approximate time. I also want you to record any upsetting incidents." He paused to make eye contact with her. "You will submit to every request, or I will make you submit. "I want to be clear here. I will let you go if you are unable to submit to my direction. I have needs to be met as well, and ultimate control is one of them. If you can't or won't do it, this won't be a successful pairing."

She bit her lip and nodded.

"I won't tolerate provoking behaviors because you're looking to be disciplined. Remember, I have been where you are."

"Yes, Sir."

"I will be totally honest with you, although there may be times I choose not to share things with you at all. But rest assured, the things I do share will always be the complete truth. In return, I expect you to be completely honest with me, but you do not have the choice to withhold information as I do. You will keep no secrets between us. This won't work for either of us if you have parts of yourself that you hold back from me. In return, I'll give you what you need--structure, unconditional acceptance and relief in the ways you need it."

He rose from his chair and headed toward the bathroom. "Strip." The one word command was all he said before he stepped in and closed the door behind him.

Chapter 13

Shane turned on the faucet at the sink and regarded the trickle of water that escaped. He plugged the basin and waited for it to fill while he gave Jordan some time for his words to sink in, really sink in, before they went any further. This way she had all the information, and if she changed her mind, no harm, no foul.

Fuck. Who was he kidding? If she changed her mind, it would be a huge letdown. He'd waited a long time for the woman on the other side of that door. He splashed his face with water and met his reflection in the mirror. He'd give her the time it took to shave his two day's growth of whiskers and brush his teeth before they got down to the heavy-duty work of forging this new relationship. They were as perfect a fit he'd ever seen. He was sure the session they'd have today would be spectacular.

They would help each other. His chest heaved with the ragged breaths of nervous anticipation. His heart was already committed.

When he exited the bathroom, he found Jordan standing nude just a few feet away. She nervously ran a hand over her stomach. The sight instantly transformed him into what they both needed. He silently accepted her surrender and took her into his care.

Shane walked around her slowly, examining her body. He became acutely aware of the sharpness of her muscle definition and pronounced protrusion of her skeleton on her small frame. She was too thin.

He rubbed his gaze along the curves, taking in every nuance. She had a collection of scars marring her pale skin, shoulder, thigh, arms. He felt a low growl at the base of his throat. He should have stayed and introduced himself to her father.

Her eyes were big and brown, and they blessed him with a glimpse of her soul. He stopped directly in front of her. "Look at me."

When he looked intently, he saw her past in there, hiding behind the distractions she tried to provide herself. He found it incredibly hard to believe that no one else had ever cared enough to delve further with this woman. All these years on her own, single, and she'd never opened herself up to anyone but Dennis. And he bet that had been a tremendous struggle.

"Present yourself." He kept his expression flat.

Her eyes flashed momentarily. What was that? Fear maybe. She lowered herself to her knees in front of him, placing her forehead on the ground and her arms stretched, palms up, in front of her.

He felt her anticipation. She waited for her next command. Her breathing was jagged, her muscles tense and straining underneath her beautiful skin.

He closed his eyes and made a futile effort to tame the raging emotions unleashed by the sight in front of him. Split-second snapshots flipped through his head.

Jordan sucking his cock.

Jordan tied to their bed, her body stippled with marks from his discipline.

He wanted to take her there. He wanted to take her to paradise.

Forcing himself to return to the present, to his task at hand, he refocused. He respected the way she'd laid herself wide open and trusted, as if trusting him was easy.

Her trust would be tested today. She was leaving for Sapphire tonight and she needed a session before she left. He had to ramp up his assessment process, completing it more quickly than he would have, had there been different circumstances. He needed to ferret out her needs and find her boundaries, so this session would double as a fact-finding mission.

The first test was obedience and patience. He stood, watching her honed female body lying prostrate before him. He didn't speak. He didn't move.

Minutes passed and Shane noted the gradual relaxation of her posture. She remained quiet and still. Inactivity seemed to relax her instead of increasing anxiety as it did in some.

He lifted a dinette chair and placed it directly behind her, where her most private secrets were exposed to him. He sat silently, staring at her wide-open cunt and the sweet puckered hole of her ass. She displayed more stress in her presentation with him at this angle. The muscles of her shoulders tightened slightly.

"What are you thinking?"

She jumped at the first of his words. "I'm trying not to be embarrassed."

His inner self smiled at her honesty. He'd help her get past the threat of embarrassment first off. "There's no room for embarrassment between us."

"I direct. You comply. That's all. There's nothing else for your mind to dwell on."

"Yes, Sir," she said in a quivery whisper.

"Move to the bed and lay on your back."

Slowly she uncurled herself, walked the two steps to the bed and lay, looking self-conscious, in the center. He followed, sliding his chair to foot of the bed.

From where he sat, the view up the length of her body was breathtaking. Her breasts were sensual little handfuls with velvet tips. Her skin was pale and smooth.

He took in his fill, from her glorious closely groomed cunt to the flat of her stomach framed by sharply angular hip bones.

"Bring yourself to orgasm for me."

She lifted her head and looked down the length of her body at him.

He met those huge, sad eyes with a flat stare. One second. Two seconds. He raised his eyebrows in warning, and she broke eye contact, lowering her head.

He watched her stare at the ceiling and thrilled when he noticed that both of them were holding their breath.

It was completely obvious she'd never been told to do this before and several more moments passed as she reconciled the request in her brain.

Finally, her face and chest flushed as she slowly spread her legs and lifted her hand to the dark landing strip of hair between them. He took all of her in as she whispered her fingers over the curves of her pussy lips, hesitating for several seconds before she spread those sweet lower lips and ran her fingers through the channel between.

She speared two fingers into her vagina and pressed the palm of her hand over her clit. Muscles in her belly flexed in time with the unconscious canting of her hips, creating a fascinating dance of tensing and relaxing muscles.

Her need to take in more air parted her lips. Her pace was even and her cunt made sweet sucking sounds as her fingers plunged in and out. Her juices shone on her fingers.

A skinny mewl escaped from somewhere inside her throat, and her pace picked up. He smiled. She'd forgotten he was watching. He leaned over and placed a hand around her ankle. Immediately, she paused, but only for a moment before she picked up where she'd been just seconds before. Her hips pumped in time with her hand. She was rough with herself, invading her pussy with force.

With arms and legs spread out wide and taut muscles, she came. The tendons in her neck rose with the strain of her climax and the curl of her spine. Her cry was short, fleeting, like a gust of air.

A few seconds later, her frame went limp.

"Very nice." He stood and slid in next to her on the bed. She was beautiful with the flush of orgasm on her cheeks. He lifted her hand and sucked in a finger she'd just had inside her, tasting her, smelling her. The action made her gasp. He smiled down at her. "Open." He placed her other cream-coated finger into her mouth. "Nice, right?"

A breathy, "Yes, Sir," floated back to him.

He left the bed, headed toward the kitchen and then poured her a glass of water from the pitcher in the fridge.

"Here, drink this." Jordan propped herself up to sitting and took the glass from him. "Are you hungry?" he asked while she gulped down half the glass.

"No."

He smiled at her and nudged the bottom of the glass so she would finish off what was left. "Did you have a word or hand motion that you used with Dennis for when you were restrained?"

"Yes. Two actually, yellow and red."

Shane nodded. "Pretty standard."

"Have you ever used them?"

"No, not really."

"That's a yes or no question. Either you have or you haven't."

"I've yelled and screamed for him to stop, and sometimes he did."

"You can scream until the sun goes down. I only listen for one word. All others will simply be noise to me and will not be heeded. I expect you to use the yellow caution word before I hear a safe word. Do you understand?"

She nodded. "Yes, Sir."

He walked over to the dresser and opened the top drawer. "Okay. I want you to go to the restroom while I get set up here."

She lay there quietly while his back was to her. Then he heard the rustle of the sheets.

Dennis had a beautiful collection of equipment, a little of everything. His gaze landed on a few items that would be perfect to establish the appropriate dynamics of their relationship. He'd already seen the restraints attached to the bed frame.

He grinned. They were one of the first things he noticed when she'd invited him into her home, into her life. Somehow, even then, he knew the course of his life had taken a drastic turn.

He tossed items onto the side table and walked around the bed, waiting for her to exit. He didn't have to wait long. When the bathroom door opened slowly, he took Jordan's hand and sat on the bed, pulling her into his lap. She was relaxed, keeping her body posture open to him as she turned and laid her cheek on his chest.

He scrubbed his fingers over the brush of the buzz cut on the back of her neck. This was the calm before the storm. He cocked his head and looked down at his acquisition. He had to restrain her to further his assessment of her boundaries, strengths, and weaknesses.

She wasn't going to just let him do it. He would have to prove his physical dominance over such a strong woman. It was expected, common almost, for a dominant to have to prove himself the first time. With her issues and alpha-female personality, he would be very worried if she didn't resist him this first time.

"Remember your safe word," he rumbled. And that was the only warning he gave before he sprang to action, sliding her body off his lap onto the bed. He tried to get his body positioned over her. She fought him like a wild animal, wedging her legs between them in an effort to push him away with her feet. Her arms waved wildly to avoid the capture of her wrists. She screamed an unholy cry as she fought with all her strength.

"I changed my mind," she shrieked. "I changed my mind. Let me go!" She tried to wedge her knees between them again, and he was forced to let go of an arm to keep her legs from getting there.

"I hate you," she bellowed, thrashing and jerking underneath him.

He was impressed by the magnitude and the fierceness of her fight but when he finally caught her arms and looked down at her face, his stomach turned. Her eyes were squeezed tight while she shrieked her pleas to be left alone, but Jordan was no longer there with him. She was purging her demons.

With one wrist in each hand, he drew her arms over her head and then put his full weight on top of her, covering the fighting jerks of her arms and legs completely and inhibiting her attempts to escape his hold. They were cheek to cheek.

"Shhh...I got you," he murmured into her ear. He doubted she heard his exact words over her own commotion, but she'd heard something because her cries ebbed.

"Your Sir will take care of you," he growled.

Her jarring resistance began to languish and her shouts eventually subsided into sharp, fast breaths breezing past his ear.

"Your Sir will always catch you when you fall."

Soon, she was quiet with only an occasional sniffle. Seconds later, the body beneath him went slack. She surrendered. "Good girl."

Quickly, he spread her arms wide and then secured first one wrist and then the other. Leaning over her, he placed both hands on either side of her face. "Open your eyes, Jordan."

She watched him while he bound her legs to the corners of the bed.

He understood where her head was as she continued to kick and thrash as much as the restraints would allow, testing them.

The restraints were the first stage in her process of releasing all of them in a safe way. He picked up the flogger he'd pulled from Dennis's drawer and started striking her on the tops of her thighs. The evenly spaced moderate stokes applied to her sweaty, gleaming skin held him in thrall. He moved his strokes up to her breasts and impacted the quivering flesh, leaving pink stripes here and there. He took his time painting those pretty pink lines over all of her exposed flesh.

A long time later as his strokes eventually softened and slowed. She'd endured the flogging without uttering a peep.

She opened her eyes, and their gazes met immediately. Her pupils were dilated, almost completely taking over her chocolate-brown irises. Her once straining muscles were loose and warm.

Her expression was raw. The doubts about her own sanity and an absurd conviction that he wouldn't want her anymore were reflected in her eyes.

From his own CALM Therapy sessions, he knew this moment and the stone-cold feeling of dread that accompanied it. "This is what I want. Anything less would be unacceptable," he said to her, knowing this moment would cement the bond between them. His heart stuttered while he found the right words. "You're mine now. I'll never leave you as long as you need me."

His brain screamed a warning but his heart already recognized the first inklings of love. He felt the gravity of his situation increase in proportion to the depth of feeling he'd already developed for her.

Her gaze was unfocused. Her sight became insight. She closed her eyes to him, hiding her relief at his words as tears tumbled from the corners into her hairline.

Shane resumed flogging her down one side of her body and up the opposite.

He knew she was nearing the next phase of her session when her quiet tears were replaced by moans.

Her massive emotional dump was being beaten back by the endorphins her body released. Shane paused only long enough to place a clothespin on each of her nipples before he picked up the flogger again and with precise skill coaxed more of the feel-good chemicals into her bloodstream. Every slap of the leather evoked an answering groan and another level of release. Her muscles trembled.

There was a great disconnect between the refined mind and the baser place where she was now. Now that she was there, where she kept her rogue cannonballs of self-doubt and pent-up pain, she could set it free, releasing it all into the air like helium balloons floating away until they were so small they disappeared.

Shane set the flogger down and peered intently at Jordan. A shaft of sunlight slanted through the window, turning her hair into a halo of illuminated strands. Her face was smooth and peaceful. His heart squeezed. She was beautiful.

She'd fallen into the correct physiological state to begin the next phase and apparently, so had he because he could not want her more...on any level. She was made for him, her ying to his yang. He stilled, feeling like this was a significant moment in his life, the consummation of their new arrangement. Well, the closest he would come to consummation.

He pulled the butt plug from the side table, lubed it, and then crawled up between her legs, trailing his index finger up the inside of her thigh as he did. He was rewarded with a guttural moan.

He rimmed Jordan's rear hole with a lubed finger. She was relaxed, pliant.

Slowly he inserted the small plug and another raw noise emanated from the back of her throat. He leaned into her and hovered over the small strip of hair at her pussy, breathing on the place where her clit peeked out at him from between her peach-fuzz pussy lips. She rolled her hips and groaned.

"Sir," she said with a barely there whisper. He swiped a finger through the channel of her tiny lower lips. Her response was urgent, a greedy movement to gain as much pleasure out of the action as possible.

Shane left the bed and picked up the flogger again. She needed to be worked for one more turn. She was too present, hanging on to the last vestiges, not truly giving up all of her control yet.

"I want it all, Jordan. Trust me to give you everything you need." He walked around to the four corners of the bed and checked her restraints before he started the methodical stripping of the last of her will.

Her thigh's and breasts glowed pink in the late-afternoon sun by the time he was done. The visual feast of Jordan bound, writhing, with his marks on her body and her cunt weeping for him, struck him with force. She needed him. The grease that quieted his own squealing emotions began to flow. He'd felt the power of dominance before, with other men's subs, but those experiences had been puny compared to the absolute fucking power that electrified him at that moment. It was a rush...cubed.

Ridding himself of the flogger, he selected a vibrator, and turned it on its lowest setting. Shane was rock hard at the sight of her delicate cunt with the cute stripe of supershort brown hair rising from her mound.

As he moved onto the bed between her legs, she moaned a complaint at the loss of the pain almost a full minute after he'd stopped flogging her. He smiled. The delay was a good indication she was near the state she needed to be. He grazed the tip of the black phallus between her pussy lips and rested it at her entrance.

She was responsive, raising her hips as much as she was able in an effort to get more of the fat dick inside her. She writhed feverishly as he slowly advanced the dick-shaped vibrator, watching her opening stretch to accommodate it, her lips becoming taut around the rubbery phallus. They held on tight as he pulled it out of her.

Beautiful, she was stunningly beautiful with the flush on her cheeks and chest and her tight little body arching, begging for more. He absorbed every moan and tremor as she responded and began the process of tensing again.

He wanted to give her a slow build because he knew the longer he held her back, the better the catharsis of her release.

He was sorely sorry he'd told Patrick he wouldn't fuck her.

He was captivated by the sight of the black dick penetrating her pink flesh and how her cunt lips caressed the length of it during the slow advance and retreat of the fat vibrating phallus.

The base of the butt plug taunted him when she moved her hips to match the rhythm of the pumping motion.

This was it. The payoff of what he did. His cock was rock hard as he surveyed *his* submissive. She'd submitted wholly. It was a rush to hear her beg and cry and a need fulfilled to experience the total trust and surrender of this powerful woman. It was the ultimate high in a world that offered him no control of his own circumstances. He was profoundly moved.

He pumped the huge fake cock harder and faster and gazed down her body to her face. Jordan's eyes were closed and her lips parted. The grasp she had on her wrist restraints turned her knuckles white.

Shane scooted himself back and lowered his head to the wildly undulating sweet spot between her legs. He closed his lips over her clit and his teeth grazed the erect knob. "Oh God," she screamed. Then she begged for permission to come. "Please, Sir. Please. I can't hold it back any longer."

Her movement stopped for several seconds while he relentlessly lashed her with his tongue and fucked her hard and fast with the vibrating cock until she erupted. Her body jerked involuntarily and the blast of a throaty shout resonated through the room. She was an explosion in a deceptively innocuous package, like a cherry bomb.

A fervent possessiveness and an intense need to protect sparked somewhere within him.

Finally, when her response slowed, he pulled away from her, unfettering her from the restraints and checking the condition of her skin underneath.

She drooped, lying limp on the mattress. Her wrists were chafed from her wild thrashing. There would be marks on her for a few days.

He covered her with the blanket and she rolled to her side, assuming the usual fetal type position he'd seen her in several times now. He sat with his back against the headboard and pulled her into his lap, rearranging her and the covers, and held the tiny bundle of woman in silence. Her teeth chattered and her muscles twitched. Shane stroked her and held her tightly.

When she opened her eyes, he reached for the glass of water on the bedside table and brought it to her lips. She drank obediently and then burrowed back into him, closing her eyes again.

"I'm sorry," she whispered. "It's been years since it's been like that. I came without permission."

"There's nothing for you to apologize for. Today, I meant for that to happen. I wanted to see how long you could hold it. Everything in this session was the way I chose it to be. Your body was under my control. Your pain. Your pleasure. It was all exactly as I wanted it. As it always will be in every session until it's time for me to release you."

She didn't respond. She just made herself smaller and snuggled into him more closely.

This was what she sought, an oasis in the eye of the storm. He gloried in the refuge he provided for her. He was prepared to be this for her forever.

Chapter 14

The half-moon beamed in the cool Atlanta night, giving Jordan a clear picture of Patrick waiting in the alley when she and Shane entered. The brothers shook hands and spoke a conversation between them with their eyes. Then she noted that Patrick's palm wasn't empty when he shoved it in his pocket. Shane had handed off something to him when they'd shaken hands.

"Jordan." Patrick leaned into her and placed a gentle kiss on her lips. "I missed you."

Shane interrupted the sweet moment between them. "Tomorrow night, I'll wait for a half hour, between twelve thirty and one in the morning. If you don't meet me then, I'll assume there's no message for Amber. Sound good?"

Patrick nodded. "Tomorrow."

Shane's gaze momentarily flicked toward her and her stomach lurched. She didn't want to leave him. She took a breath to speak and began to form the word "wait," but he'd read it in her face and shook his head before he silently stepped out of the alley, leaving her alone with Patrick.

He turned to her. "Ready?"

"Yes."

He took her hand, pulled her into the night and then got her settled into the backseat for the last few hours of his shift. She tried to stay awake as long as she could in the cool darkness of the car because she'd already decided that she would change her sleep schedule to match with Patrick's night-shift job as much as she could. Plus, if she only went out at night, she thought she'd have a better chance of not being noticed while in Sapphire.

Her mind ticked through a mental list of everything she wanted to get done over the next two days. She felt like herself again, strong and confident, for the first time in a while.

When Patrick finally got off work, the sun had almost fully risen, turning the eastern sky increasingly lighter shades of blue. He drove silently to his parents' house, pretending she wasn't hidden away in the backseat. But as soon as she was in the house, Patrick shut the kitchen door behind them and kissed her.

"God I missed you," he said as he pulled her toward him.

He burrowed his fingers through the short hairs on the back of her head, while his other arm wrapped around her waist. He held her tightly. She arched backward from the forward advance of his lips. He groaned his pleasure.

Then Kate cleared her throat from across the room and Patrick let loose another groan, but this one was a protest.

Patrick released his grip on her and acknowledged his mother's presence. "Mornin', Ma."

"Good morning you two." She looked to Jordan. "Hungry?"

She nodded. "Very."

"I'll make us all breakfast. If you'd like a shower, I have some clean clothes for you in Patrick's room."

"Thanks, Kate." She turned to Patrick. "I'm going to clean up."

Jordan heard Kate moving around in the kitchen as she walked from Patrick's room to the bathroom. She left him lying on his bed and had a feeling he'd be sleeping when she returned.

She was okay with that. He needed a nap and she needed some perspective. This was going to be her routine now, and she'd have to be able to transition from one zone to another without getting disconcerted.

She hated being separated from her Sir. She hated it with Dennis and she hated it now. She pressured herself to brush off the residue of her new situation in Amber. And the worry she carried about what Patrick may or may not think about her had to take a backseat to the job she had been assigned.

By the time she'd showered, eaten and updated Kate with the plans she and Xander had agreed upon, it was time for the first official meeting of the Sapphire Zone Resistance.

Thanks to the cover of the Irish Heritage Club, the Sapphire Zone resistance meeting took place at dinnertime and looked more like a social event than a group of people plotting to take down the Gov. There was food and refreshments and the loud chatter of a large group of women when they entered the space. The noise immediately began to dim as they walked through the door and made their way through the crowd.

Their first order of business was to choose leaders and organize their zone's different divisions. The group voted Kate to colead with Jordan, and she would be the head honcho when Jordan was in Amber.

After that piece of business was concluded, Jordan talked with the entire group, discussing goals as well as identifying the teams she and Xander had deemed necessary in the meeting she'd had with him two days earlier.

Kate's efficiency astounded Jordan. Because of her personal knowledge of every person in the room, Kate got to work assigning people to the teams she felt they were best suited. The woman was a whirlwind and had the job done in less than two hours.

Then, Jordan and Kate met with every team leader, identifying their initial duties and ultimate goals. Kate had chosen Patrick to help head up the missions team

It was late night when Jordan and Patrick rode in the rear seat of his parents' car back to their house. He was quiet, too quiet. So far, they'd not spoken a word about what he'd learned about the therapy and if it would affect their relationship.

She'd hoped. God she'd hoped that when she returned to Sapphire, she'd find the man she left, waiting for her. But now, the sinking feeling in the pit of her stomach told her something was different.

Whatever. She swallowed past the lump in her throat. Shit. She was going to cry. Turning to look out the window, she gathered herself and took a deep breath.

She told herself it didn't matter what he thought. And then she spent the rest of the ride trying to harden her heart and thicken her skin. She absolutely refused to let anything detract her attention from resistance business.

When they arrived, Aaron excused himself for bed. Kate lowered herself into a chair at the kitchen table and motioned her over. They still had quite a bit of information to get through so Kate was completely updated and in the loop. Jordan's heart fell when Patrick approached the table and gave her and his mom a kiss on the cheek. "I'll leave you two women to it. I'm tired and going to bed."

Jordan watched him leave, only turning her attention back to Kate after she couldn't see him anymore.

Less than a minute after he'd left the kitchen, Kate derailed their conversation about safe houses and started down a new path.

"I think my son is falling for you"

Jordan looked up to meet Kate's gaze. "I don't think so. Not anymore."

"I thought I detected a slight change between the two of you since last time you were here." She looked at Jordan speculatively. "How does Shane fit into this different dynamic? I understand he's staying with you."

Jordan swallowed, and the loudness of it was almost comical.

"I'm not trying to pry, but if you need some advice about either one of my boys…" She didn't finish the sentence. "Are you a fallow, Jordan?"

That was an awfully personal question and would have been considered rude if they were in the Amber Zone. "No. I'm not."

"So you like children?"

Jordan looked Kate O'Connor in the eyes. "Sure, I like them, but I couldn't eat a whole one."

The woman met her gaze, her eyes were blue knives whittling away the armor to see what was inside. She smiled. "I like you," she announced. "We're going to get on just fine. If you ever need to pick my brain about either one of them, just let me know."

Kate was shrewd. She would be a good leader. "Thank you, but I can't." Her throat started filling with that damned lump again. She shook her head. "I'm not sure what's going on myself yet." She pasted on a smile. "Now let's figure out how to get close to General Morgan."

Kate nodded and then turned her attention to her notes. "We can't just go in there shooting. The chance of anyone getting next to him is slim. And the chance of that person getting back out alive is slimmer."

"We have to get to him in a way that won't call attention to us, and the assassination needs to be quiet enough it won't trigger alarms while we have people in the compound.

"Patrick can get into the Peacekeepers Compound, but he's with his unit when he goes there. The chances of him getting away and then getting close to Morgan…it would be insanity."

Ideas were proposed and ruled out, others were kicked around and around, but none resulted in any feasible plan.

Kate rose from the table and padded over to the kitchen cabinet. She pulled out two short glasses and then filled them with a clear liquid she poured from an unlabeled bottle. When she returned to the table, she handed Jordan one of the glasses and clinked the rim with the glass she kept for herself. With a swallow chased by a hiss, she threw back the contents of the glass.

Jordan should have known by the whiff of kerosene she got a second before the liquid splashed on her tongue that the innocent-looking liquid would be noxious. It burned her esophagus as it traveled down to her stomach, and she felt like she was breathing fire. "Holy God." She wheezed.

"One of Aaron's friend's makes it. Another?"

Despite Shane's dictate about alcohol, Jordan nodded and Kate went about refilling the glasses.

"Maybe we're approaching this from the wrong angle," Jordan said, slumping back in her chair. "We need to be thinking about getting to him through his family or a friend, someone he'd meet without being too concerned about how much security was around."

"The man's single. Who do you think he's wettin' his willie with? A man like that, so full of himself, he's fucking someone." Kate slid another glass of the liquid hell across the table to her.

"If he has a regular woman, maybe there's a way to get near him through her. But I've never heard of him having a lady friend."

"Maybe he's not into ladies." The two women cackled, clinked glasses again and swallowed back the homemade booze.

Jordan set her glass on the table. "Hmm. He could like guys. I have no idea."

Kate's eyes glinted with mischief as her gaze flew up to the clock on the stove. "Two in the morning. Go wake up Patrick, see if he'll join us while I put some water on for tea. We'll pick his brain."

"Kate, you're evil."

"God knows he's had me up at this hour more than once. It's time for him to return the favor."

Jordan laughed. "I like your style."

"Right back at ya."

With only the light from the kitchen spilling through to the corridor, Jordan tread softly on the cushy carpet. It was so dark by the time she entered his room, she could barely see. Walking closer and finding the edge of the bed with her hands, she knelt beside it.

The room was too dark to distinguish his features but she waited for her eyes to adjust, listening to the steady rhythm of his breathing. Her heart ached. She hadn't realized how intense the feelings she had for him were.

She laid her head on his chest and her hand found his face, caressing his cheek. "Patrick," she whispered. "I need you."

His arms came up and curled around her. "I need you, too," he whispered back.

"You have to get up. We need to pick your brain."

"No." He pulled her closer and scooted her body so she ended up straddling him with her head still positioned over his heart.

"Your mother is waiting for us."

"She can wait," he said running a palm over the curve of her ass.

She grinned into the darkness. "No. You can wait."

Placing her hands on his chest, she pushed herself up. She wanted to lean over and give him a quick kiss, and in the moment's hesitation she took to have the thought, Patrick raised his hand to the nape of her neck and pulled her down until they were nose to nose.

"Fuck, I'm hard for you. Come on, put a man out of his misery."

She gave him that quick kiss, finding his soft lips in the darkness and then did some maneuvering to exit the bed. "We'll be in the kitchen."

Patrick joined them, dragging ass but sweet as always as his mother picked personal facts about General Morgan from his brain.

Jordan admired the way Kate's mind worked, following her train of thought as she teased enough information to form a loose plan from both rumors and fact.

Jordan was engrossed with the navy-blue eyes scanning back and forth between Kate and her when something brushed against her pants underneath the table.

She glanced at Patrick. He was totally engrossed in the debate he was having with his mother.

When she felt the whisper of movement again, it was on the other side of her body. Jordan scooted her seat away from the table and glanced underneath. When she caught sight of black fur, she yelled, "Oh my God!"

She jumped from her chair. "Oh my God." She gasped. "There's an animal in here."

She glanced up to Patrick, who was already standing and then Kate.

"Don't worry, Jo. It's my cat." Kate walked to the animal and scooped it up off the floor. It was shiny black with intelligent green eyes that stared back at her.

She met Patrick's gaze, heart racing and anger rising. "Dammit. That thing scared the hell out of me." Kate let the cat jump out of her arms and it advanced on her. "Shit, Patrick! Grab it."

Patrick laughed and finally moved to grab the animal by the scruff of the neck, stopping it in its tracks. "His name is Sylvester. Come on," he encouraged her. "Touch him."

He stroked the cat's back and it arched up into his palm.

Now that he had the animal under control, Jordan reached out slowly, and grazed Sylvester's smooth coat with her fingertips. He attempted to nuzzle into her, but Patrick kept a tight hold. "He likes you," Patrick said.

Kate yawned and rose from the table. "I suppose this would be a good time to pack it in. I'm going to bed."

"Thank you," Jordan said when Kate gave her a hug. Then Patrick got one as well before she left them alone.

Jordan turned her attention back to the cat. "How did I miss that thing the last time I was here?"

"Cats are independent creatures. He probably wasn't in the mood for socializing."

"Are they safe...friendly?"

"For the most part, they don't really have a desire to please like dogs do. They're smart enough, but they look at any human that presumes to tell them what to do with disdain. They do what they want, when they want. Period. Ma says dogs have masters and cats have staff." As if to prove a point, Sylvester escaped from Patrick's grasp and padded his way silently, tail curling in the air, out of the kitchen.

"He's kind of cute."

Patrick pulled her toward him. "So are you." He positioned her on his lap. "I think it's way past time for us to go."

The warm air from his words sent a shiver down her spine. He wrapped his arms around her, gathering her up so that every part of her was on his lap. They spent some time in silence and during the lull, Jordan realized how tired she was. She broke several of Sir's rules, alcohol, sleep...at least she was eating well. She rested her head on Patrick's chest and closed her eyes. "I could fall asleep right here."

"Go ahead. You're going to need your rest," he growled and then stood with her still wrapped tightly in his arms. "I'm taking you home and having my way with you."

She giggled several times during the harrowing drive. It was obvious he couldn't get her there fast enough.

When they arrived back at Patrick's apartment, he turned on a tiny lamp that gave them just enough light to climb their way up the winding staircase. The loft bedroom was cloaked in dark shadows. Patrick clapped his hands twice and the bedside lamp responded by popping on.

"Oh!" Jordan giggled.

"Try it," he urged her.

She clapped her hands turning the light off, then on again. Then she burst out laughing.

"I know, I know. It's called The Clapper. I saw it in a special display at the store and I had to get it. It's perfect for this room, don't you think?"

She sighed. "Absolutely perfect." Feeling warm and happy without a tsunami of body chemicals overwhelming her was a weird, different kind of wellbeing.

He turned to face her in the shadowy room and began to unbutton her shirt. Slowly, the seconds ticked by as he took his time revealing a little more of her with each button. She looked at the top of his head as he lowered himself to one knee and unfastened her pants and tugged them down toward her feet. She used his shoulders to steady herself as he rid her of her pants and panties completely.

She stood nervously before him, fully naked. His gaze raked over her body, taking her in. When he stood though, his expression had changed. He walked a slow circle around her, and she felt a soft touch to her thigh.

"You have bruises." His words were terse, his eyes angry. She looked down at herself and was reminded of her melt down and the resulting session with Shane. The cuts on her knees from the broken glass she'd groveled in were scabbing, and she had tiny bruises speckling every square inch of her skin along the front of her body. The abraded skin around her wrists and ankles was raw from her session too. When she realized what she must look like to him, anxiety followed.

"What the fuck? Did you do this? Or was it Shane." He advanced on her and she stood her ground. She would never again cave to a man's aggressiveness unless she gave her consent for him to do so. She lifted her chin. "What Shane does is not your business."

He stopped cold. "I love you. Can't you see that? I can't stand all these marks on your skin."

"I need these marks on my skin," she grit out.

He looked down at her with worried eyes. "Jo." He shook his head. "God, baby, I don't even know how to respond to this."

He shook his head and released a long sigh. Stepping close, he took her hands and placed a gentle kiss to first one bruised wrist and then the other. His palms skimmed up the outsides of her arms, while his gaze searched out all the other little marks and bruises. She couldn't quite decipher the expression on his face. It seemed to be a mix of anger and anguish.

He swept her up in his arms and deposited her on the rich mocha duvet. Standing next to the bed, he loomed over her. She was scared. Scared he would think she was crazy and reject her.

He rubbed his hand over his face and sighed. "Fuck, Jo, I'm going to soothe every single mark away, every damn one."

She shook her head. "No, Patrick. Just pretend they're not there and lay down next to me...please." She looked him in the eye. "Please," she whispered so softly she wasn't sure he'd heard, but moments later, the length of him stretched out next to her on the mattress.

He wrapped an arm around her. "Come closer," he whispered.

She snuggled into him in a way she'd never done with anyone before, throwing a leg over his body and laying her head on his pectoral. She listened to his heartbeat as he held her tightly.

It was progress.

It was perfection.

It was a moment that made her believe someone could love her.

Chapter 15

Jordan wandered through the empty safe house checking all of the cabinets and looking through closets to pass the time until Jaci arrived. She was glad for the solitude. She'd been feeling like she needed some time alone.

For over a month, she'd alternated two days with Patrick and two with Shane.

With every new day in Sapphire came a lifetime of new experiences and new feelings. For the first time in her life, Jordan's positive feelings overshadowed the darkness of her past.

Patrick loved her. He knew about the CALM Therapy and loved her anyway.

They never discussed it--not once since that first night he'd found bruises on her. Jordan knew he put it out of his mind because it upset him, but there was nothing she could do to change that.

She felt back in control because of Sir's care and structure at home. She loved to curl herself into a tight ball and nuzzle next to him when he watched the video feeds. Sometimes, he sifted his fingers through her hair. Sometimes, she relaxed so completely, she fell asleep. He was her serenity. The absolute constant in her rapidly shifting and chaotic life.

Alone in their apartment, she lived the carefree life of a child, safe and sheltered. There were no worries about tomorrow. She lived totally in the moment because, more than anything, she knew her Sir would take care of her. She was his prized possession. He reminded her of that fact often. This was the very essence of what total submission was to her. She gave everything up to him, and in return she lived her life with a slight high that released the tension in her shoulders and made her aware of the first deep breath she'd taken in a while.

The anticipation of when she might repay him for all the burdens and worries he took off her shoulders grew with each passing day. She saw his erections during their time together. One day, he wouldn't hold back, and he would use all of her. And though he never said it, she knew he loved her. She'd never felt more loved in her life, not even with Patrick.

She was in love with them both. It was foolish, she knew, but both O'Connor brothers had gained entrance into her heart, one with a quip and one with a whip. Patrick's sweet words could coax the sugar out of a bowl of punch. He made her see the lovable woman who'd always been inside. The one she'd never had enough courage to let out.

Shane sliced through her tough outside layers and made her accept herself in a way she never had before.

They provided the cornerstone she needed to begin healing in earnest. The fifty-fifty split of her time in Amber and Sapphire created a perfect balance, stabilizing her life in too many ways to count.

Now, as their mission plans were coming together, Jordan's thoughts turned to the future. She feared a change. And there *would* be a change.

At some point, she was going to have to make a choice between the brothers because her half time in each zone wouldn't continue indefinitely.

Her chest squeezed tight at the thought of it. Lately, much of her time had been spent attempting to shake that fear away, telling herself she'd cross that bridge when she had to and not one second before. She wanted to love them both for as long as she could.

Jordan gazed in amazement out the windows, soaking up the view in every direction. The Onyx Zone was overgrown. Houses drowned in dense brush and tall grass.

The tunnel to the other side of the wall around New Atlanta hadn't been one hundred percent finished, but a person could squeeze through if they had enough courage to do so. Lack of courage was not an issue for her.

Jordan couldn't wait to get a look at the outside world, and she knew that once the word spread, many would want to make the journey across. Once all the supports were in, that tunnel was going to be well used.

The resistance had encountered a handful of people living just outside the wall. Normal, friendly people, not the crazed savages the Gov invented to keep people afraid of the zone outside the city walls. The sheer enormity of the lies and psychological manipulation they'd been subjected to, keeping them afraid and compliant, hit her as she stared out into the surrounding neighborhood. Every single person in New Atlanta could have their own city if they wanted to. The wildlife was abundant, and she didn't doubt for a moment that given the right circumstances a strong, healthy person could survive there. It was paradise, a Garden of Eden.

When Jaci slid open the large glass door leading from the backyard into the house, a huge feeling of relief washed over Jordan's tense muscles. She needed this time with her friend. She needed female advice, judgment-free advice from someone who knew most of her secrets.

The women hugged each other before sitting at the kitchen table.

"How's the repop coordination going?" Jordan asked.

"Good. There's a lot more to it than I thought, but I think my team is starting to get a handle on it. The first hurdle has been overcome. We have several vehicles up and running so when people start leaving Amber, we have a means to get them where they need to go."

"So you're relocating away from New Atlanta?"

"Yeah. It makes sense. If people are leaving, they're not going to want to be too close to what they're running from."

"But total isolation isn't good either."

Jaci nodded. "We've found an area about forty miles from here. It's perfect. The houses have enough land to farm and access to water. We've cleared the road to get there, and we've cleared most of the houses in that area of remains, mapped and documented their size and location. To do it right, giving everybody a decent chance of making it on their own, is a massive undertaking." She smiled. "I'm excited for the people who are going to show up at their new homesteads and find them prepared, stocked with water, food and wood for heating and cooking and rifles to hunt with. God, Jordan you can't imagine what's out there. This world on the other side of the wall is saturated with guns and ammunition, wildlife, fruit trees. There are massive stores that have what seems like unlimited amounts of brand-new things, from blankets to cars. It's amazing. We've also found things the resistance can use like body armor and night vision. It's awesome, Jordan. We can all be happy out here."

For a moment, Jaci seemed inflated, floating on a vision, and then she relaxed and returned to the real world. "It's going to take a lot more work. But it's doable. My latest scheme is to get some chickens in the pens of some of these farms. One of the resistance members works at the egg-processing plant and we've been working on a way to get eggs that will produce chicks out and into Onyx." Jaci looked over toward Jordan and waved a hand. "You must think this is ridiculous compared to everything you're doing."

"Huh. Actually, I was thinking I wanted to be on your team instead of having my own."

"How's everything going in Sapphire?"

"Did Xander tell you that the vast majority of the Sapphire resistance is women?"

"Of course. He's proud of you and your women."

Jordan smiled a rare smile. "I'm pretty proud of us, too."

"Speaking of women, did you hear the rumor that Morgan was keeping the women that would have been sterilized and transferred to Amber in his jail on the Peacekeeper's Compound?"

Jordan nodded. "I'm the one who started it. Patrick got a message from Rock confirming Morgan has two women down there now. What I'm wondering is what are they doing with the men? They're not being delivered into Amber anymore and Morgan sure as hell isn't going to let them stay in the Sapphire Zone unless they're in jail. But Rock says they're not."

"So what are they doing with them?" The women looked at each other both speculating as to what the answer to that question was. "I don't even want to think about it." Jaci sighed. "It's too disturbing.

A comfortable silence fell between them until Jaci spoke again. "Xander told me about the breakdown you had and about the therapy. Why didn't you tell me? I obviously would have understood."

"I always thought it was something…I don't know, sick. Like only people who are unbalanced need it. I didn't want people thinking I was crazy. Besides, I've hidden it so long it was just the normal thing for me to do."

"What are you doing now that Dennis is gone?"

"Shane stepped in."

Jaci's eyebrows shot up and a sly smile spread over her face. "Why don't you get Patrick to do it?"

"You make it sound like there are people lining up for the job." She shook her head. "No. Patrick is playful and fun…and romantic. Not really the personality profile of a dominant. Shane is none of those things. He's serious, protective--" She looked at Jaci and whispered, "Sexy."

"Oh God, Jordan, you're in love with both of them."

Jordan's stomach jumped unsteadily, hearing Jaci say the words out loud. "Yeah. I am. They're both so wonderful, in totally opposite ways, but still stunningly wonderful. I've tried to choose one but whenever I see the other twin, I fell back in love all over again.

"It's normal to fall in love with your dominant. Regardless of what's going on with Patrick, wouldn't Shane be the right choice?"

"You'd think, but I've discovered a totally different part of myself with Patrick. He brings out a playful side of me. Life is fun when I'm with him." She met Jaci's gaze. "My life has never been fun. It feels so good, normal. God, I'm getting the urge to cry just thinking about it." Her voice wavered. "How lucky am I?"

Jordan shook her head. "And their mother, God Jaci, she's awesome. She's exactly what I've always wished for in a mom. We're friends now, but ultimately, she's going to hate me for pitting her sons against each other, and she'd be right to do it."

"You're not the only person responsible for this three-way thing that's happening. They've had a hand in creating what's going on. Don't take all the blame."

Jordan felt like she was going to cry as the real reason her world felt like it was going to crumble around her came to mind. "I lied to them, Jaci. I told both Patrick and Shane someone else would be bait on the mission coming up."

Jaci gasped. "The Morgan mission? Shit, Jordan, why?"

"I was trying to avoid a month's worth of their objections. It seemed like a good idea at the time, but now, I have to tell them. God, Jaci, I'm scared. I've never been so scared in my entire life."

Jaci stood, pulled Jordan out of her chair and hugged her hard. "Whatever happens, just remember I'm here for you and you're my best friend. You can talk to me about anything."

Chapter 16

The door to Patrick's apartment crashed open and Jordan threw down her bag full of firearms with a *clang*.

Patrick had spent the drive home telling her exactly what he was going to do to her when he got her alone.

He wasn't messing around.

She ran into the living room, laughing and evading capture while he started unbuttoning his Guard uniform. He advanced on her until he'd backed her into a corner with no avenue of escape.

"Stop! I need to talk to you before the meeting," she yelled and then squealed as she tried to run out of the corner.

"Talk later. Monkey-love now." He lunged at her, wrapping an arm around her waist and began his efforts to free her from her black t-shirt.

"No," she said a little too loudly. She evened out her tone and slipped out of his grip. "Later."

He scowled "Promise you're not going to get too busy."

She nodded. "Promise."

He grunted and then reluctantly stepped back and plopped himself on the couch. "Okay, what's so important that it's cutting into my playtime," he grumbled.

She stalled, looking at him, reluctant to say the words she'd practiced so many times in her head. "I am going to be the bait in the mission tomorrow, not Alissa. And before you say anything, nothing is going to change that fact."

That he immediately understood the full magnitude of her deception was readily apparent. His jaw clenched. "You were planning this all along." He stood, and the features on his face turned hard, and his blue eyes were stone cold. "You never intended Alissa to go, did you?"

"No."

"Does my ma know this?"

Jordan nodded.

He turned his back and walked away from her, grabbing his keys from the table where he'd dropped them.

"Where are you going?"

"To my parent's house. I'll come back and get you before the meeting."

She wilted. She'd been hoping for a miracle. A reaction that didn't include him walking out on her. She told herself this would be okay, that he just needed some time to assimilate the new information, and Kate would help talk him down and smooth things out.

Her heart was in her throat as she walked to her backpack, scooped it up and handed it to Patrick. "Take this, people are waiting for the guns."

He took it from her and paused, shaking his head. He looked like he was going to speak, but he closed his mouth and shook his head again.

"Oh, wait." She pulled the backpack out of his hands. "I have fresh panties in here." She unzipped and fumbled around inside. Her journal fell to the floor. "Dammit." She set the bag on the table to prevent other things from spilling out while she dug for her underwear, then zipped the pack up when she was finished.

She looked up to hand the pack to him and found Patrick reading a page in her journal.

His gaze lifted from the book and flashed at her. Rage tinged his face red. "You tell him how many times we fuck?" He threw the journal onto the floor at her feet. "Does he keep track of how many times I cum in your mouth, too?" he sneered.

"Sir needs to know. It's a part of the--"

"Sir? Sir," he shouted at her. "You call him sir?" he bellowed.

He crossed his arms and stood there gawking at her with a disgusted expression and eyes that burned her with the contempt they held in their depths.

In that instant, Jordan's soul contracted and her walls flew up. After all this time, it only took a moment for the easy comfort she relished so much when she was with Patrick to vanish.

For the first time since she started splitting her time between zones, Jordan's emotional defenses stepped in to protect her. Inches thick armor, honed and hardened from the realities of her life, slammed into place.

She stood tall and lifted her chin. "Have someone pick me up for the meeting. And I'll be going back to Amber tonight so don't forget about me when you leave for work." Then she turned her back on him and walked away.

He must have seen the change in her, understood he'd crossed a line, and sighed. "He's my brother, Jo. Please tell me this wasn't a flight of fancy, something to pass the time while you're trying to rule the world."

Jordan sat, propped her elbows on her knees and cradled her head in her hands.

She had to tell him. She'd get no better opening than this.

She looked up and met Patrick's gaze. "I love you, Patrick. But I love him too."

* * * *

The past month of two days in Amber and two days in Sapphire seemed to be what Jordan needed. And Shane had never seen Patrick happier

Shane was miserable.

He was in love. He hadn't been able to keep enough emotional distance to prevent himself from falling in love with Jordan. She was irresistible and there wasn't enough control in the world that would have held his heart back from her.

He sat in the empty room as the sun began its descent beneath the horizon, casting late day rectangles of light onto the crumpled sheets of the bed.

The door to the bathroom opened and Fern stood in her bra and panties, scanning the room for the rest of her clothes.

Shane had been benefriends with Fern for years and lately, he'd been calling her regularly to relieve the lust that boiled in his blood every time Jordan was in the room with him.

He'd kept his word to his brother. He hadn't fucked Jordan and he hadn't made her suck him off. But his willpower was nearing his breaking point and even the meaningless releases he'd been fortifying himself with were becoming dangerously close to being ineffective.

He watched Fern dress. She was a gorgeous woman and a wildcat in the sack. But today, he'd had a difficult time getting his dick hard so he could fuck her.

"This isn't working for you anymore," she said as she sat on the edge of the bed.

He shook his head. "No. It isn't."

"What are you going to do?"

"The same as always. There's not a whole lot of options for me."

"I don't understand why you're just giving her to your brother. She obviously needs you more than she needs him."

"Maybe. But he loves her and she loves him."

"And you love her."

"And she doesn't love me."

"How do you know that?"

"Because she has a sweeter, funnier version of me to love."

Fern stood, grabbed her purse and strolled over to him. "Sweet and funny are not all a girl looks for in a man." She leaned over and kissed him on the cheek. "See you in a few days."

Shane stood and walked Fern out, then returned to the stark loneliness of the apartment.

Later tonight, when Jordan arrived, the room would be filled with her presence and the apartment would feel like a home again. But right now, it was cold and empty. His heart ached when she was away.

He made the trek to the alley expecting to give and receive information with Patrick, but Jordan was there instead, and she'd come alone, without Patrick as her escort like every other time she'd crossed.

She was quiet on the hike back to Circle City. Shane didn't ask about what was on her mind. Their division between her resistance authority and his home authority worked exceedingly well. He would ask when they were in the solitude of their apartment. If she couldn't talk about it because it was privileged information she had to discuss with Xander first, he treated the stress and left the topic of what caused it for another time.

As soon as Jordan stepped over the threshold of their apartment, she began removing her clothes. "May I go to bed please, Sir?"

They made eye contact, and he brushed aside the short wisps of hair on her forehead with his thumb. He scanned her stance. She looked defeated and exhausted. "No, not yet. Present."

Jordan removed her clothes and knelt in her present pose.

"Are you okay?"

Something serious was going on. He walked to the dinette and opened the bag, looking for the journal. "Where's your journal?"

"I don't have it anymore," she mumbled.

"Rise to kneeling and tell me what's going on."

Jordan straightened and looked up at him with her huge brown eyes. "I got into an argument with Patrick."

"About?"

She swallowed and he saw the struggle taking place within her. Her face turned cold, blank. "We were arguing because I told him I was going to be the bait for the mission tomorrow, not Alissa."

Shane straightened and crossed his arms over his chest. Silence stretched as his mind worked to create the appropriate response to the bombshell she'd just dropped.

He'd had a suspicion this would happen but he had to stick to his agreement about her command and her authority outside their apartment. He was the grunt.

And then--he saw it. The moment her eyes latched onto a tiny silver hoop peeking out from underneath her knee. She snatched it up, turned it over in her hand and opened her fingers. It glinted where light touched the metal.

His heart went into free fall when he saw the transformation of her face. She looked to him with accusation "You have women here when I'm gone?"

"I do." The words were raw and his heart broke when he saw the crushing blow they delivered.

"But you're *my* Sir."

* * * *

"It's my place to service you, please you. I don't understand." She looked up at him. "I would give you any part of me. You don't need to have anyone else." Jordan stood and began dressing. She turned to face away from him until her shirt was buttoned.

Her Sir stood silent behind her.

She faced him to read his expression when she spoke her next words. "I thought you loved me back. It felt like you loved me back," she whispered.

"I do love you."

She shook her head and walked a wide curve around him on her way to the door.

Her ears rang a high-pitched tone and the blood drained from her face. She braced her hand on the wall to steady herself and slipped her shoes on.

When she met his gaze again, she made sure she looked collected and emotionless. "You made me feel like I was important to you."

"Jordan. We need to talk about this."

She ignored his words as she finished putting on her holster, grabbed her gun from on top of the dresserand holstered it.

She was confused. Then, her confusion turned to shock when she realized he wasn't going to stop her from leaving. There was a rapidly growing pit in her stomach and dread was tying tight knots in her chest.

Jordan paused just before opening the door. "I'll see you the night after the mission. Or," she added in a carefully controlled voice, "the night of the mission if things go wrong."

Then he let her turn and leave the apartment. She closed the door quietly behind her.

As soon as her feet hit the pavement of the courtyard, Jordan ran. It was stupid, she knew, but she couldn't stop herself. She took a play from Jaci's playbook and squatted for a night in building twenty-eight. Somehow, having Shane and Patrick in her life during the past weeks heightened her feelings of isolation on the rare occasions when she found herself alone now.

She spent the night staring at the ceiling, trying to sleep. She never felt more alone and hollow inside than in those still hours, lying on a bare mattress in the abandoned apartment.

Her insides twisted in knots anytime she let her mind wander to the O'Connor men. She was woefully inexperienced when it came to love, but she thought she'd felt it from Shane too. She set herself up to be hurt. She knew when she started with these brothers that the whole thing was going to end up a mess. Yet she chose to do it anyway.

When late morning finally came, she met with Xander in the back room of the Wellness Center. For five hours, they pored over the entire assassination mission plan, detail by detail. When they were done, Jordan didn't return to the apartment.

Her thoughts were focused now. She needed to stay that way. She took a deep, cleansing breath of the crisp fall air. Jordan the soldier, the leader, was going to murder a man.

Chapter 17

Jordan was not afraid to die, and in many ways, she'd welcome it.

Aaron O'Connor stepped to her side. He was dressed in one of Patrick's Guard uniforms. "Are you ready for this, lass?"

Jordan nodded wordlessly. All around her were women, armed and unarmed. All with a special task in this mission. All risking their lives. Her throat was too tight to speak.

Kate O'Connor stepped up to her husband and kissed him. It was not the kiss of an old married couple. Aaron wrapped an arm around Kate's waist and twined his fingers aggressively into the thick knot of red hair at the back of her head. Jordan looked away, feeling like she was intruding on an intimate moment.

She turned and walked a few steps away, but still, a few seconds later, she heard them exchange I love yous and then Kate's instructions to her husband. "Take care of our girl here. I'm not sure either one of our boys will be the same if anything happened to her."

Jordan held in the "Yeah, right" perched on the tip of her tongue.

Then Kate turned and spoke loudly over the low stream of murmurs in the room.

"Gather around everybody." She motioned with her hands. "Come on. Get close."

Everybody moved in, clasping their neighbor's hand and looking to their leader and friend.

"I…" Kate looked at the floor for a few moments and when she looked up she had tears in her eyes and her words shook as if they were forced through a knotted throat. "I took some time thinking about the words I wanted to say as I sent everybody off today." She looked down again and wiped her eyes with her sleeve. I chose an old Irish blessing that I'm sure most of you know. I just couldn't have expressed my own feelings any better. So--" She grasped Aaron's hand and then traveled the few steps so she could hold Jordan's with the other and began the blessing as her gaze scanned over every person in the room.

"May the road rise up to meet you.

May the wind be ever at your back.

May the sun shine warm upon your face,

And the rain fall softly on your fields.

And until we meet again,

May God hold you in the hollow of his hand."

She looked around the room at everybody gathered there. "Good luck, and no matter what happens, use the tree. Two minutes until we move out."

Adrenaline pumped through Jordan's veins, and her system gobbled it up like candy. Her senses seemed to have sharpened in the crisp night air. As each team fanned out in the direction of their specific assignment, she gave a mental nod to Patrick for the idea to use distractions to draw the guard farther away from the location of the actual mission. His absolute planning from beginning to end was insanely coordinated. There were contingency plans for the contingency plans.

Their walk wasn't long, and when she and Aaron finally arrived outside the Peacekeepers Compound, Jordan shed her black shirt, pants and shoes before slipping through the slice in the fence.

She wore only panties and a razor blade taped to her abdomen, just below her panty line. Her heart thrummed loudly, and she tried to control her short, rapid breaths while she watched Aaron slip through behind her.

Jordan spotted the guardsman walking a woman toward General Morgan's private quarters. He was early tonight. Their timing had been almost too close for comfort.

Out of her peripheral vision, she saw Aaron pull his knife out of its sheath. They stood just outside the circle of light projecting from the single spotlight attached to the front of the building. When the guard stopped at the metal door and pulled his keys to unlock it, Aaron crept silently toward him.

The woman saw Aaron, and then Jordan behind him and immediately said something to the guard, drawing the man's attention completely away from the direction they approached.

The kill was quick and silent with just a momentary flash of Aaron's knife reflecting the light before the soldier hit the ground.

Aaron quickly dragged the dead man into the darkness around the corner of the building, and the frightened woman followed him. Jordan held a finger to her lips, grabbed her arm and led her to the slit in the fence, holding the metal apart as the woman slipped through. When Jordan released the fence, the woman turned to look at her.

"Aren't you coming?" It was a desperate whisper.

"No. Take this road." She pointed away and to the right. "We have someone waiting for you about five minutes away. She'll take you to a safe house."

The woman nodded. "Are you going to take my place?

Jordan nodded.

Their gazes met. "He will rape you."

Jordan gave her a gentle verbal push. "Go now."

She hesitated for only a moment more. "Thank you."

Jordan watched her retreat. It took only seconds for her form to completely disappear into the darkness.

"You ready?" Jordan jumped at Aaron's words coming from behind her. She nodded, and they cautiously walked back to the metal door. The key still protruded from the lock. Aaron turned it and twisted the knob. "Good luck. I'll be right here."

She stepped into the threshold and the door slammed loudly behind her. Another metal door was in front of her. She heard a slight buzz, releasing the locking mechanism and she pushed that door open.

Jordan felt awed by the over-the-top luxury of the General's residence. The bloodred carpet cushioned her bare feet as she stepped farther into the room.

Immediately, she caught sight of Morgan sitting in a living space off to the left. He sat on a dark leather sofa, watching the day's news feed. At first, he didn't acknowledge her entry. He was focused intently on the video clip of himself. She couldn't see the video, but she heard his latest speech coming from the speakers.

He was dressed in jeans and nothing else. The video feed illuminated his pale skin, defining the musculature of his shoulders and arms. It amazed her how the outside of a person could be so beautiful while monstrous evil lurked within. He leaned forward in his seat and grabbed a short glass with ice and a honey-brown liquid from the table in front of him. Still, he ignored her.

She took in the rest of the room. It was opulent with rich fabrics of red, rust and cream, crystal vases with fresh flowers, and on the far side, the biggest desk she'd ever seen. There were no other exits and no windows. She spotted several small cameras observing different areas. One, at the far end of the hallway to her right, was fixed on her.

One of the things that Patrick brought up and they had discussed at length was that Morgan was a predator. He would stalk his prey before devouring it. Cameras fit that behavior. His eyes were riveted to the video feed. He was watching her right now. She felt it.

She stood quietly, looking nervous for another minute more, when he finally turned to catch her with those ice-blue eyes. He looked at her wrist first. "A Sapphire. It's not often that I have such a treat. Why are you in my jail?"

"I was caught on the street a few minutes after curfew."

He smiled at her and it triggered a feeling of trepidation deep in her gut. The man was insane. "You won't make that mistake again, will you?"

Jordan looked at the ground. "No, sir."

"Do you know why you're here?"

"Yes, sir."

"Lift your chin. I want to see your face." He smiled another psychopathic maw when she met his lunatic gaze. "Are you going to be cooperative?" His eyes sparked. "Or do I have to tie you up?"

Jordan licked her lips seductively and then looked down at her feet again. "Cooperative," she whispered.

"Go to the bedroom down the hall and to the right. The bathroom is off the bedroom. Clean yourself up and then wait for me on the bed."

Jordan left the room quietly and walked down the short hall, hearing the soft whirr of a camera trained on her. The bedroom on the left had to be his bedroom. It was huge, luxurious. It looked lived in.

She walked into the room he'd directed her to. It looked like a guest room, but she knew it for what it was, his raping room. She walked through and entered the bathroom, shutting the door behind her. It carried the lush red theme of the rest of the residence with a floor of white marble veined with the same dark scarlet of blood. Deep red towels and accessories punctuated the rest of the room. She turned on the water and stood there, looking at herself in the mirror. There had to be cameras in there, too, though she didn't see one. She took deep breaths, trying to calm the furious racing of adrenaline-laced blood through her veins. She leaned over and placed an arm on top of the vanity and rested her head on top of it. Hopefully, while he looked at her from the camera somewhere above her, he wouldn't catch her other arm underneath her body, ripping the tape from her skin and unsheathing the razor blade from its cardboard holder.

She gripped it tightly between her thumb and forefinger, just how she'd practiced it over and over again. She was good at concealing the blade in a hand that looked natural and relaxed.

If he took his pants completely off, she'd strike while his legs were still tangled up in them. If he was only going to unbutton and unzip, leaving his jeans on, she'd wait until he was close enough to have a reasonably good chance at a clean strike at the neck.

Jordan turned off the faucet and opened the door an inch, peeking out to make sure the room was still empty. She exited the bathroom and, as she sat on the edge of the bed, she hid the blade under one of the pillows.

Jordan donned her mask of helpless and sweet while waiting there, and experienced a fleeting sorrow for all of the women who'd been there before her.

Her muscles were tense and twitchy, and her breathing came fast and hard. Her insides rioted while she sat as still as she possibly could.

She was ready to strike, primed to do some damage and ready to run.

Morgan entered the room with a gun in his hand. He held it down at his side as he stood at the doorway, scanning the room. "Let me see your hands."

She showed him.

He nodded and advanced on her, unbuttoning and unzipping his jeans with his free hand. He stopped in front of her. "Open your knees." She complied, and he stepped between them. "Come on, girl, wrap those legs around me."

Jordan tilted her head up slightly just as she'd practiced it and whispered, "I'm scared." She glanced at his gun for just a second then met his eyes. "I've never done this before."

He flashed an evil grin. "A virgin?" His eyes danced as she nodded. He was excited by the revelation.

"You'll have bragging rights then. All your little girlfriends will be green with jealousy when you tell them who took your innocence." He set the gun down on the night table next to his right hand and grabbed the front of her panties. Jerking hard, he ripped them away from her.

She was wide open and exposed to his greedy inspection, and she held her breath. A low growl emanated from his chest as he gripped his cock and angled the turgid and bulbous purple end toward her entrance.

She caught his attention with a whisper. "General Morgan?"

He stopped and looked up from her pussy to her face. Asshole.

"Will you kiss me? Please?"

Her words were a whisper with a perfectly added quaver of fear. She noted the quick dart of his eyes to her sapphire tattoo. Ah yes, he would never kiss an Amber.

His gaze softened, and he trailed a soft caress on her cheek. Jordan closed her eyes and moistened her lips by peeking a shy tongue out and sliding it over her top lip. She would not give him the time to think as she continued to nudge him into position with her practiced seduction and indomitable will.

His exhale breezed against her face a moment before his lips met hers. She widened the reach of her hand until she'd grabbed the razor blade. Then, she sliced at his neck with force.

Some instinct alerted him to the attack, and he was already jerking away from her by the time the blade sliced through skin. Instead of his neck, she flayed open the left side of his face.

"You bitch," he screamed. She bunched her legs between them, got a foot on his chest and shoved him with all the force her muscles could muster, sending him sprawling to the floor on his ass.

Blood poured profusely, through the hand covering the gash on his face

She sprung from the bed, leaving his screaming curses behind.

In an instant, she was at the exit. The handle turned, but the door swung inward, momentarily halting her progress while having to swing it wide.

A shot sounded from behind her and the pain in her right hand was instantaneous. Aaron was there in the cubby space between the doors when she entered.

There were two more shots while Jordan frantically pulled the door closed with her good hand and yelled, "Go!"

They ran into the night with Aaron taking her rear.

There would be transportation less than a thirty-second sprint down the street. She slipped through the fence easily and lurched toward her pile of clothes.

When she fell, it was face-first.

Then she passed out.

Chapter 18

Patrick sat, staring out the window at the border guard station. The plan to meet back at his parents' house would only stay in place if Jordan was successful in killing General Morgan. If she failed, they would all move onward over the border into Amber, having Patrick set fire to the border crossing station before joining them at The Holistic Wellness Center. From there, they would move forward, through the underground tunnel to the Onyx Zone. The surveillance cameras at the Peacekeepers Compound and at several other places would enable the authorities to eventually identify the parties responsible. Neither Jordan, his father or himself would ever be able to live in New Atlanta again.

Patrick stared at the window willing nobody to come.

When he saw his parents' car pulling up to the border crossing, he opened the vehicle gate and ran outside.

The car's trunk was open when he got to it, revealing two red plastic containers of gas. He grabbed them, closed the trunk and ran to the driver's side.

His inside's turned liquid when he saw Jordan's unconscious body in the backseat.

Aaron got out of the car. "Come on, boy. She'll be fine." He grabbed Patrick by the arm and directed his attention away from the car and toward their task.

Together, they lifted the containers and carried them into the building. Aaron unscrewed the caps and tipped them over, spilling the liquid in the center of the turnstile area. "Go on, Patrick. Get in the driver's seat. I'm right behind you." Patrick nodded, whistled loudly to wake up his sleeping partner in the break room and backed up toward the Amber Zone exit door.

Aaron pulled out the box of wooden matches from his leg pocket and caught sight of the half-asleep man emerging from a side door. "Run boy or you're going to be toast," Aaron said to him as he backed up and drew the red tip of the match over the strip on the little box. He waited for the Guardsman to get close to the Sapphire side exit before he threw the lit match into the room. A flash of light accompanied the *whoosh* of sudden conflagration.

In a few seconds, both men were in the car. Patrick drove away and glanced once in the rearview mirror to witness the sight of his old life burning to the ground behind him. "What's wrong with Jordan?" He repeatedly tried to look over his shoulder while driving.

His dad grabbed the wheel from the passenger seat. "Boy, you're going to get us killed driving with no headlights and looking into the backseat." He scooted closer. "Switch."

Patrick let go of the wheel and awkwardly climbed out of the driver's seat as his dad slid underneath him.

"Shane said this road dead ends at Circle City. He should be waiting for us there," Patrick said as he turned and knelt on the front seat to face his mother and inspect Jordan's body. She was covered with the Guard jacket he'd lent his father. Bare ankles and feet peeked out one end. His mother cradled her head and stroked her hair. Patrick reached out to lift the jacket but his mother caught his wrist. He looked to her.

"Patrick." She shook her head. Her expression was grim, her lips pressed into a tight, white line. "You've got to keep your focus. If you want to help, take your shirt off. She could do with something covering her. Patrick started stripping before the sentence was even completed, taking his jacket and uniform shirt off and then pulling his t-shirt over his head.

He handed the shirt to her and watched his mother lift Jordan's head off her lap and position the head hole at her crown. When he leaned in to help, she slapped his hand away. "Go on. Put your clothes back on. I'll handle the rest."

Their gazes locked and for the first time since he was a teenager, he was tempted to argue with his mother's instructions.

Reluctantly he listened and began to redress, but his laser gaze didn't leave Jordan as he did it. The peeks of skin he was able to discern were stained with blood.

His mother laced one of her arms though the sleeve of the shirt then looked up at him expectantly. "Give the woman some privacy before I tan your hide."

Patrick turned and faced the windshield, buttoning his shirt. "Ma, I've seen her naked before." He got no reply. "What is it? You're making me more worried."

"I'm just covering her."

"There's Shane," Aaron said, interrupting the tense moment between them. The car slowed.

When Patrick saw Shane, he knew the feeling swimming in his brother's stomach because he'd had it himself only a few minutes before.

Everybody opened their doors as the car rolled to a stop. Kate slid from underneath Jordan and stepped away from the car, and Patrick dove into the opening, pulling Jordan half out of the door. Shane was there a second later catching Jordan's lower half.

"What the fuck happened?" Shane growled.

"Shane," his mother said. "She'll be fine. Just a flesh wound, that's all. Let's get going. Now!" she ordered, snapping the men into action.

Patrick and Shane worked together wordlessly to position Jordan in Shane's arms. He turned and walked through the lobby of an apartment building. It was bright and crowded but quieted substantially as they wove through small groups of people with Jordan cradled in Shane's arms. Then they exited through another set of doors.

Patrick felt as if he'd walked into a movie. Even in the drab beginnings of winter, the beautiful garden setting they entered was gently lit and peaceful. Once they'd started on the path that wound through the garden, their pace slowed.

"Is everything in place here?" Kate asked Shane.

"Yes. We're all set at both border crossings. When Guard tries to come through, they'll be met by the Amber Resistance. Here we are."

They walked through a dark, empty building all the way to the back exit and then Shane stopped. He jerked his head toward the metal door. "Jaci's waiting for you. I'll follow when my part is done." He handed Jordan to Patrick.

Kate grabbed Shane's arm. "Your part is done. You got us here."

Shane shook his head. "No, Ma. I'm a member of the Amber Resistance. I belong out there with everybody else."

He opened the door, revealing the night. "Go on. I'll be right behind you." With barely a pause, Shane clapped a hand on Patrick's back. "Take care of her." Then disappeared in the direction they'd come.

"What happened?" Jaci asked as she approached them and caught sight of her best friend's limp body in Patrick's arms.

"She's been shot in the hand. She's going to need a doctor," Kate answered.

Jaci looked at the older woman. "You must be Kate. I'm Jaci." Jaci offered her hand to his mother who took it and then introduced him and his father.

"Patrick." Jaci nodded at him.

Turning her attention back to Kate, Jaci said, "Unfortunately, there are no doctors in the Amber Zone. I've been training as a nurse. I only just started, but I'll do my best to help. Let me run back into the building and grab some things."

She was back less than two minutes later with a black bag on her shoulder. The group followed her through the gardens to the farthest raised garden bed. She looked at Aaron. "Can you help lift?"

The wood frame of the raised bed was on a hinge and the entire structure lifted and propped open on one side, revealing the entrance to the tunnel. Jaci lowered herself in first and turned on a solar flashlight. His parent's went in next, and then Patrick handed Jordan down to his father and followed close behind, releasing the wood bar that held the frame open and closing the entrance to the tunnel.

It was dark down there with only the narrow beam of the flashlight to guide them. They were entombed by the red soil of the area. The hair on the back of Patrick's neck rose and a shot of apprehension washed over him in response to the tiny, suffocating canal they walked through. After several minutes, they hit the dead end of the tunnel. Metal rods were embedded in the soil like rungs of a ladder so people could climb out easily.

"I'll go first," Patrick said. "You guys work together to hand her up to me. Once I've got a good hold on her, I'll pull her out."

Patrick emerged into an overgrown, fenced in yard and pulled Jordan's unconscious body out of the hole shortly after. Jaci led them to the back door of the house and into a bedroom.

He laid Jordan on the bed.

"Okay, let's take a look," Jaci said as she began to unwrap Jordan's hand. Looking up at his mother, she asked, "Could you grab a basin, washrag and fresh water from the bathroom?"

Kate nodded and left.

Patrick turned his attention back to Jordan's hand now free of the wrapping.

"How could one bullet do so much damage? God." Jaci stepped back and looked away. "It looks like the bullet entered her hand in the side... here." She pointed.

Fingers dangled and shards of bone stuck out of the mess that had once been Jordan's right hand. It was beyond repair. He glanced up and met the stoic gaze of his father. His parents must have known that already because there was a tourniquet cutting the blood flow.

"It's going to have to come off," Jaci said. "I don't think I can do this."

She was white as a virgin's wedding dress and looked ready to pass out. "Sit your ass down before you fall down," he ordered.

She looked at him with desperation. "Oh, God, Patrick."

He grabbed her by the shoulders and looked at her eye to eye. "I need your help, Jaci. Keep it together."

He snapped his head around. "Da, we're going to need something to cut it off with. Something sharp and serrated would be best I think. Or maybe a cleaver if you can't find anything else."

Without another word, Aaron left Patrick and Jaci alone, hovering over Jordan's body. "I'm not sure I can do this," she repeated as she turned to rummage through her bag. "At least I have sutures and some antibiotics." She gasped and straightened. "Wait. I might have something that will help." She ran out of the room, leaving Patrick alone with Jordan.

He leaned over her and pressed a kiss to her lips. "I'm sorry, Jo. I'm so sorry for what I said. I'm not mad anymore." He tried to swallow away the tight, burning lump in his throat. "God, please," he hissed in an anguished whisper.

His desperation was cut short when Jaci reentered the room, paging through a book. "Here." She flopped it in front of him. "Directions."

He glanced down at the old medical textbook. "We'll do it together. Just don't lose it on me.

The procedure of removing the remainder of her hand, cleaning all the bone fragments out and pulling over the flap of skin to sew the wound closed lasted three hours. It was nearly dawn when Jaci got to her feet. "Pulverized garlic, spread thinly over the wound will stave off infection. Clean her up. I have to go back to the Wellness Center for what I need."

He nodded, but she was already down the hall by the time she ended the sentence.

Patrick looked to his parents. "I need some time with her."

Kate walked over and laid her hand on his shoulder. "She's going to be all right." His mother placed a kiss on the top of his head, and then she and his father left.

The room was silent. He looked around at the blood-soaked towels and shards of bone lying in disarray next to her on the bed and in piles on the floor.

He picked up a gallon jug of water, poured some of it in the ceramic bowl at the bedside table and soaked a clean rag. He began with her face, drawing the cool cloth across her forehead, and then he leaned over to place a kiss there. He did the same with her eyes, cheeks and lips.

His heart broke at the thought of how she'd feel when she woke up and found her right hand missing, and fear trickled down his spine at the thought of how she'd feel about him, knowing he was the person who took it. He didn't know whether she would forgive him for this.

Patrick gently pulled her good arm out of the bloody t-shirt, stretched it over her head and carefully threaded her injured limb through the armhole last. He rinsed the washrag in the basin and began cleaning her chest. Over and over again, he threw the dirty basins of water out the window and began again with fresh, cleaning every inch of her body.

He shook his head. There was too much blood.

She might still die.

He tried as hard as he could to swallow back the emotion, and the desperate begging that circled over and over inside his head.

Oh please, no. Please, no. The internal pleas wrenched from his heart while his shredded soul was paralyzed by fear and regret.

Wash.

Rinse.

Repeat.

By the time Jaci returned, Jordan was clean and the linens underneath her had been changed. He watched as she applied the poultice and covered the wound with gauze. "I'll be back later. I want to get back to Circle City to find out what's happened since we left." She cleared the area, putting her medical equipment back in her bag and with a quick wave was gone.

Chapter 19

Jordan's hand bellowed her heartbeat like great thumps of an internal bass drum ticking off seconds of excruciating agony. She attempted to drag her eyes open and felt the momentary resistance of eyelids that were glued shut.

Finally the gunk gave way to the dry scrape of eyelids. She was in an unfamiliar, but beautiful room with pale pink walls and painted bedroom furniture. From the color of the walls, her first instinct told her that she was in the Sapphire Zone.

But then she knew she wasn't. She was in Onyx. In the safe house.

Her brain came online a little at a time, she remembered the mission they had attempted the night before. Morgan had been right there, inches away from her and she'd missed his neck altogether.

The assassination attempt had failed. She'd failed.

The magnitude of this failure hit her hard. Every fear and vulnerability that had crossed her mind in anticipation of this mission struck her all at once. Every life that was irrevocably changed, like Patrick, Kate and Aaron's, every person left exposed because of their ties to Kate's Irish Heritage Club, flashed through her head. All of it was in play. The burden of her failure now lay squarely on the shoulders of the people left behind in New Atlanta. How many people were going to die because she'd missed that psychopath's neck?

Jordan closed her eyes to her beautiful surroundings. She wanted to sleep again. There was bliss in unconsciousness, no unbearable pain, emotional or physical. But now, sleep would be impossible. The throbbing agony of her hand was too severe.

She struggled to lift her arm, trying to get a look at how badly it was injured. When she focused on the blood-soaked padding that surrounded the end of her arm, her stomach lurched and her mouth began to water vigorously. She swallowed and breathed deeply to stop herself from being sick.

She looked again, only because she so clearly felt the pain and throbbing of it. But there was no denying the hand was gone.

Her head spun with rapid-fire thoughts, each one worse than the last.

Her right hand.

Her writing hand, shooting hand.

She was disabled.

She tried to sit up, using her uninjured limb to lift herself, when the warm grasp of a soothing hand cupped the back of her neck to assist her. She looked over to find Patrick's ocean blues searching her face with concern.

"Patrick," she croaked.

"Shh. Let's get you propped up so I can give you some water."

He lifted her to sitting against a stack of pillows so she was a little more upright. He was away from the bed in a flash, walking over to a small table with a glass and water pitcher.

Dazed, she looked down to her left hand and right stump resting in her lap. Her head spun and eyes fluttered as she struggled not to faint. A flash of heat flooded her face and immediately perspiration beaded on her upper lip and forehead. She groaned.

Patrick approached the bed with the glass of water and sat next to her on the edge.

"Shane?" she whispered.

Patrick's eyes were bleak as he lifted the glass to her lips. "Drink this. Slow sips. If you go too fast, you'll feel sick." As she took the time to take in the cool liquid, her mind raced. He hadn't answered her question. Shane wasn't there. Something went wrong with his part of the plan.

Panic sloshed the newly introduced water in her stomach. She groaned again, pushing Patrick's hand with the proffered glass away. Jordan breathed in gulps of air, trying to prevent herself from vomiting. As she doubled over from the cramps in her stomach, her eyes landed squarely on the stump of her arm.

She lost it then, vomiting up the burning mixture of water and stomach acids.

Patrick was prepared and held a towel under her chin, catching the majority of the rancid liquid. "It's okay, Jo. I got you." He hovered over her, cleaning up the mess with one hand and rubbing the top of her back with the other. Jordan rolled herself to her side and curled into herself, covering her head with her arm. The stump lay gingerly over her ear.

Sylvia Ryan

Patrick slid into the bed behind her, molding his warm, hard body against hers. He brushed his hand through her short hair on the back of her head and soothed his hand over her shoulder and arm from his position behind her. "It's going to be okay. Everything is all right. Everybody's safe."

It seemed like an eternity before she felt like she could open her mouth without vomiting again.

"Where's Shane?"

"He never left the Amber Zone. He wanted to stay and stand with the Amber Zone Resistance against retaliation."

"I need to speak with Kate," she rasped.

Patrick sighed. The warm air from his breath warmed the top of her head. "She couldn't stay here. She was worried about Shane and crossed back into Amber so she could get an update."

"How long have we been here?"

"About thirty-six hours."

Totally out for more than a day, and she still felt barely able to move.

"Who did it?"

"You're going to be--"

"Who fucking cut my hand off?" she shouted at him.

He stopped short and whatever words that lay on the tip of his tongue, he held tight.

"I did."

Silence.

"You'll be fine as long as you don't get an infection. Jaci did some of her holistic stuff and also brought over some antibiotics that she'd found in a pharmacy close to here. They're about twenty years past their expiration date, but we'd like to give them a try anyway."

Disjointed thoughts whirled through her half-lucid mind throughout the day.

She was in pain and numb at the same time. It was a hell of a cocktail that ebbed and flowed, tossing her in and out of consciousness, making time vacillate. Sometimes large chunks passed when she'd closed her eyes for just a moment. Other long periods of consciousness limped along at an agonizing rate.

Patrick was always there, whispering encouragement and taking care of her.

Two more days passed quietly between them with no word from anybody.

When Jaci finally showed up, Patrick left the room, giving Jordan some rare moments without being watched and cared for like an invalid.

She barraged Jaci with questions about what was going on in the city, about Shane and Kate but got no vital information.

"I haven't been in Amber since I arrived with what we needed to do your amputation." Jordan watched Jaci's eyes flick over to her stump and then back up to her face. "Xander didn't know how bad things would get and wanted me safe." She sat on the edge of the bed. "I'm sorry about your hand."

"I'm sorry, too." Jordan reached her good hand out to hold Jaci's. "It couldn't have been easy for you to help Patrick take it."

She shook her head. "It was the hardest thing I'll ever do, I think."

There were a few beats of comfortable silence before Jaci squeezed Jordan's hand tightly. "Everything about this has been hard. I've been trying to keep busy. It seems like there's so many things I don't want to think about right now. The work to get everything up and running for you guys is a blessing. My team has more than a hundred people now." She smiled. "And they're working like a machine. I can't believe how much we've completed in the last week alone.

"These last two days, I've been rushing them to get your new place one hundred percent done so we can transfer you there and free up the room here for others that may need to flee the city."

"When will it be ready?"

"I'm thinking tomorrow. I've got transportation lined up."

"I can't leave without knowing what's going on with Shane."

Jaci nodded. "I'm feeling the same way about Xander. I'm dying to get an update and know that he's safe. I'll tell you what, if Kate and Aaron don't show up before tomorrow morning, I promise I'll risk Xander's wrath and cross back over to get us an update. Deal?"

"Yeah. Deal." Jordan smiled. "Thanks."

"Can I get you anything?"

"No. I'm good."

"I have to go. There's still ten or a hundred things I need to do today."

"Can you tell Patrick I want to be alone for a while when you leave?"

She nodded. "I'll tell him, but I'm not so sure he'll listen. I don't think he's left the room or even slept since we brought you here."

"I need some time alone to take all of this in and try to figure out how this is going to work once Shane arrives."

Jaci shook her head slowly. "Shane wouldn't want you worrying about the stuff between Patrick and him." She leaned in close, meeting Jordan's gaze and whispered, "Trust him to take care of it when he gets back."

"I know."

"You know, but you're not doing it. If you truly trust him, you'll honor your bond with him even when he's not here. That means no worrying."

"He's not here, though. I need him and he's not here," Jordan rasped through a tight throat.

"He will be. What you need to do in the meantime is take care of yourself. Sleep. Eat. Heal. Relinquish everything else for now." Jaci leaned over and kissed Jordan on the forehead. "And I've got everything covered for you in Onyx. I'll be back tomorrow. You'll have news by then. I promise. Rest now, okay?"

Jordan nodded "Yeah, okay." She tried to accept the reassurance and push away the gnawing doubt. She'd walked away from him. Now, she couldn't blame him if he didn't show.

* * * *

It looked to be late morning when Jordan opened her eyes the next day. Multiple voices in the other room were muffled, but she definitely heard more than one male speaking. Jordan pushed the covers off her body, slowly slid her legs over the edge of the mattress and placed both feet firmly on the floor.

She felt shaky, but it wouldn't stop her from leaving the room that was beginning to feel like a prison.

She pushed herself to her feet. Four steps to the door, eleven steps down a hallway toward the voices, and she found herself standing in the doorway of the kitchen where Kate, Aaron, Patrick and Jaci sat around a glass-top table.

A loud scrape on the wood floor preceded Patrick's jump up, sending his chair tumbling backward and landing on its side behind him. "Jeez, Jordan, what are you doing out of bed?"

"I heard voices. I thought maybe Shane was back."

Kate ushered Jordan toward the chair Patrick had placed back in its upright position. When he tried to hover, Kate pushed him back. "Go on, boy. It's been nice chatting with Jaci on what she's been up to, but I have an official report to give. So if you'll excuse us please." Kate glared at her son, and for several seconds Jordan thought there was going to be a standoff. But then he nodded and slipped out the back door with Jaci following on his heels.

Aaron nodded at her. "Good to see you're up and around."

"Thank you."

"I'll be in the next room if you need anything."

"She doesn't need you breathing down her neck," Kate said. She looked down at Jordan, smiled, and then looked back to her husband. "That will be all, grunt."

Jordan laughed as Aaron shook his head and left the room. "Thanks. I needed that."

"My pleasure." She settled herself across the table.

"Shane?"

"He's fine. He's in one of the units trying to prevent the Guard from coming in and slaughtering indiscriminately. The Amber resistance has put the Guard at a disadvantage. Every time they try to cross into Amber, they're met with a unit that has more guns, more ammunition and geared up in body armor they don't have. But it doesn't seem like they're ready to give up trying at this point.

"Morgan's got to be superpissed. He's stitched up from the corner of his eye to his lips. He looks hideous, evil." Kate smiled. "Now his outside is as ugly as his inside.

"Shane said he'll exit Amber as soon as this siege was over. He said he had to stay and do his part so he'd be able to live with himself later. He told me to tell you this message word for word, 'Rules are to be followed.'"

"That's all? Does he know about my hand?"

Kate nodded. "He does." She sighed. "I doubt that's all he wanted to say to you. But it was all he was willing to say to his mother." Kate met her gaze. "He's in love with you, too."

Jordan shook her head. "I'm not sure about that, but I'm definitely in love with him." She put her head in her hand. "I couldn't stop it."

"Do they know about how the other feels about you?"

"I think so. They pass notes back and forth to each other." She snickered. "They think I don't know." Jordan lowered her hand and glanced over at the other woman.

Kate pursed her lips. "Interesting." She had a million-miles-away look in her eyes.

"Interesting?"

"Yes. It's interesting that they've both chosen to fall in love with the same woman.

"I'm not sure 'chosen' is the correct word."

"No. Chosen is the right word. Listen, Jordan, you're the newbie here. These men shared a womb and every minute of every day for the first twenty-one years of their lives. They know exactly what's going on in the other man's head. They don't even have to think about it. It's second nature. They are more attuned to each other, even in different zones, than you'll ever be with either one of them. So, yes, chosen *is* the right word." Kate smiled at her. "What, you thought you pitted them against each other?" She leaned in, sure to catch Jordan's confused gaze. "If anything, it was the other way around."

Jordan's mouth fell open.

"I don't know if it's true with other twins, but with them, nothing was as cut and dry as mine and his. With them, it was always ours. There was never much separation between them. They liked the same things. If one twin had something, the other wanted it too. But instead of fighting it out like normal brothers, they had this unspoken symbiosis that always seemed to satisfy any issues between them. In their entire lives, I've never seen them raise a hand or even a voice at the other.

"I guess what I'm trying to say is that this isn't happening because of something you've done wrong. I knew both my boys would fall in love with you as soon as I heard Shane had moved into your apartment all those months ago, and at some point they knew it too."

She shook her head. "Jordan." Their gazes met. "Don't worry about this. It isn't on you. It's on them. They'll work this out." Kate reached across the table and patted Jordan's hand. "You have other things to worry about." She stood. "You look white as a ghost. Let's get you back into bed before Patrick sees you like this."

With a strong arm around Jordan's waist, Kate practically carried her back to the pink room and inviting womb of the ultra-soft sheets. After getting Jordan situated, she stood back and smiled. "I have a letter from Xander." She pulled a folded envelope out of her back pocket. "I'm going to help Jaci and the men pack up the rest of the items we're taking with us to our new homes. I'll leave you to read it." She handed the envelope to Jordan and exited the room, closing the door behind her.

Her hand shook as she awkwardly ripped open the top crease of the envelope, holding the envelope down with an elbow and running her finger along the fold.

Jordan,

Unless I hear differently, I'll assume our worst-case contingency plan of action will be initiated as soon as you're able to do so. Jaci has everything ready for you, and I think you'll be happy in your new home.

If, for some reason, Patrick and Shane choose to move on instead of staying, let me know and I'll send some men out to you. You'll need someone to maintain law and order once the refugees begin to arrive.

Rock will secure a drop house near your new home. He'll leave the supplies he continues to collect while he's out on his missions there. Since we no longer have Patrick at the border guard station, the drop house will also be used to exchange information back and forth from Amber to the resistance in Sapphire. I will get the information regarding its exact whereabouts to you as soon as I have it.

From now on, a unit will run out to you once a week to share news and later, deliver refugees and any supplies we can help with.

We've had a large number of Amber Zone citizens step forward to join the troops covering the border, and with their numbers added, we've had no problem keeping the Guard out of Amber so far. We'll keep things under control in here. You do it out there.

I have no doubt that we'll come out on the right side of history and your sacrifice to this cause will not be forgotten.

I wish you well in the new adventures that wait ahead.

Good Luck,

X

Jordan looked away from the letter toward the window. "Well that's that." She threw the letter aside. She'd known already that she'd never be back to New Atlanta. She allowed her mind to wander through the conversation she had with Kate, and Shane's reminder to follow the rules.

She sighed, letting out not only air, but the angst that had been building over the past twenty-four hours. She should probably be gearing up to take over the reins of this massive next step in their plan.

She slid down in the bed and rolled onto her side. Her stump rested on her hip while her gaze still searched the view through the window. It was wild out there. She closed her eyes and listened to the sound of the birds calling to each other and daydreamed about the possibilities of this new life.

She eventually dozed, spending the rest of the day falling in and out of sleep with the pain dictating how long she'd remain in the sweet state of unconsciousness.

Chapter 20

Jordan sat next to Jaci as she drove the pickup truck down the two barely cleared tire tracks that passed as the road. The crews had removed large debris from their path, but the vegetation had a good foothold and only now was starting to give up some of its ground for the vehicles that have been streaming back and forth for a month now.

"Xander and I have talked about the setup in the Onyx Zone quite a bit over the last couple of months, figuring out the particulars to make this work. I've brought a manual detailing all the planning. What's been done, what's next on the list.

"We wanted this frontier to be organized, done right, so less people die and more people, maybe the next generation, would have the confidence to strike out further on their own. Everybody will pass through your relocation center, spending some time scouting out available properties and choosing which their group will go to. They'll also have the choice to join a group that's already established themselves, if there's an opening. Along with each location, there's an extensive library on one specific area of expertise. The adults on that homestead will become as knowledgeable as they can about that particular specialty. There's hundreds to choose from, medical, agriculture, animal husbandry, gas engines, solar technology, plumbing and waste disposal. I could go on all day. Anyway the homesteads all have enough land to grow food during the summer and keep animals. Plus they are in close proximity to places they need to access in order to learn and practice their skill. For example, the homestead charged with learning how to get the water running into the homes again is walking distance to the water pumping station. The medical homestead is right next door to an old hospital and the house itself is stocked to the brim with every medical textbook we've run across. The homesteads span out in a full circle with your homes and the relocation center in the middle of them all."

Jordan listened to Jaci go on and on about the planning and work her team already completed in the Onyx Zone. The whole enterprise was well thought out and organized with impressive detail. Jaci's team was doing everything they could possibly do to ensure the new pioneers would survive. Jordan was impressed at the sheer magnitude of details Jaci rattled off and she gained another perspective and a new level of respect for her friend.

"We're here," Jaci sang. Her excitement was cute. But when Jordan's attention turned from her friend to the property in front of them, her breath caught in her throat. The truck pulled around the horseshoe-shaped drive of an elementary school.

"This is the relocation center, the clearinghouse for the people coming in. But it's more than that. It's downtown, town hall, trading post and where the law will be if there's trouble. It's really an ingenious plan because as the homesteads succeed and grow outward in concentric circles, there's a link back to somewhere more civilized if it's needed."

The truck's door squealed open and Patrick reached in to help Jordan out and steadied her as they walked through the front door of the school. An office sat to the left of the entrance door. Beyond that was a large open space that had corridors fanning out in different direction.

The focal point was a huge map adhered to the far wall.

Jordan began to walk toward it when Jaci's gentle touch on her shoulder stopped her. "Hold on."

Jordan turned to look as Jaci strode to beside the door and rolled a wheelchair in her direction, stopping behind her. "Sit."

"Is there anything you haven't thought of?" Jordan asked, thankfully settling herself in.

"I can't take credit for the chair. One of the team members found it in the clinic and cleaned it up for you."

Patrick took the handles and rolled her further inside.

A you-are-here arrow identified the clearinghouse, and over a dozen homesteads around it were indicated with thumb tacks that had a number written on the end of the white plastic base. The counter beneath the map held numbered files, presumably filled with information regarding each homestead and the area of expertise the inhabitants were expected to become proficient at.

"Every white pin indicates a home that's ready for inhabitants. The red pins are ones that are currently being prepped but aren't ready yet."

Even with the O'Connors, you're going to need a few more people to run this operation. I think it will soon become apparent how many more you'll need and what jobs you'll need them for.

"There's a neighborhood behind the building. We've prepped two homes for your group. They're big, and you guys can split up as you see fit. She turned to face Kate. "Of course, if anybody in your family doesn't want to stay here, they have first choice of homesteads."

Jaci turned back to Jordan. "This building contains the relocation center housing, trading post, farmers market, town-hall meeting room, clinic and secured rooms for a jail, if needed. I'd like to house people with specialized and necessary skills like doctors, dentists, solar energy and cistern installation, to the neighborhood behind this building with you guys at first. Their central location will serve everybody until more come.

"We've outfitted thirteen guest rooms. Each room can hold up to four people." Jaci walked down a long hallway and opened one of the doors, revealing what appeared to have been a classroom at one time. The room was bigger than her entire apartment and held two big beds, a couch and dinette set. "There's solar panels on the roof. They provide enough charge to light the common areas at night."

"Nice," Patrick said.

"Jordan, you'll be running the Relocation Center and oversee all the services in this building. Yours is the final word here."

Jaci turned a corner and large double doors greeted them. "It used to be the gymnasium but now it's the trading post and market." She opened a padlock that secured the thick chain around the handles of the double doors and pushed one of them open. "We were hoping you and Aaron would take charge of this area," she said to Kate.

The room was well lit by panels of glass in the ceiling and high windows along the outside wall. The group stilled for several moments and took it all in. There were empty tables lining the room. To their right, a newly constructed wall that bore the sign General Store above the door filled everybody in on what was on the other side.

"So, people who have goods can come here to trade and barter outside the store. And if they can't barter for what they want, they can use money to buy it at the general store."

Jordan was rolled through the door of the store. She was impressed. Behind the counter was shelf after shelf of every kind of necessity she could think of.

"When we first started out here, our teams went from house to house looking for specific items. Coins, anything farming or gardening related, generators, matches…there's really too much to even mention right now. We took shelving from the school library and stocked this place to the brim." Jaci turned to Kate. "What do you think? Would you like to run it?"

Kate nodded. "I would."

The group took several more minutes to wander and absorb everything.

"Are you ready to see your place?"

Jordan nodded. "Yeah. Then I need to rest for a while. I'm beat from sitting up so long."

Patrick's voice sounded from behind her. "There's no rush, Jo. We have forever here." Jordan looked up over her shoulder at him. His eyes were bright and his smile was even brighter. It was obvious that he was happy to be there.

"You're right. Let me lay down here for a little while before we go anywhere else."

"Okay. You rest. I'm going to take Kate and Aaron to their house." She motioned for them to follow her. "I'll come back for you two."

Jordan and Patrick ended up alone in the large entry room. He pulled her up out of the chair and laid her down on a comfortable brown couch. She watched Patrick move around the room, finally ending up at a table that held a large water dispenser and cups. He filled a cup and brought it over to her.

"Come on, baby, let's sit you up so you can take your pills."

He helped her to sitting and handed her the cup of water before he dug in his pocket, producing a couple of the many pills he made her take every day. Her hand shook as she lifted the cup to her lips.

"This is too much, too soon for you," he grumbled. As he watched her drain the entire cup of water.

"I'm fine. I just need a few minutes."

"I wasn't expecting all of this. Were you?"

"Yeah. When Jaci and I spent the afternoon together at the safe house, it was obvious she'd thrown herself into this job. And with a crew of about a hundred people, I knew it wasn't going to be half-assed."

"It makes me sick to think about where we could be by now if the Gov had set its priorities on something other than the Repopulation Laws," he grumbled as he continued to eye the map on the far wall.

Jordan shook her head. "This will be better. It's Gov-free here…" Her next thought hit her full force. "We're free."

Goose bumps raised on her arms as she looked to him. "We're free."

Patrick lifted the top portion of her body, sat and pulled her into him. "You're free to have as many babies as you want."

Jordan swallowed hard. The statement he'd just made was massive, a bomb that blew away the restrictions she'd lived with all her life, opening up possibilities, but also reminding her of Shane.

As he sat holding her at the beginning of their new life together, the air thrummed with the unsaid. Patrick had to be as aware of the predicament they'd be in when Shane arrived as she was. She assumed it was at least part of the reason he'd set aside what was between them and hadn't so much as kissed her on the lips since they'd arrived in the Onyx Zone. And with the notable exception of the statement he'd just made, dreams of the future Patrick used to share had been left unmentioned. He didn't have to tell her why. It was mutually understood. They were in limbo until Shane arrived.

When Jaci returned, she was alone. "You ready for the best part?"

"Better than this?" Jordan asked.

Jaci nodded. "I can't wait to show you." As they exited through the back door into the rear parking lot of the relocation center, Jaci pointed out the house on the right. It was gigantic. A mansion. "That's Kate and Aaron's house."

She pointed to the house on the left. "That's yours."

Jordan's breath caught in her throat as she took in the two-story brick building, surrounded by a sleeping forest and a colorful carpet of fallen leaves. She was speechless. Jaci stopped pushing Jordan's chair and stepped up next to her. "Did you ever imagine you'd live in a home like this?" Her voice was laced with just as much awe as Jordan felt.

"No. I could never have dreamed up something so beautiful." She looked up at her friend. "Thank you."

"After what you did to Morgan?" She smiled. "Call us even. Come on." Jaci pushed Jordan to the edge of the cement at the back of the school and then stopped long enough for Patrick to pull her out and carry her through the yard up to the front door. He carried her over the threshold and set her down gingerly.

"Can you walk?"

She nodded. "Enough to look around and get to my bedroom."

Jaci walked them through the lower level, showing them the modifications they'd made, including the installation of a wood-burning, cast-iron cook stove and a toilet rigged to a cistern on the roof that actually flushed, using the force of gravity to fill the tank.

"There are solar panels on the roof here, too. Not too many though. Just enough to give you light in the evenings and maybe charge some small electronics. Come on out back. It's the best part."

She slid open a glass door that exited into a backyard completely enclosed with wood fencing and occupied by chickens and rabbits. "The eggs hatching into chicks were a miracle. Only about ten percent hatched and survived. The rabbits were easy. We set a couple of humane traps, caught some wild ones and now we're letting them do their thing. You should be overrun with rabbits any time now." She laughed and Jordan laughed with her.

"Jaci, I don't know what to say."

"You don't need to say anything. All of this is purely selfish. I want you around when I move into the neighborhood. I'm thinking that house over there." She pointed to another home to their left that was almost completely covered by ivy.

"Just FYI, that plant attaching itself to the houses and climbing everything gives people a terrible, itchy rash. Don't touch it without gloves. Some of my guys found that out the hard way." She shook her head. "It was really awful. Their hands, arms and faces were covered for over a week."

They stood for a minute taking it in when Jordan began to feel the drain of all the activity. She swayed slightly while a high-pitched tone rang in her ears and the blood ran out of her face. She made an effort to hide it, not wanting to show her weakness, but Patrick was way too close to not notice.

"Come on. Let's get you to bed," he said, sweeping her off her feet and carrying her up to the bedroom. The room was huge with windows lining the outside wall and a sitting area across from the bed covered by a beautiful quilt.

"The washroom is in the far corner." Jaci pointed. "The sheets are clean."

Patrick laid Jordan on the bed and then looked down at her with concern. "You okay?" He held his hand to her forehead and then her cheek, checking for fever for what seemed like the hundredth time.

Jaci moved to the bed. "I hate to go so soon, but I've got to make a run out to one of the homesteads. I'll check back tomorrow, if I can. The next day, if I can't do it tomorrow."

Jaci hugged her.

"Thanks for everything, Jaci," Patrick said, and after she gave him a hug too, he walked her out

Jordan spent the rest of that day and several of the following fighting exhaustion and dealing with the never-ending treatment of her stump. It oozed and bled, needing constant dressing changes so the bandages wouldn't become putrid and infect the healing wound. And the pain, it never went away. What Jordan had assumed would be an easy recovery as long as she didn't get an infection, turned out to be a nightmare. The hand that wasn't even there anymore cramped and burned. Shooting pains attacked her unexpectedly. The blissful respite from the pain she experienced in days of deep, healing sleep, began to elude her as she became stronger.

Every morning she and Kate met and discussed the projects for the day. And then, they all left her to complete assigned tasks essential to their survival out in the Onyx Zone.

The O'Connor clan made it perfectly clear everything other than getting well was somebody else's responsibility. She had to wrestle away easy tasks like unpacking her clothes and organizing the cupboards and drawers in the kitchen from Kate on the first day she felt well enough to do the smallest of tasks.

During the days, when everybody was busy, she walked the rooms, making a sincere effort to keep her mind off of Shane. When he returned, she'd tell him how much she loved him and needed him. Until then, she decided to put the scary issues that remained in limbo out of her mind, trusting that when he returned, he would take care of the new set of problems facing them now that the brothers were in the same zone.

But solitude had a way of working on her mind. As days passed, it became harder to not worry why he still hadn't come.

She tried to prepare herself emotionally for the outcome of the devastating decision the brothers would probably make together. Deep down inside she knew what that decision would be. Patrick's comment about babies pointed out the obvious. Shane couldn't give her a family, couldn't give Kate grandchildren. He would bow out of the equation.

She knew he would. Or maybe, that was what he was doing now… bowing out.

She looked down at the stained wadding at the end of her arm. Or more likely, he was disgusted by the thought of her stump.

She was. Why wouldn't he be?

More and more every day, the thoughts stewed while she wandered endlessly in her new home. The impending loss grew and festered as each day passed without Shane's return.

This was what living without him felt like.

Complete emptiness and an exponentially burgeoning despondency afflicted her to her very soul. The morbidity of the thoughts and feelings she kept caged within her flourished like a sickness, taking over her body and her mind until she had little motivation to care about much else. Her depression was gaining ground.

After a week in her new home, the uncertainty created by Shane's absence threatened to unhinge her.

And then the thought came. It was the Hiroshima of thoughts, a late entry, a game changer that almost tipped her over the edge of sanity. Shane stayed in Amber to be with the woman he'd been seeing…the owner of the earring.

The irony of the situation didn't go unnoticed. She was drowning in the deepest wave of depression she'd ever experienced and it was caused by the loss of the only man who could help rid her of it.

Finally, she knew it was time to move on. Time to put on her big-girl pants and start living her life again. If Shane showed up, great. If he didn't, she'd make it without him.

She walked to the relocation center and found her office. In another time, when the building had been a school, it was the principal's office. She spent the rest of the day reading the operations manual Jaci had drafted for her. The woman's organization was impeccable and the manual covered everything from the building's operations and upgrades, to how to care for baby chicks to maximize their survival rate.

By the end of the day, Jordan felt better emotionally. Staying busy took her mind off Shane. She only thought about him a hundred times a day instead of a thousand, and she was tired enough to crawl from her office to her bed without worrying about lying awake because of all the rest she'd gotten during the day.

Jordan repeated her long days holed up in her office, reading, learning, preparing to be the cornerstone of this operation. The success of the relocation center was imperative to the resistance. She wanted to make sure the people seeking refuge with her would leave with a solid foundation of knowledge and the necessities to see them through the rest of the winter.

Jordan's days got longer and her withdrawal from the rest of the O'Connor family grew. In the moments between tasks, when her mind wasn't occupied with the business at hand, she tried to avoid thinking about Shane. When she did, she got trapped in daydreams that hurt too much. She fought hard to prevent the depression from debilitating her.

In the quiet moments, she considered the Gov's stand on the Repopulation Laws. The perspective that Ambers were diseased and crazy obviously had some merit, because no matter how hard she tried to fight it, she'd been just able to keep her head above the drowning flood of despondency she'd inherited from her loser parents. It incensed her that the only thing those people gave her was this defect. She was a disgrace, handicapped in mind and body, and neither impediment would ever mend. They were her burdens for life.

After hiding from everybody in her office for a couple of days, she looked up from her desk to find Patrick standing in the doorway. "Jo." He shook his head. "Baby, we need to talk."

"No, Patrick. Just…no. I don't want to talk."

He walked over to stand directly across from her desk. "You didn't eat your dinner."

She glanced at the plate sitting on her desk. "I forgot. I've been reading." She mustered a smile. "You'll be happy to know that I now feel confident I can deliver a baby, both human and barnyard animal.

"I also developed a daily chore list for you." She slid a piece of paper across the desk. "Read it and make changes as needed, then return it to me."

He walked around the desk, turned her chair around to face him and leaned in to clutch the arms. He hovered above her, forcing her to tilt her head up to meet his gaze. "Jo, stop. Just stop," he hissed. "Running yourself into the ground is not going to get him here any faster." His stormy eyes swirled with anger.

"I don't know what you're talking about."

"The fuck you don't!" He pounded his fist on the desk beside him and she instinctively flinched at his show of aggression.

"I'm sorry." His tone was immediately softer. "I didn't mean to scare you. I'm frustrated. You're not eating. You barely sleep in bed anymore. I feel like I'm losing you."

She stared at him stony faced. "You didn't scare me, and I'm not going anywhere."

"Do you need a session? I could try--"

"No," she said quickly. "I do not need a session." She glared at him. She thought she was doing a pretty damn good job of keeping herself together after losing her hand and her Sir.

At the sound of someone clearing their throat, Jordan looked over Patrick's shoulder and found Rock leaning, arms crossed and tattoos proudly displayed, in the doorway. She smiled. "Now there's a scary sight."

"Right back at ya." He strode across the room and shook Patrick's hand before he settled on the other side of her desk. I made the trek to check out your digs and this is the welcome I get?"

"I've got a few things to get done. I'll leave you two to catch up," Patrick said, still sounding hot under the collar as he strode out of the room.

"Lemme see." Rock raised his hand palm up and looked at her expectantly. She left her stump in her lap. "Lemme see." The low rumble of his voice sounded menacing but she knew Rock was about as dangerous to her as a cotton ball. She rolled her eyes at him before she placed her forearm into his hand with her stump in full view.

He examined it on all sides in the bright rectangle of natural light coming in from the setting sun. "That's bad ass." He grinned at her. "I want to make little attachments for the end like a flashlight or an arm gun, something like that. Would you wear it if I made you something?"

"Only if it's really precision, state of the art all the way. I don't want any rubber-band bracelets with a bottle opener and a pocket knife taped to them."

They laughed together. It felt good to have a genuine laugh. It had been a while.

Rock met and held her gaze. "Patrick's really worried about you."

"Patrick can get over himself. There's nothing to be worried about."

"That's a load of crap and we both know it." He leaned forward, his face held a determined scowl. "If I had to pick my ass off the floor and brush myself off, so do you. You don't get to check out because you're feeling sorry for yourself."

"You're an asshole, Rock."

He nodded. "That fact is not in question."

"I'm not feeling sorry for myself."

"Then what is going on?"

"Shane." She shook her head. "I'm not sure he's coming back."

"Listen, the Amber Resistance is still holding the Guard at bay. You should expect to have him walking through the door in a day or two after that situation is resolved. When that happens, all of your pieces will be in place. Then it's time for you to start doing your job. People are counting on you. Are you understanding me here?"

Jordan bowed her head and looked down at the hand and the lack of hand in her lap. "Yeah. I got ya. I don't get to check out."

He nodded. "Good."

"You were at the safe house?"

"Yep. I stopped in on my way out here."

"You're welcome to stop back anytime. As a matter of fact, you don't have to go back at all. We have rooms ready."

"No. I still have work to do inside New Atlanta. Plus, when I leave, I think I'm going to try to get as far away from this place as possible."

"Don't blame you a bit."

"I gotta go if I'm going to hitch a ride with one of Jaci's crew." He stepped around the desk, got down on one knee next to her, and wrapped his arms around her.

"Everything is going to be okay," he murmured.

"Come see me again?" she choked out.

"As soon as I can. Promise."

Chapter 21

Patrick was failing, and he needed reinforcements.

Little had he known when he rose in the small hours of the morning and made his way out into the clear, cold night that his desperate grasp for help would end like this. The only thing he'd really been thinking was he was losing her, watching her crumble a little more every day and had no idea how to stop the spiraling free fall.

He didn't know if she was mourning the loss of her hand, if she was missing Shane, or if she burdened herself with the failure of the mission to kill Morgan. She didn't say much to him even when he turned on the charm full throttle. When he'd tried to talk to his ma about it, the normally opinionated Kate O'Connor said, simply, "Give it time."

He'd been desperate as he turned the key of the truck, and the motor sparked to life. It seemed noisy in the quiet of the night, riding back toward New Atlanta.

He only spent an hour at the safe house before he turned back toward home. He expected to be back by early afternoon.

Patrick looked down at the old-fashioned wristwatch he had to wind every morning. It was one of the small treasures left from the family that lived in their home all those years ago. It still worked perfectly, showing it wasn't even eleven AM, and he was only a few miles away from the relocation center compound.

He looked at what sat next to him in the cab of the truck and smiled. While at the safe house, he'd left a message to be sent to Shane about Jordan and got talked into this return passenger when he'd confided his feelings of worry for Jordan to the woman currently staying in the safe house, awaiting transfer to the relocation center.

He pulled into the yard and turned the engine off before he pulled his sleeping passenger off the seat and carried his charge into their home.

Jordan wasn't in the kitchen, so he made his way up to the large master bedroom suite upstairs. She was sitting up in bed but her eyes were closed. He set the small, now totally awake and squirming, puppy, down on the bed. The dog's brown-and-black tail wagged its whole backside back and forth while it walked excitedly toward Jordan. It stopped and sniffed the bandages that covered her limb and then whined before plopping down next to her. It tipped its head to the side and perked her ears up when Jordan finally opened her eyes and focused on the hairy bundle. He knew he'd found something when the surprise…and fascination flashed over her face.

"Pam, the woman you saved from Morgan that night, is waiting with her boyfriend at the safe house. He breeds the Guard dogs. He brought his dog, Sweetie Pie, who is the mommy, to move out into the Onyx Zone with them. And this little girl he brought especially for you when he heard you'd been injured. He said once he gets here, he'll finish her training to be your service dog."

"I don't need a service dog."

"I thought the same thing at first. But, she'll be good protection for you when Shane and I aren't with you. Plus, how could I say no? He saved this girl from the Guard just for you."

They both examined the curl of brown-and-black fur. The puppy gazed at Jordan as intently as a little one with heavy lids could do after a long car ride. "This is going to be her first night away from her mama. He said to expect some crying. He gave me the basics for care but he said all she really needs right now is love and soothing from her new pack leader, you. It already looks like you've got a new best friend."

Jordan smiled and whispered, "She's so cute," as she raked her fingers her fingers against the lay of the black fur on the puppy's back.

"You're so cute," she whispered so as not to disturb her. "What's her name?"

"She doesn't have one yet. Naming her is your job."

Jordan's eyes widened with that news. "Hmmm. That's going to be hard. Got any suggestions?"

"I thought about that all the way back here. How about Liberty?"

Jordan was quiet for a few moments and she smiled at him. God he'd missed that. "I like it. Maybe I'll call her Libby for short."

Chapter 22

Shane sat on the top of an old split-rail fence in front of the new Onyx Zone relocation center, trying to get his bearings and also trying to figure out how this very complicated situation between his twin and the woman he loved was going to play out.

He promised her on their first day together he wouldn't walk away from her as long as she needed him. If she didn't need him anymore, he had already prepared himself to walk away.

Because of her injury, the unique opportunity to care for her twenty-four hours a day for nearly two weeks had dropped into Patrick's lap. He gave Patrick the time to have her with him. With her injury, she'd be forced to rely on him, and the dynamics of their interactions would be very similar to how she'd been living with him. Jordan could bond with Patrick in a way she needed to bond with the man who was going to be her husband. The situation was exactly what she needed to shift Patrick into position of the dominant man in her life. It shouldn't have been that difficult since he and Patrick look exactly alike, and she loved Patrick already.

He rubbed a hand over his chest. It felt tight, like his body didn't want to breathe anymore. The past week and a half had been the hardest in his life. He fought the compulsion to run to Jordan, to care for her, every waking second of every day.

The only thing that kept him away was his love for them both. He wanted them to find their joy together. It was the right thing. The only thing that made sense. They would marry and have babies. Jordan would get the normal family she never had. His brother would share his life with a spectacular woman. His mother would get her grandbabies.

And he would watch it all with a smile on his face and excruciating pain in his heart.

Just as it had been when they were a constant presence in each other's life, Patrick found him and sat next to him, overlooking the tall pines, dense vegetation and the last vestiges of a colorful rain of maple leaves, blowing in the fall gusts of wind.

"It's good to see you." He slapped Shane on the back and they sat on the top rail of the old fence in silence for a while.

"How is she?"

"Falling to pieces." Patrick raked his hand through his hair. "The last ten days, God, I don't know what to do to snap her out of it. Her retreat from the rest of us is frightening. I've never seen her like this." Patrick glanced at him, shaking his head. "I've done everything I can think of to snap her out of it. But words, no matter how positive or encouraging, have done nothing. She just isn't the same woman."

"She needs a session."

Patrick shook his head. "I asked her. Told her I would do it for her. She said no."

Shane needed a few minutes to process this new information. He had been absolutely sure she'd be able to make the shift, putting Patrick into his place in her life.

Shane's worry took over. "Have you been holding her, soothing her, comforting her?"

"No, she'll barely let me touch her let alone do any of those things."

"Shit." Shane rubbed his eyes with the heels of his hand and blew out a long rough breath. He'd made a serious mistake. Jordan hadn't bonded more closely with Patrick as he'd thought, and now he knew his absence probably slowed her adjustment to her new disability and her new life.

"She needs a session."

"It's hard to believe a session will make much of a difference."

"It will make all the difference. For Jordan, sessions are like hitting a reset button. No matter how bad the depth of the hole she's in, she pops back."

Shane hooked Patrick's shoulder with his hand and spit out the words that weighed heavily on his mind. "I can't hold back from fucking her any longer." Shane turned his head and met his brother's gaze. "I can't do it anymore."

"I'm not askin' you to. Holding back all this time." Patrick grinned wide. "Must have been hell on ya." Then he laughed. "That's going to be the shortest fuck in history once you get your tiny willie in there." Patrick laughed some more.

Shane smiled and slid off his perch on the top rail of the fence, turned to Patrick, and jammed his fist into his brother's nose.

"Ow!" Patrick shouted and covered his face with his hand.

"That's for making me wait." He sat back down on the fence. "You don't know how much trouble I'm in because you made me promise not to fuck her."

"Yeah?" Patrick was grinning again from ear to ear. "Tell me about it."

Shane ignored him. "You should stay for the session. As a matter of fact, I encourage it. She'll be worrying about what you think of the therapy, the sessions, and she's got too much on her plate right now. We need to include you as soon as possible. No more secrets."

They sat in silence for a few more minutes before Patrick jumped off the rail and motioned to Shane. "Come on. I'll take you to her."

Shane nodded and walked with his brother into one of the homes behind the relocation center. "Ma and Da are next door." Patrick pointed to the house on the right.

At this point, Shane was barely interested in what Patrick had to say. He'd been away from her too long, and the knowledge that he was going to see her again in mere moments turned off all the other questions he'd turned over and over in his mind during the time he spent keeping the Guard out of the Amber Zone.

When he entered the room, she sat facing away from him. Her form was slightly hunched over. He could tell she'd lost weight with just a glance of her back. The knobs of her spine poked out underneath the black t-shirt she wore. He wanted to punch Patrick in the face again for not making her eat.

She looked over her shoulder, and Shane laid eyes on Jordan's face. He recognized her desperation and, automatically, he transformed into what she needed. "I come home after eleven days and you greet me sitting on your ass?"

Jordan bowed her head then slowly walked toward him and lowered herself to her knees at his feet, pressing her forehead to the floor. "That's better."

His heart clenched as he took in the sight of her. She was definitely thinner.

"Take the bandages off. I want to have a look at what's mine." He watched as Jordan awkwardly stripped the gauze away. He stepped next to her and held his hand out. She hesitantly placed her forearm in his palm and looked away from him.

Shane lifted her chin and met her gaze. Her tears fell back, rolling toward her ears. She was waiting for him to reject her because of her injury. He saw it in her worried, tear-filled eyes. He knelt next to her and leaned in until his lips brushed her ear. He ran his hand down her back and over the curve of her ass. "Still beautiful," he whispered. And that was all it took to undo her completely.

A long, loud groan escaped. Now that he was there, she'd allow herself to feel everything. She crumpled to the floor, releasing another desperate sound, a keening wail of pain like none he'd heard before.

Shane scooped her up and cradled her in his arms as he walked to an armchair, sat and rocked her like a baby. "I got you. I'm here now." He surrounded her with his arms, his hands petting and caressing. "Shh. Shh."

Jordan wept uncontrollably. Big, racking sobs followed one, after another, after another while she tunneled herself into his embrace as if she wanted to crawl underneath his skin.

Patrick stood watching them from the corner of the room. His mouth hung open, a frozen expression of astonishment on his face.

Shane met his twin's gaze. "Stay or go, Patrick, but make the decision now and stick with it." The words had teeth. It was unintentional on his part. He was beside himself and crazy with worry.

Patrick closed his mouth then and lifted his chin, squaring his jaw. He sat, and Shane turned his attention back to Jordan.

This emotional dump was the best of the therapy at work. Once the bond was established, pain wasn't always necessary for catharsis. Just his presence and the structure that came with it triggered the meltdown. She felt safe to let go, and she trusted him to catch her. He held her tight for a small eternity as the feeling of warm, wet fabric on his chest grew from her tears.

When she'd finally settled, Shane brushed the hair away from her face. Her eyes were red and fringed with wet, spiky lashes.

"Have you been taking care of yourself?"

Jordan broke eye contact and looked down at her stump then looked up at his eyes to see if he was looking at it. "No. I…I haven't felt like it."

"Haven't felt like what?"

"Eating. Sleeping."

"What did I say the last time you didn't follow your rules?"

"If it happened again, you'd tan my hide," she whispered.

"Well? Let's get to it." He twirled a finger. "Roll over." Her jaw dropped and she took a moment to process his request.

"But--" She looked over her shoulder at his brother. "Patrick. He's here."

"He made his choice, Jordan. Things can't stay as they were. We're both here. We'll adapt accordingly."

She continued to hold Patrick's gaze, and to his brother's credit, Shane saw only love in his expression.

"Now," he growled, "I advise you to roll over before your discipline doubles."

Shane knew he was giving her the power to choose how much pain she needed. He hadn't been there at all and had no idea how close she was to losing it. But he knew her well enough to know if she rolled over, she didn't need a session as badly as if she overtly displeased him. He waited a beat, two beats, and then she scooted off his lap.

She stood, glaring at him with her hand on her hip. He had to consciously keep his jaw from dropping open as she stood there in a stance that connoted strength and power.

He noted her slight tremble. Her breathing was rapid and shallow. "I needed you," she sneered.

He smiled at her and then looked over his shoulder to level a stare at Patrick. It's message was unmistakable. "Don't move." The "or I'll kick your ass" was implied.

Patrick nodded and Shane turned back to Jordan.

* * * *

Jordan watched the silent conversation Sir was having with Patrick. Two seconds later, he lunged, wrapped an arm around her waist and in no time at all, he sat on the bed with her struggling face down and rear end up, in his lap. Two more quick moves and she was restrained between his legs, feet on the floor, bending over his left thigh.

The sound of the first stinging slap to her ass resonated through the room. "Let me go," she screamed. "Stop!" she screamed again.

"I hate you!" *Thwapp.*

"I. Hate. You!" she bellowed, using every last molecule of oxygen from her lungs. *Thwapp.*

"You left me here. I hate--" *Thwapp.* "You-u-u," she sobbed, followed by a huge gulping sound escaping from her throat as she tried to take a breath. *Thwapp.*

"Stop," she shrieked. "You have no right to come back here after eleven days. Eleven days!" *Thwapp.*

She sobbed until her lungs were empty again "I lost my hand, and you left me." *Thwapp.* "I lost my hand, and you left me-e-e." Jordan attempted to kick her feet and thrash around again. He tightened his hold on her until she couldn't move anything and gave her five more swats.

"That was for not listening to me when I instructed you to roll over," he said in an even, calm tone. "This is for not following the rules. Count." He spanked her again.

"Let go of me." Her voice was raw. She was tired from thrashing. After five more strikes, she finally started counting.

By the time Jordan counted, "twenty," she didn't feel as angry. She wasn't thrashing or trying to kick him, but he still hadn't let her go.

She closed her eyes. "Sir." Her voice shook.

"Yes?"

"May I be released, please?"

"Yes, Jordan. After you get the second half of your punishment. Don't forget, you decided to double it with your behavior. Will you turn around and bend over the other leg. This hand hurts. I'd like to use my other one."

Jordan obediently followed directions and braced herself for the second half of her discipline. She cried loudly, wailing after each spanking on her rear end.

Sir didn't make her count this time and it was a good thing, because her thoughts turned within as the rest of her anger fled.

A rush of relief bowled her over. Shane was safe. Shane was home. And even though everything else in their lives had changed, nothing had changed between them, hand or no hand. Brother or no brother. They were solid, as before. As always.

Quiet tears still brimmed and then overflowed out of her eyes and took an interesting trail over her forehead into her hairline. She slumped, exhausted.

Sir finally finished her discipline and turned her over in his lap.

She curled up again and he tucked his chin on top of her head. She felt so safe there with her head on his chest, listening to his heart beat, feeling the gentle sway of him rocking her ever so slightly back and forward. He smelled clean, like he'd just taken a shower. "Are you ready to serve my needs now?"

"Yes, Sir."

A gasp sounded from the other side of the room, reminding Jordan that Patrick was there too.

Shane stood and deposited Jordan unceremoniously on the floor. "Present," he ordered. She shifted to her knees and leaned forward, placing her cheek on the wood floor and her arms extended in front of her.

Sir walked away from her to the other side of the room opposite the bed at the sitting area. The brothers sat in silence, neither speaking for several minutes. The quiet soothed her, helped her to recover from her loss of control. It was odd. She'd spent so much time in that room during her recovery, and when Sir wasn't there, the quiet hadn't been soothing at all.

"So what would you like to do about our girl here?" Sir asked.

"I don't feel like there's a whole lot of options."

Jordan didn't need to strain in order to overhear their conversation, she heard them loud and clear. No secrets. Never any secrets with Shane. She turned her head slightly so she could glance surreptitiously.

"You can give her children."

"And you give her something that I've come to realize is more important than children." Patrick paused. "I need to be more than a sperm donor to the woman I love."

"Stop being a dick. It's not like that, and you know it," Shane spat.

"Yeah, well, I guess at some point we both knew this situation wasn't going to last forever."

There was a long silence that followed. It was comfortable, peaceful in the room.

"We still have the issue of Ma and the others that will be passing though this place. She should marry one of us."

"I thought the same thing and told her so. She seems intent on not doing that."

"At the very least, she should take our last name."

"Mmm. I agree. Okay. Jordan O'Connor it is," Shane said.

"What about Ma?" Sir asked.

"Ma wants us happy. She'll be fine."

Sir hesitated. She heard him shift in his chair. "Are you sure?"

"I was serious before. I kept my promise to you. I've never fucked her. But I don't think I'll be able to stand it for much longer. Once it's done, I can't take it back."

Shane had made a promise? He wanted to fuck her instead of that woman? Her brain fired, flooded with rapid-fire snippets of her life that now made so much more sense because of this new information.

There was silence again for a while until it was broken by Shane. "Jordan needs her session."

"That wasn't it?"

"No. That was punishment for not obeying me." Shane's footfalls vibrated the wood floor beneath her cheek until they stopped close to her head. He'd returned his attention to her, and her body trembled under his scrutiny. Then he walked away from her again.

Her emotions rioted. How ridiculous that her feelings of abandonment appeared mere seconds from the removal of Shane's attention. She'd felt safe and special when she held his full attention.

Minutes passed and as always when she remained presented to him for long periods of time, Jordan relaxed. Her emotions settled. Maybe everything was going to be okay. They had worked out an arrangement or something. God she hoped.

Jordan was so deep inside her head she was surprised by the naked feet on the floor in front of her when she opened her eyes. Then Shane's crop waved into her view.

"Go to the bed and lie down. On your stomach please." She shuddered at the tone of his commanding voice. It was a harbinger of the coming frenzy and the splintering away of that part of herself she so desperately needed to set free.

She couldn't help herself. As she got to her feet she spared a glance toward Shane and was shocked to find him completely naked and fully erect. "Oh God," she huffed. Then, Jordan heard the slice in the air right before the crop striped the backs of her thighs and her breath left her.

When she turned to crawl into bed, her gaze landed on Patrick, who still sat in the armchair with his ocean blues focused on her, absorbing every detail of the scene.

"Come on, baby. Crawl on." She swung her head around, and Sir recaptured her attention.

She gazed up at him. He was so deadly sexy with the blue-fire eyes scorching her skin. She would finally serve him the way she'd wanted to for so long, giving him everything. Her Sir came back to her, didn't leave her. She was desperate to please him so he'd never leave her again.

"I won't leave you again," he growled into her ear. "Lay down on your belly, arms and legs spread."

Confusion swirled through her senses, and as she attempted to speak, her lips wanted to remain slack instead of forming the movements needed. "Did I say that out loud?"

Sir settled his weight on top of her, pressing her into the mattress. His arms covering her arms. His legs slanting over hers, pinning her. "No, baby. I just know the way your mind works."

Jordan waited, ready to feel the familiar restraint at her wrists and ankles.

Then, the thought came. Cuffs and rope were useless with her stump. She sucked in a huff of air. He would never again restrain her as he used to. The bombshell was followed by a visual picture. What she saw in her mind's eye constricted her throat.

What must she look like from Sir's point of view? The flash of her form beneath him materialized in her head and then twisted her stomach. She was so much less now.

"No. *You* do not decide what *I* think is sexy."

She jumped when Sir spoke so close to her ear from behind.

"How many days did you worry about something that took me less than ten minutes to work out?"

Jordan hesitated, knowing how unhappy he would be when she gave him her answer. "Eleven, Sir,"

"I'm disappointed in your choices." The low rumble of his words vibrated her back. His breath gusted past her ear. She was trapped, caught with his body heavy on hers.

"I'm sorry,

"Do you love me, Jordan?"

She nodded and closed her eyes, noticing the thick spear of Shane's flesh prodding at the opening of her pussy.

"Do you trust me?"

"Yes. But I know what you tried to do, leaving me like that."

The head of his cock penetrated and then advanced at a slow pace.

"I did what I believed was the right thing at the time."

"How can I trust you when I know you tried to give me away?"

"Because I wanted you both to be happy, I gave the two of you a chance to be together without me, a chance you both deserved. So we'd all know for sure what would have worked and what wouldn't. That was the first and last chance anyone will ever have to take you away from me. Do you understand?"

"I love you, Jordan," he said when he finally filled her. Sir's throaty words cut through her fears, her pain and her failures.

"Never again, baby. You'll never be without either one of us again. We're three from now on."

"Yes, Sir."

He groaned as he began a slow beat of thrust and retreat. "Forever."

"Promise me, Sir. Promise me."

"I promise, baby." Shane fucked her slowly while maintaining complete control over her entire body.

"I've waited a long time for this, Jordan. To feel your cunt sucking me in." He was gentle. His kisses to her shoulder were soft. She closed her eyes and reveled in the complete satisfaction she felt serving her Sir. She was finally allowed to serve him the way she'd always wanted to. The slow penetration of his cock filled her fully. He was too slow. She needed him, more, faster.

But he knew that already, she was sure. Still, the pleasure mounted. "Oh, God." She heard her own cries faintly penetrating her consciousness.

She turned the remaining pieces of herself over to the force of the cock pumping inside her. Moments later his hand snaked underneath her and a finger slid between her pussy lips, parting them and then just rested there. The slight rocking effect of his thrusts on her body moved her clit over the finger resting directly on top of it. She cried out her pleasure as he rammed into her. Quicker, and then quicker still until Sir fucked her at a furious pace.

On the precipice of orgasm, she stiffened, tightened her muscles, fighting the climax that was right there.

She waited. Waited.

"Please!" She pleaded and he still made her hold. "A-a-a-ahh. Please." She bellowed in a stuttered shriek between his thrusts inside her.

"Come for me." He rasped at her ear and thrust into her several more times before she shattered, crying out her pleasure. She turned her head and met Patrick's gaze at the far end of the tunnel where she currently existed, hoping she'd just fall into it completely. Disappear forever in the wonderful fog. Jordan surrendered it all to Sir, crying out one last, keening wail. It was her expression of relief, acceptance of his love, and hope for the future. It marked the end of New Atlanta, the end of her past. It was her life starting anew.

It was the most perfect moment of her life.

Chapter 23

At dawn the next day, Shane walked down to the same place on the fence he'd perched the day before. It would become a habit. He knew it already. There was something to be said by starting the day overlooking the unbelievable portrait of nature. He looked forward to enjoying the continually changing land season after season, year after year.

A moment of cockiness zinged through him. How long before Patrick sought him out there? He bet himself less than fifteen minutes. If there was anything he could count on in this world, it was that he and his twin would keep each other on a short leash. And now, after his years in the Amber Zone, he knew neither one of them would survive another long separation.

He thought back to the night before. It was beyond obvious that Jordan needed the therapy and Patrick had done well as a spectator.

Speak of the devil. Behind him, Patrick's steps crackled fallen leaves on his approach.

"Jordan still sleeping?" Shane asked when Patrick sat on the fence next to him.

"No. She's up. Said she hasn't slept more soundly since before the mission."

"She'll be better now. The partial session yesterday should alleviate the majority of the depression until she's physically able to take a full one."

"Just like that?"

Shane nodded. "Just like that."

"What I saw last night, it wasn't the Jordan I know."

"She never wanted you to see that part of her. She's always been afraid you'd think she was crazy. It was her biggest fear. Probably still is. She's going to be extremely sensitive to your words and body language today, so don't put your foot in your mouth. If she gets it in her head that you think less of her because you're shocked or disturbed by last night, it will mean big trouble for all of us."

Patrick sighed and nodded. "How do you want to work this?"

Shane looked up into the deep blue eyes of his twin. "Like yesterday, I guess. We'll have to make a few changes to accommodate our new configuration, but she's been with both of us for months. She loves both of us. It will be more of an adjustment for you and me than it will be for her. Actually...the adjustments will be mostly yours because she's happiest with a session every three to four days and has a tendency to not take care of herself properly without structure and discipline on a daily basis at home. So yeah, you're the one who'll be doing the most adjusting because her home environment should remain as stable and structured as possible.

"I'll adjust," Patrick said. His voice was thick, hoarse. "I'm just glad we're back together. You're different now, though."

Silence rested heavily between them as Shane tried to get a grip on the emotions welling up inside him as well. He swallowed hard. "God, I missed you." He released a quick breath and shook his head. "When I first got to Amber, I was so lost...the total disconnect from you. It was hard. I was packed in with hundreds of people around me all the time and I thought I would die of loneliness. Finally, I recognized I was wallowing in a headspace that was the equivalent of a shithole. I had to toughen up. That's when I sought out the therapy. Without it, I don't know what would have happened to me." He took in a long, slow breath of air, maybe his first of many years. "After that, I had a thick skin. I was tougher. The whole experience changed me."

Patrick met his gaze, nodded and then smiled. "It was a year before the impulse to find you, to be by you, began to fade. I kept wondering if that was what it was like for people who weren't twins. If they felt so alone like that. No matter." He put an arm around Shane's shoulders. "The O'Connor boys, together again. Ma's goin' to be in heaven."

"How do you want to handle the Jordan situation with Ma?"

Patrick ran a hand over the short scrub of hair on the back of his head. "Ma loves Jordan. They're friends and partners in crime. And you--I doubt you'll do any wrong in Ma's eyes for at least a year or two." Patrick stood. "Come on. I need some tea. And maybe we can talk to Ma without Jordan around."

Shane matched Patrick's stride as they crossed to their parent's home. "I don't think we're going to need to tell her anything," Shane said. "I'm pretty sure she already has a good idea of how we feel. The rest is none of her business."

"I suppose. But when has that ever stopped her before?" The brothers looked at each other and burst out laughing.

When they got close enough, both men spotted Kate O'Connor watching them through her back patio door.

As they approached the house and climbed the porch stairs, their mother opened the door. "Shane!" She wrapped her arms around him and held him tight.

"I knew you were home when I woke up and found Jordan in my kitchen, smiling with a cup of tea waiting for me. She's already given me my duties for the day." Shane's mother winked at him and then grabbed him into a tight embrace. "What a difference a day makes."

After letting him go, his mother hugged Patrick. "She's looking for you both. And Shane, you need to see your da before she's got you busy for the rest of the day."

"Kay, Ma. I was planning on it." Shane followed them to the kitchen. Jordan looked up from her papers when they entered. Patrick kissed her. "Good morning, Jordan O'Connor."

And Shane followed with a kiss of his own. "How's our girl this morning?" He enjoyed watching as her cheeks turned crimson, and she looked down at her paper nonchalantly, though it was obvious she was avoiding eye contact.

Shane watched his mother's reaction closely. Her eyes fell on Jordan then moved to Patrick and then finally settled on him. She blinked expressionless, once, twice, and then gave him a slight nod. He smiled at her and nodded back.

Patrick had been right. There'd be no questions.

"I'm going to drag your father out of bed while you eat some breakfast and get your assignments for the day from the boss here." She patted Jordan on the shoulder before she left the room.

"The woman we rescued from being raped by Morgan"-- Jordan picked up a sheet of paper and looked down at it for a moment-- "Pam, has been waiting with her parents and boyfriend over a week for us to get up and running. Patrick, I'd like you to make sure our guest rooms in the Relocation Center are ready to go. Take Shane with you. He needs to get the lay of the land and learn the care of the animals we have out back as well."

"You need your dressing changed first," Patrick commented.

Jordan shook her head. "I don't think so. After I clean up, I'm going to leave it open to the air. It doesn't seem to be leaking anymore. I think it'll be okay." She swallowed and looked away from them both. "Might as well get used to looking at the damn thing. It's not going to get any prettier.

"While you're at the safe house, pick up the bulbs Jaci has waiting for us there. They need to get into the ground before it gets too cold so we have onions, garlic and whatever else she's collected for us come springtime."

They all talked through their tasks for the day and ate breakfast before they parted ways. Shane shot an inquiring look over his shoulder at Jordan before he left the room.

"Go on. I'll be fine. I'm just going to do a walk-through of the relocation center, grab some paperwork and then me and my girl here"-- she pet Libby who was sitting faithfully next to her chair-- "have some bonding to do."

"I'll see you later?"

She smiled, and the sight of it allayed his reservations about leaving her alone. "Yes, you will."

* * * *

Later that day, Jordan was too tired to do anything else when she climbed the stairs up to their rooms. Liberty was on her heels with a tail wagging so enthusiastically that it jiggled the entire rear end of her body. Jordan chuckled "Lib, I don't think I've ever seen anyone as excited to be around me as you are." She patted the bed. "Come on. It's naptime for both of us." Libby jumped up, watching as Jordan covered herself to the armpits with the sheet and blanket. Moments later, she felt Liberty circling and then dropping herself so that she lay against Jordan's body.

They napped together and apparently it was for some time because the next time Jordan opened her eyes, the sun had set and the room was dark. Libby was still parked next to her, but moved when she realized that Jordan was awake. The ball of furry cuteness moved to stand next to her head and licked her face nonstop until Jordan half laughed and half squealed for the animal to stop. She did after two more good licks, one of which sent Liberty's little puppy tongue halfway up Jordan's nostril.

It wasn't much after that when Shane entered the bedroom. The scrape of a match preceded the flame Shane held to the wick of a candle, before blowing it out and setting it carefully in the metal candleholder.

"I thought I heard you making noise up here."

Jordan moved to greet him properly.

"No. Stay there. You look comfortable."

She smiled at him. "Thank you, Sir."

He sat on the side of the bed and pulled Jordan into his lap. Libby got up, turned and dropped so that her body was up against Sir's.

"Did you get the group?"

"Yes, everybody's back safe and sound."

Liberty wagged her way over to them and sat closer. Shane shook his head. "Her mother is enormous. Scariest dog I've ever seen. But amazing, too. She's not like the scary animals we're used to seeing in the Amber Zone. She's smart, and she follows word commands like they do. But she's also calm, majestic almost, and I swear watching her with Pam and Eric, it seems like she has the ability to love. I told them to meet us for breakfast tomorrow morning so he can start working with you on training."

She smiled. "Good." She was anxious to get started and couldn't help the excitement she felt when thinking about the friend Liberty would become.

"How are you feeling?"

"Both my stump and my heart are feeling better."

"Good."

"Where's Patrick?"

"Making the rounds, checking on the animals. He'll be up in a minute. I wanted to talk with you alone." He cocked his head and then reached up to brush a thumb over her bottom lip. "Our circumstances have changed with Patrick back in our lives full time.

She nodded.

"He and I have talked about how we want things to go here, and I want to make sure you agree to these new rules. I also need to talk with you about any limits you might have." She opened her mouth to speak but Shane held up a hand. "No. I'll tell you when you may speak. Listen first.

"With tomorrow's installation of a door and dead-bolt lock, the upstairs rooms will be our own. When you are up here, all submission rules apply. You and I will interact as we always have. For the time being, it is also how you will interact with Patrick. After some time, he will change the rules to suit him, but mine will always be what they are now. If it's warm enough, you're to be naked. And I wouldn't count on Patrick changing that rule. He wagged his eyebrows at her in a very un-Shane move. I'll give you sessions as needed. I will no longer be holding myself back from you during sessions. In some sessions, Patrick will participate also." He lifted her chin so that she was meeting his gaze. "Do you have a problem with any of these changes?"

She shook her head. "No, Sir."

Do you have any new sexual limits due to this new configuration?

"No, Sir."

"If you begin to have anxiety or form a problem because of the change, what will you do?"

"Tell you, Sir."

"When will you tell me?"

"Right away, Sir."

"Good. Any questions?"

"Should I call Patrick Sir, too?"

Shane shook his head. "No, baby. I'm your only Sir. I'm just letting him partake of what is mine."

"So, I have permission to have sex with him?"

"Yes, when he wants it. When you want it, you have to get my permission."

Shane flashed a look over his shoulder in the direction of the door. "Ma is going to want you to marry one of us before babies start coming. When Patrick asks, I encourage you to say yes."

Jordan's heart twisted. "No, Sir. I will never do that. I'll never do anything that would make it seem like I love one of you more than the other. I love you both too much."

"Jordan, any babies you have will be Patrick's." He paused at the sounds of Patrick walking in the door downstairs. His Adam's apple bobbed with the big swallow he took before speaking again. "He should be the legal father of his own children."

Jordan remained steadfast, looking him directly in the eye. "No."

A second later, Patrick walked into the room and the topic was closed for discussion.

Chapter 24

Jordan climbed the stairs to their rooms deep in thought. Sir had been home for more than a week. She didn't exactly know why, but she'd been testing his patience since he arrived, and hadn't had much free time to devote to trying to figure out her motives.

And now, the "permission" he'd given to marry Patrick riled her up more and more every time she thought about it. She knew she viewed the situation in a wholly negative light. He wasn't trying to give her away again, even though it felt like it.

Lately, she always felt like she was at a slow simmer, just a few bits of bad news away from boiling over. She'd been releasing some of the anger in subtle ways, mostly disrespectful, over the last week. Today was no exception.

Sir had made her new rules very clear. He was responsible for her well-being. Period. Eating, sleeping, sessions and until she's one hundred percent healed from her amputation, the work she was allowed to do was his decision, not hers. Everything else outside their rooms, she was her own boss…and theirs.

Today, she'd completely defied him, and had been caught red-handed carrying fire wood after Sir told her she wasn't strong enough to do heavy work yet.

She had punishment coming. She smiled a wry smile. The whole missing a hand thing made him kind of soft. She'd gotten away with an awful lot of misbehavior since he'd joined them out in Onyx with little discipline.

She sat upstairs in their room in the candlelight. The house was still and quiet. She'd expected them to be waiting for her, ready to pounce when she emerged from the washroom, but the room was empty when she returned.

The wait was unnerving. There was nothing to do except speculate how the evening was going to play out. Her heart fluttered while her stomach did backflips at the images that flashed Technicolor in her mind's eye.

As the candles flickered, something on the floor caught her eye. She stooped to get a better look at the new restraints installed to the frame at the foot of the bed.

Downstairs, the side door to the house opened and the men's muffled voices rose from below her.

"Shit." They planned something. She walked around in a circle while her mind reeled. She didn't know if she was ready for this.

The muffled voices became clear as they opened the door at the bottom of the stairs.

No time.

The bedroom door opened and Jordan fell to her knees and presented for her Sir.

Patrick walked through the door first and bent to run a finger down the curve of her spine as he walked by. "How's my Jo today?"

"Good," she answered from her position on the floor.

Shane walked past her without speaking.

"I'm going to wash up a bit," Patrick said, walking toward the bathroom and then shutting the door behind him.

"Stand up, Jordan."

She lifted herself to her feet and stood in front of him naked, nervous.

"So I take it from your disobedience that you feel like you're a hundred percent?"

"Yes, Sir."

He nodded. "Good. Tonight I'm going to give *you* a hundred percent." He walked over to his drawer and pulled out big handfuls of items, spreading them out on top of the dresser. He stood with his back to her until he settled on the item that was in his hand when he turned around.

"Come here." His eyes blazed.

She rose to her feet and approached him cautiously.

"You're angry. I get that. And so far, I've let you get away with your eye rolls and generally bad attitude because my first priority is to care for you and in my estimation, you weren't strong enough to receive the discipline you deserved. Apparently, that is not an issue any longer. So, it's time."

"Time?"

His smile turned wicked. "Yes, time."

"For?"

"For your discipline." He turned and tapped a finger on the sheet of paper on the dresser. "Don't worry. I kept track." He referred to the paper. "For your smart mouth." He held up a ball gag. "Open."

She did, and he placed the ball in her mouth, connecting the straps at the back of her head. He stepped away and cocked his head as he admired the sight of her with the contraption in her mouth. "Very nice. Let me hear your safeword."

"Re--" She couldn't make the "d" sound around the ball in her mouth.

"Good." Looking at the paper again, he picked up a blindfold. "Let's put a stop to the eye rolling when you think I can't see you." He walked behind her and slipped the soft fabric over her eyes and then swatted her bare ass. "I don't expect to ever see that again," he rumbled close to her ear.

"Yes, Sir," she whispered.

He gripped her upper arms and walked her backward a couple steps. "The bed is right behind you, lean back and rest your rear end on the edge and spread your legs wide."

Jordan did as she was told and seconds later, her ankles were restrained in the position.

Patrick stepped out of the washroom and crossed to the sitting area by the window. Then she heard Shane join him.

"Alright, I can already see the appeal."

"This, right now, looks like the therapy is about sex. But it's not. It's about making her stop, whether she wants to or not. The total lack of stimulation to her senses allows her to gain some distance from the pressure and responsibilities of her daily life. It's a rabbit hole she drops into at the end of every day, and when she's there, she can be exactly who she is without fear of rejection, criticism or judgment. I've seen the worst of her and love her unconditionally. It's honest. More honest than any other relationship I've seen, except maybe ours."

Jordan never heard Sir describe how he felt about her, what she meant to him. She was touched and felt a little guilty for her brattiness toward him since he joined them on the Onyx Zone.

"For me," he went on, "it's about absorbing the power this magnificent woman needs me to take from her, trusts me to take from her. She gives all of herself to me, and her complete submission to my word fills my need to be important to someone. I'm needed. My life is better because she's in it."

"Now that we're in Onyx and you have total control over your life, do you think the need to dominate will fade?"

"I have no idea, but my guess would be no. I'm hooked on this, hooked on her. I'm not sure whether there will ever be a time when she doesn't need me. If that happens, I'm not sure I'd be able to walk away. I love her, Patrick. It's just a different type of connection. A different flavor of love."

The room fell silent, and Jordan relaxed as the silence stretched.

"Jesus, she's gorgeous standing there waiting for us." She wasn't sure who'd said it. With quick, short sentences, Jordan occasionally had difficulty identifying which man was speaking if she wasn't looking at them.

Somebody walked over to her and sucked first on one nipple and then the other. Then he walked back to the sitting area.

"Very nice." It was Patrick who spoke. She detected the slight roll of his R.

Jordan relaxed into the absolute absence of sensory input leaning back slightly and placing her good hand on the mattress behind her.

"This is nice. I could do it every day," Shane said.

"Yeah, I agree."

"I think Jordan needs to know we know about her parents and how hard it was for her growing up. I don't want to start our lives together pretending there's a secret she's keeping when she isn't."

Jordan jerked her head up and...couldn't do or say anything. The two of them schemed like schoolgirls. She would remember this. Oh yes, she'd remember and someday, when the opportunity presented itself, they both would pay.

"I think she'll be a good mother, despite the shit for brains that raised her," Shane said.

"I'm ready to start a family. I don't want to put it off," Patrick said. "God, I hope she's fertile." She heard mirth in his tone. He was teasing her...or baiting her. She wasn't sure.

"She sure don't look it. Look at all those bones sticking out like popsicle sticks under her skin."

"Yeah." One of them sighed, presumably, Patrick. "Soon." Jordan heard the smile in Patrick's voice and had to smile along with him.

She heard the sound of someone walking to the dresser. Sir probably. He stayed there for a while before she heard the sound of him walking toward her.

His hand spread the cheeks of her ass and a lubed finger pushed into her. He added a second digit a minute later and manipulated the hole.

Jordan groaned.

A moment later, the fingers were gone and the cool end of a plug slid into her ass.

She groaned again as the object continued inside her, filling her ass slowly, stretching her rear hole. It was too big, too much girth. She was just about to scream when it popped into place. Then Sir retreated.

"Man, look at her nipples. I don't think I've ever seen them that small and tight," Patrick said.

She sensed movement and a few seconds later her nipple was pinched. She recognized Sir's favorite nipple clamps. He called them the alligators because of the toothy openings. "Aahhh." She screamed around the ball as the clamp pinched the other. He gave the chain connecting them a sharp tug, making her scream again.

"That's better." Sir said. "Let's get back to the details of Jo's therapy."

"Alright. What if I want to fuck her and end up screwing up a session you had planned?"

"Hmm. Good question. I usually know in advance when she's going to need one. And after a while, I think you'll be able to tell when she's due. Until then, I'll let you know as soon as I've decided she's got one coming like right now."

She groaned into the silence of the room. She felt their eyes roaming over her tortured nipples, the flat of her stomach, her traitorous clit, peeking out and seeking more of their attention. She never had a session when Sir was so angry at her. It boosted the adrenaline racing through her veins. Suddenly, she wanted to take back the disrespect she'd been giving him. Being keyed up like this was too uncomfortable. She tried to speak. Tried to let him know she'd try not to take her upset and bitterness out on him, and he didn't need to be angry anymore. But with her mouth overfull the words transformed into unintelligible sounds.

She heard him advance on her. Seeking fingers curled past her begging clit and wiggled the butt plug peeking from between her cheeks. The miniscule movement was a tease and her body reacted to it by rushing more blood to her lower lips. Her girl parts were heavy, her vagina clenched and found nothing to grab onto. Then she received a pinch to her clit. She grunted and blurted out, "Stop it." It came out more like "aahi."

"You do not have permission to speak," Sir rumbled directly into her ear. Her stomach flipped. His words were ice cold.

With her lame attempts and making things right between them, she'd only succeeded in rousing more of his anger and disapproval.

He pinched her clit again and in an instant she was steamed again. Belligerent because of the teasing and upset with herself because she couldn't seem to stop her contentious hostility and disrespectful automatic responses.

"ow uh ker." The words left her overfilled mouth before any thought was given to them.

Sir's progress back to his chair stopped.

"You did not just call me a fucker," he spat.

He returned to her and she waited for the swat. It didn't come right away. She'd crossed the line and she knew it. Oh God, what was she doing? This was insane.

Instead of coming back to her, he continued to retreat. The absence of his attention was worse than any punishment she could have received. She was wired. Her emotions were everywhere and she felt the explosion within herself building.

It was a long time before either man spoke again.

Finally Patrick broke the silence. "We need to turn her around. I want to see that ass."

Moments later, each man worked at the restraints around her ankles and then removed the nipple clamps. The resulting surge of pain as the blood returned to her nipples was agony, but she didn't utter a peep. A hand grabbed her forearm, turned her around to face the bed and leaned her over until her chest met the covers.

"You stay there," Sir growled. His footsteps retreated.

"Much better."

"She's never been this disobedient before."

He was right. She didn't know why she had this impulsive need to strike back at him.

"She's still mad at you. She'll get over it."

"She better get over it tonight. She's on very thin ice right now. One more peep and she'll be sleeping in the bed next door…alone."

"Look at that beautiful pussy." Sir's rumbled words eased her a bit.

"Prettiest thing I've ever seen."

"Have you fucked her in the ass yet?"

"Nope. Never got around to it."

Sir grunted.

She wasn't expecting it when Sir's paddle connected with her ass. He paddled her ass for a good long time. He didn't make her count the number of times the paddle met her ass, and she was oddly preoccupied with how the strikes shifted the plug lodged inside her. After a while, her thighs began to quiver with the strain of holding up her weight, spread eagle like that.

Still the slow, evenly spaced swats continued, heating her rear end.

Finally, her legs had had too much, and she put the full weight of her body on the mattress.

That state of being Sir brought to her during sessions approached at a slow crawl. She craved her fix. The anesthesia that numbed her depression, her anger. It was always total relief.

She no longer tensed anticipating the next strike. No need. Her body didn't feel it much anymore.

The next step, she needed it. Needed to be fucked. Needed to come. Her body was already aroused and preparing for what was next while her brain switched to autopilot.

She moaned when the paddling stopped.

"Your ass looks pretty pink," Sir whispered into her ear. Her pussy lips quivered, anticipating his cock.

Silence.

"It is a thing of beauty, shall we?"

And then, they were on her. Hands stroked her everywhere, her calves, her back, her cheek. The flat of a velvet tongue sealed over the entrance of her vagina and then rubbed over her needy clit. The heated mouth attached to it, sucking it in, flicking the very peak of it with the tip of a tongue. Even in her half-dazed state and blinded by the black seclusion provided by the blindfold, Jordan knew the sharp swipes of Patrick's tongue. She got lost in the steady cadence of his lashes, tensing as the pleasure began to build.

Two sets of hands continued to roam her body as Patrick brought her close to orgasm with his mouth. Her insides turned liquid, and her heart hammered double time. She released a stuttering breath and drew one in the same way. She was overwhelmed, her brain not able to focus on everything that was happening.

Just as she was coming close to orgasm, hands made her stand upright. Her legs almost gave out. She was disoriented when one of them guided her to the side of the bed, and then nudged her to crawl on.

"Lie on your back, Jordan."

She did as was told and rough hands adjusted her position before strapping ankle restraints onto her. Then another restraint was threaded underneath her and fastened her arms down against her body.

Spread wide with her arms cocooned to her side, she was theirs to do with as they wished.

Somebody straddled her waist. "Now that you're feeling a hundred percent, I have a few things I'd like to say." It was Sir. His words were clipped. He was definitely not pleased with her. "First, I can't tell you how disappointed I am after all this time of being your Sir, you actually believed I would leave you. The fact I gave you my word I'd stay with you as long as you needed me, and you chose not to believe it, is an insult. An insult I'm going to make sure doesn't happen again." She lifted her chin, trying to look strong and brave for a moment but Sir's laugh sliced through her. "Where do you think you are, little girl, with that pride you're trying to show off?"

She was being Jordan the leader, not the Jordan who belonged to Sir, the naked, raw woman who sought refuge in Sir's embrace, who flung off the weight of the world when she was kneeling at his feet, feeling his fingers sift through her hair.

Jordan panicked a little. She was having trouble doing that since Sir finally joined them. She hadn't been able to totally let go of her anger.

She was so fucking angry, every minute of every day. She was angry at herself for not killing Morgan, at Sir for leaving her, at the loss of her hand, at the world for being so horrible.

"This is not acceptable."

She sagged, no longer trying to look proud and strong. Instead she imagined she looked like an old broken-down, sagging-in-the-middle, bones-sticking-out-from-under-the-hide mare.

"I don't want pretend Jordan. I want my Jordan," he snarled into her ear. "You defy me by holding her back from me. I want her now!" he roared.

A burning streak drizzled onto her breast. "You are mine, Jordan O'Connor."

Jordan felt the sizzle of the letter *m* on her breast.

"Don't ever insult me with that type of thinking again," he growled.

The letter *i* followed like a string of fire on her skin. "I will never let you go."

The approximate shape of the letter *n* covered her breastbone and a slight rise to her other breast.

"You are mine!"

Jordan jumped. The air from his words blasted her face.

She groaned, but even she wasn't sure if it was in protest to the hot wax streaking over her nipple in the approximate shape of the letter *e*, or in relief upon hearing his claim of ownership. Two slices of fire underlined the word. She felt him lean in and then he clamped his hands in her short hair, pulling her head to the side and exposing her neck. "You are mine. I will not leave you as long as you need me. Don't ever doubt that again."

He murmured the words close to her ear and a ticklish chill ran down her spine.

"Say 'yes, sir.'"

"Yes, Sir."

"Good." She felt him lean to the side and then heard the soft *thud* of the candle on the side table.

"I'm doubly pissed that you didn't follow the rules while I was away. You've embarrassed me with your disrespect in front of others. I've allowed you to be angry. You're human, and I wouldn't dare tell you you can't have feelings. But it's over now. And you will let it go. You'll take your punishment tonight and it will be done with." He paused "Period!" The one word shout made her flinch. "Do you understand me, Jordan?"

"Yes, Sir."

Then he left her, cold and exposed, both inside and out. She wanted to cry. He was so angry at her. She thought about what she must look like to them in the candlelight. "Mine" in big letters written in wax over her chest, her arms bound to her sides and legs bound spread eagle. And of course the piece de resistance, the ball gag and blindfold.

Her heart's mad pounding just added to the heaviness of her pussy. She could feel the swollen wetness open to them. It was there for them to do anything they wished.

Jordan had lost the ability to judge time, but it seemed like forever until her legs were unfastened. Patrick took her blindfold off, and the sight of his sexy blue eyes greeted her.

"On your knees," Sir said from behind her as Patrick climbed onto the bed in front. Patrick was naked and hard, and his midnight-blue eyes were serious and hot as his gaze roamed over her form. She knelt between his legs and then was lifted from behind.

Sir accomplished a maneuver in seconds, and Jordan found herself chest to chest on top of Patrick. With the slight cracking and crumbling sensation of the wax letters on her chest, he wrapped his arms around her and kissed her hard before grabbing hold of her hips and scooting her lower until his cock slid inside her.

Yes. She sighed at the complete contentment that came with being loved by Patrick. And he still loved her, even after what he'd seen of her sessions. She saw it there in his eyes.

She rested on the warm cradle of his chest. She couldn't touch him, couldn't express how much it meant to her that he still loved her. Her arms were still secured to her sides and her mouth was still overfull.

Patrick wrapped both of his strong arms around her, placing one hand flat on the top of her back and the other petting from the crown of her head to the nape of her neck. He stroked her over and over again. "It's okay, baby, we're here with you," he whispered. "We both love you." He soothed her and her muscles began to relax.

She let go of her tenuous grasp on the present and receded into herself. She was high. Her body buzzed as her mind fled to elude reality, burying her thought processes deep in her own experience.

Her body was rubber and the world beyond it was gauzy.

Without warning the whip of the cane slicing through the air sounded a millisecond before a streak of pain ran across her ass. Jordan whimpered and tightened her ass to escape the next blow.

The motion moved her on Patrick's cock, and when Shane hit her again, the action was repeated. Patrick stroked her back, and held her to him with the hand at the nape of her neck when she attempted to move. With each stroke of the cane, Jordan dragged in another breath of air, stroked Patrick's cock with her pussy's needy clench and ground her pelvis against him, stimulating her clit. It was his groans that kept her with them, instead of turning inside herself completely.

But still, the familiar fog that surrounded her brain during sessions rolled in, heavy and thick. She lost herself in it.

The bed sagged behind her, and the anticipation for what was next kept her on edge.

Sir was behind her, entering the bed between her legs.

Mercifully, the straps from the ball gag loosened from around her head and then, finally, it was removed from her mouth. Sir covered her with his lean, muscular body. "Behave yourself."

With a tug, he popped the buttplug out of her ass and a second later the blunt, satiny rod of Sir's cock bumped up against her anus.

"Aaahh," she cried out as Sir's cock popped past her circle of muscles and inched in slowly. She groaned at the continuous advance of him inside her and felt as if she would have to use her safe word in just, one, more, second. She cried out into the fog that swirled around her and then again, louder as his cock ruthlessly continued its advance. Then finally, he was fully seated. His body curled and covered her back. His head was close to hers again. The breeze from his exhalation wafted over the back shell of her ear.

"You do not have any thoughts of anger or pride when we're in this room. Your thoughts should only be about how to please me, not about you."

"Yes," she said into the fog. Her mind was mush.

He completely withdrew his cock and then slid it into her forcefully again.

She shouted a choked cry and then another with each savage penetration until eventually, arousal began to outpace any other feelings she'd had.

Shane covered her with his sweat-slicked body and pumped her ass, grunting with each stroke.

His heavy weight on top of her tiny body made her feel safe. She was in a safe cocoon between the two men she loved. Men that loved her.

They fucked her hard, alternating penetration.

"Breathe, Jo," Patrick whispered.

She let out a breath and took in another.

Then she let go of thought altogether. She was safe totally surrounded by the hard heat of these two men, their grunts and groans floating like sweet music into her ears, touching her soul from the beauty of it. The pleasure those sounds brought her was beyond sexual. It felt like it was the ultimate acceptance of who she was. They knew her, what she carried inside, and still loved her.

Beneath her, Patrick groaned. His hands, dug into her hips, moved her faster, rubbing her clit at the base of his cock. They pistoned her between them, hard and fast until she was submerged in the pleasure.

"Come for me, Jo. I want to hear you scream, baby." Sir's words came short and ragged. Her pussy clasped Patrick tight and she teetered on the verge of the highest high, the most glorious release. She floated… waiting. "Do it!" he barked. The words were so far away, but her brain heard them. Sir wrapped his hand around her throat, pounding her ass hard, and she lost it. Her body convulsed. She wailed her release, her pussy fluttering like butterfly wings around Patrick's cock and her ass clamping down on Sir.

She froze, a euphoric, shuddering recipient of everything they had to offer. Jordan was vaguely aware of the men's cum flooding inside her as her orgasm waned, and then her awareness fled. She was wrecked, limp, done.

Someone released her arms, laid her on the cool sheets. She was near sleep when Patrick lifted her and put the rim of a glass to her lips. "Drink."

She did, and then he laid her back down.

Her men held her, kept her warm, surrounded her, and as she emerged from hard core mix of brain chemicals and sex, the sweet confirmation that they both were with her rectified her world, pivoting it onto a different axis, making everything right. She closed her eyes and barely registered the sweet words whispering through the room before she fell into the oblivion she'd been searching for since she left New Atlanta.

Chapter 25

Christmas 2075

Jordan watched as Kate stood to offer the blessing and everybody's hands linked with the person on either side of them. The motion was automatic for the three O'Connor men sitting around the table. Shane put his hand on her thigh and squeezed it tight since he couldn't take her hand. One day, this family's traditions would be second nature to her too.

"May the Good Lord bless you as your dear ones gather 'round.

"May your laughter be hearty, and love and joy abound.

"Thank you Lord for everything you've provided for this family."

Jordan listened to the chatter and *clink* of serving utensils against the bowls and plates, They all sat around the table, literally stuffing themselves with the special meal Kate made and talking of plans for the improvement of their homestead.

She looked down at Libby who sat at her left hand. Her training wasn't complete yet, but already she was a significant addition to Jordan's life, providing constant companionship and complete adoration. The innocent, unconditional love the animal had for her softened her in ways that felt unfamiliar. And as an added plus, the fierce protection Liberty displayed whenever a stranger got too close made both of her men rest easier as Jordan went about her daily work of running the center.

The O'Connor men made a routine of connecting at the end of every day, sitting in their chairs, talking and enjoying her nude submission. During the past month living with them, she'd found that Shane and Patrick were not just close, they were uncanny in their ability to know where the other was, what the other was thinking, and they always seemed to be on the same page.

The O'Connor brothers were just as close with each other as they were with her. Every relationship within their union was soul deep and intimate on a level she'd never seen before. There was comfort in knowing that the two men in her life would never become disenchanted with the other. It seemed to give her the extra security she needed so she could truly be comfortable with how they lived. She understood now why Kate thought they chose to fall in love with the same woman instead of this unusual triangle being something that just happened.

Kate O'Connor was fast becoming just as much "Ma" to Jordan as she was to her sons. The feeling of having a mother, at times, seemed almost more significant than the love she shared with Patrick and Shane. Almost. She was thankful that she would have a good role model to help her do the right things and make the right choices when her children came.

The journey culminating into this moment had been almost debilitating in its harshness. But as she looked around the table at the people she loved, she acknowledged all the pain had been worth it because it landed her there, with them. Her family.

She picked up her knife from the table and tapped the edge of her glass to get everybody's attention. "Uh." She cleared the emotion out of her throat. "I have something I wanted to say." She made eye contact with every one of the four gazes that landed on her. "Uh." Jordan had waited almost two weeks for this moment, but now that she was in it, she found her throat had closed tight and tears swam in her eyes. The words she'd practiced were lost.

She swallowed hard and just let it fly.

"I think I'm pregnant."

The room seemed to explode. Chairs slid across the wood floor. Kate made a sound that sounded terribly close to a squeal. Patrick pulled her out of her chair and wrapped his arms around her. Her cheek lay on his chest. He looked over her shoulder at his brother, and she felt Shane's hesitancy as he stood behind her. Patrick extended his arms past Jordan and pulled Shane into them behind her. The three stood, holding each other.

No words were necessary. They'd talked about this. Jordan had made her feelings extremely clear. They both would be "Da" to any children. She wouldn't tolerate anything else. Period. End of discussion.

She didn't care which one of them was the sperm donor and she didn't think her children would either. How could they? They had the best of the best when it came to family.

She was scared of the future. Nervous that she'd be ill suited to be a good mother. Fearful that the Onyx Zone would be no place to raise a child. Afraid she would pass on her depression and burden the next generation.

The two men in her life knew these fears. They knew everything. And they'd promised her, whatever the future held, they'd face it together.

Crying, and completely surrounded with love, she gave thanks to the God Kate always prayed to. When she opened her eyes, her watery vision focused on the hand lying against Patrick's chest and the dark blue tattoo that circled her wrist. It would forever be a reminder of the best decision she'd ever made…being Sapphire.

Meet the Author

As I sit here looking at the blank space where I'm supposed to write about myself, all I want to do is tell you more about the next book in the New Atlanta series, Being Emerald.

In Rock's story, the escalating struggle for freedom continues, but I'm more excited about the characters and epic love that slowly unfolds for this hero. Rock is close to my heart and different from any alpha hero I've written about before. His character is based loosely on someone I knew decades ago, a man who was scary on the outside and a teddy bear to anyone who really knew him. Being on the receiving end of sweetness from an intimidating giant is a memorable experience, one that stuck with me all these years. I loved that man and I hope you'll love Rock as much as I do.

Stay tuned for the next, and in my opinion, the best installment of the New Atlanta Series. And, don't forget to catch the epilogue for Being Sapphire on my website, www.RyanBooks.net and find out what ultimately happened with the O'Connor clan.

As always, thank you for reading

Acknowledgements

Special thanks to Donna Johnson for her unbridled enthusiasm, priceless opinions and sharp eyes